Too Much in the Son

For information, contact henrygraypub2022@gmail.com.

Publisher's Cataloging-in-Publication Data

Names: Peters, Charlie, 1951-.
Title: Too much in the son / Charlie Peters.
Description: Granada Hills, CA : Henry Gray Publishing, 2023.
Identifiers: LCCN 2023907000 | ISBN 9781960415042 (pbk.) |
ISBN 9781960415059 (ebook)
Subjects: LCSH: Crime – Fiction. | Impersonation – Fiction. | Mistaken identity – Fiction. | Mothers and sons – Fiction. | Fathers and sons – Fiction. | Los Angeles (Calif.) – Fiction. | Martinique – Fiction.|
BISAC: FICTION / Thrillers / Crime. | FICTION / Thrillers / Suspense.
Classification: LCC PS3616.E84 T66 2023 | DDC 813 P48—dc23
LC record available at https://lccn.loc.gov/2023907000

Cover illustration by Dailey Toliver, © 2023 Dailey Toliver

Proofreading by Helene Moore D'Auria

Made in the United States of America.

Published by Henry Gray Publishing, P.O. Box 33832, Granada Hills, California 91394.

For more information or to join our mailing list,
visit HenryGrayPublishing.com.

Too Much in the Son

Charlie Peters

Granada Hills, CA
"Select books for selective readers"

PART ONE

Martinique, 2003

1

Leo regained consciousness in the back of the panel van as it swerved over the island's unpaved and rutted roads, stones bouncing off its undercarriage, making it sound as if he were inside a tin drum. His hands were wrapped behind his back with duct tape and his head throbbed where he'd been hit. He could taste blood in his mouth. There was more blood, lots of it, on the floor of the van. But that blood wasn't his. Lying across from him on the van's rusted floor was the body of the young man whose throat he'd watched being cut a short time before.

The dead man's face was covered by a burlap bag, but Leo had no doubt it was Hoffman. He recalled the argument, the shouting and the fight. And he remembered seeing the blade slicing Hoffman's neck quickly and deeply.

It was only a few days before that Leo met Taylor Hoffman and he might have had more sympathy for him if Hoffman wasn't the reason that both he and Leo were in the van. Now he was going to watch him be buried. And more likely than not, Leo would be buried along with him.

2

Four days earlier, Leo stood at the concierge desk in the resort La Cachette where one of the housekeepers was telling him, half in the island's patois, "You are mistaken, *monsieur*, I give you your package *ce matin*." She turned to the concierge and told him, "I swear he wrong, monsieur. I give it to him after *la femme* in Room 107 give it to me."

The concierge smiled patronizingly at Leo. "Madame says she gave it to you this morning, Mr. Malone."

"Then why am I standing here asking you for it now?" Leo said.

"The fact of the matter is that I'm not able to answer that." Like many people, the concierge used unnecessary phrases when he spoke, hoping they made him sound smarter. They didn't. "At the end of the day, I trust my staff implicitly," the short man said and smiled at the housekeeper like a teacher might smile at a favorite student. She nodded her thanks to him before staring shyly, or guiltily, at the floor.

Leo was not officially a guest of the resort. But he'd left his passport in Janice Heller's room along with some clothes and cash when he went for a morning swim. If she had to leave for the airport before he got back, Janice said she'd ask the housekeeper to give Leo his things. Now the housekeeper claimed that she'd already given him what Janice had left for him. She was lying of course and Leo assumed that she'd already given his few clothes to her relatives and pocketed his money for herself. But the money or the clothes weren't important. What Leo wanted was his passport. He had no plan to go back to the States but, even so, you don't want to be anywhere without a passport.

"How am I supposed to get home now?" Leo asked the concierge.

"I can see how that might present a problem."

"I'll go up and look for myself."

"I'm sorry, Mr. Malone, but at this point in time the suite is occupied by Mr. and Mrs. Passenti. They're newlyweds," the concierge said with a conspiratorial smile as if he had any idea what newlyweds do. "Do you have any other business at the resort, Mr. Malone? Because, if not, I'm afraid Dr. Heller was the last single female guest staying with us at the moment." The concierge and the maid grinned knowingly at each other.

"I'm going up there," Leo said.

As precious as the concierge was, his access to the resort's security staff gave him the courage to step from behind the desk and stand in Leo's way. "If you go anywhere near that room, Mr. Malone, I will have no recourse but to alert security."

Leo wasn't going to fight him and the concierge knew this. So the two men stood there until a voice rescued them from their impasse. "You guys talking about this?"

They both turned to a young man who held a manila envelope.

"*Voilá*," the housekeeper said, pointing to the new man, roughly the same age as Leo. "I give it to him *ce matin* like I tell you, monsieur," she said.

The stranger was the same height and build as Leo. And even though his hair was a lighter brown and he didn't have Leo's scraggly, week-old beard, it was possible, likely even, that someone could mistake the two men. The housekeeper looked quickly back and forth between the new man and Leo and said, "*Ils sont freres*."

"*Oui*. More than brothers," the concierge said. "Almost twins."

The housekeeper nodded. "*C'est vrai. Jumeaux*."

The new man waved the envelope with Leo's name on it and pointed to the housekeeper. "This one here gave it to me this morning. I thought it was some tourist shit until I opened it." He handed the envelope to Leo who quickly confirmed that his passport was in it. So was his money. There was also a note from Janice Heller, handwritten on the resort's stationery. Leo counted the money and pocketed his passport. The note he'd read later.

"All's well that ends well," said the concierge.

The young man stuck his hand out to Leo. "Taylor Hoffman," he said.

"Leo Malone," said Leo, shaking his hand. "Thanks."

"No problem, bro."

Upon hearing who this new man was, the concierge perked up, his hands fluttering. "Welcome to La Cachette, Mr. Hoffman. I'm so sorry I wasn't here to greet you personally this morning," he said, clasping the young man's hand with both of his. "But rest assured anything you need, anything at all, simply inform me or my staff and we will see to it immediately."

"Thanks," Taylor said dismissively.

Not reading the man's disinterest, the concierge continued to fawn. "We at La Cachette deeply regret that your parents had to cancel their visit, but I will personally do everything to make your own stay here as memorable as possible."

"Whatever," Taylor said.

"*Merci,*" Leo said to the housekeeper and left the scene.

Taylor followed Leo into the lobby. "So you think they're right?" he said.

"About what?"

"That we look alike?"

"I don't know," Leo said and kept walking. But Taylor Hoffman grabbed Leo's shoulder and stopped him in front of a gaudy, mirrored wall near the entrance. Leo quickly shook off the other man's hand. He didn't like being touched by people.

"Check it out," Taylor said and pointed to Leo's scruffy beard. "Especially if you didn't have that shit on your face."

Leo looked at himself and at Taylor. Did they look alike? Who knows what anyone looks like to others? Where does your own eye go when you look in a mirror? First to your flaws—the unbalanced nose, those too-large ears, your pointy chin—to see if they're as bad as you thought? Or do you look at your strengths—your blue eyes, your full lips—none of which, flaws or strengths, are even noticeable to others? No one gives a shit what anyone else looks like. If people remembered that, their lives would be a lot easier.

Still, Leo had to admit there was a resemblance between Taylor Hoffman and himself. "Maybe we do look a bit alike," he said before he walked away.

Taylor followed him. "You staying here?"

"Not anymore." Leo walked through the front door held open for him by a tall Black man in a uniform like one you might see in a community theater production of *The Pirates of Penzance.* The doorman nodded a silent goodbye to Leo who headed to the road that would take him to his small apartment in the island's central town.

3

The shoes and cuffs of the two men sitting over Leo in the van were all that he could see of them, but their pants were the same dark green the island's police force wore. Leo recognized their shoes, too, as the imperfect rejects of an expensive running shoe donated with much fanfare by the manufacturer and the NBA star whose name was printed on their heel. They were brought here by an NGO three years after a hurricane called Heidi devastated the island's eastern shore, killing hundreds of people. *Heidi*? What idiot names these storms anyway?

When the hurricane struck the island, Leo had been working for a year on a Chickasaw reservation in Oklahoma. At a meeting about the residents' diets, Leo said that processed food had probably killed more Native Americans than any white man ever had or will. Given that one of the primary sponsors of the clinic was a multinational conglomerate whose most famous product was an iconic cookie made by elves, it was suggested Leo find another job. That same day he saw a notice on the chapel wall looking for volunteers to help hurricane victims on the island. He signed up, thinking it'd be a change for him and good for the island's people.

But less than a week after getting there, he lost his enthusiasm and not because of the work required. He was used to hard work and shitty quarters. The island's indigenous aid workers, recipients of the donations Leo arrived with, welcomed him. They saw in Leo a toughness that the other Americans, mostly high school kids looking for an experience to put on their college applications, didn't have. So Leo did what he could. But he quickly realized that the island's local leaders were as criminal as they were cruel. Canned food and clothing were readily accepted, but nearly all of the donated money disappeared. The politicians spent it on their whores who spent it on clothes they had nowhere to wear.

Leo stayed on the island, taking odd jobs, but mostly working as a guide to the tourists who came to the resorts like La Cachette. He volunteered three afternoons a week teaching reading in a local school. The kids liked him and the teachers, Carmelite nuns, were grateful for any time Leo could rescue them from the classroom.

And now, as a final mockery of Leo's good intentions, these two men in the van who'd been ordered to kill him wore the same imperfect shoes he'd brought to the island for them in the first place.

The two cops spoke in a deeply accented patois that Leo had trouble following. His head wound didn't help. But he could make out that the younger cop, who had a daughter in a class Leo taught, questioned why they had to kill him. Because their boss told them to, the other one answered. But the younger cop protested; the American had done nothing wrong. The older cop told his partner to shut up and again quoted their boss, a local police chief, who warned them more about tying up loose ends than about breaking the law.

That's what Leo was: a loose end to be tied up. But maybe he could say something to the young cop about his daughter and remind him why he came here in the first place. He could restate his good intentions, beg for their sympathy and promise both cops that he'd say nothing about what they'd done or what he'd seen. He'd give them money, American money, a lot of it by their standards. But they'd probably already taken any cash he'd had in his pockets and finally Leo decided it was better that the policemen, distracted like all subordinates by smoking and endless complaining, thought he was still unconscious while he planned what to do next.

The van went over a huge bump in the road, causing Leo to fly and linger momentarily in the air like the coyote in a roadrunner cartoon. The young policeman fell off his perch and swore. His partner laughed at him.

4

Two days before Leo met Taylor Hoffman because of the housekeeper's mistake, Dr. Janice Heller, a forty-three-year-old psychiatrist from Santa Barbara, arrived at La Cachette. Her plan was to get far away from her husband, an investment banker, who'd been arrested for something that involved a student at the public high school where Janice volunteered as a counselor.

Her first evening there, as she drank a Mai Tai at the poolside bar wondering if coming to Martinique was a good idea, a young man took the seat next to her.

The man, not much more than a boy really, introduced himself to her as Leo Malone and, being told that she'd never been to the island before, he asked if she'd like someone to show her and her husband around. Janice shook her head. She was here alone. Leo expressed surprise at that news.

The bartender, a local, interrupted to tell Janice that Leo had been showing La Cachette's guests around the island for several years and that he spoke the language and knew the islands as well as anyone did, especially the places to stay away from. "This man the best, madam," the bartender said. "Everybody, they say so."

"You like the book?" Janet asked Leo who was holding a dog-eared copy of S.E. Hinton's *The Outsiders,* a book she sometimes gave her younger patients to read.

He didn't say whether he did or didn't like it. All he said was, "She started writing it when she was only fifteen years old." Then he added, "The S.E. stands for Susan Eloise."

Janice pointed to the paperback. "You don't expect a girl called Eloise to write a book like that, do you? You'd expect her to be at a place like this."

Leo nodded. "Not Oklahoma."

This young man was pleasant enough to look at. He wasn't gigolo-good-looking, but he was fit without being muscular and unlike most men who prey on women, he didn't speak much. Words were not his weapon, if he even had a weapon. He didn't laugh easily and his smile was forced. When it appeared, it was awkward, hesitant. As they spoke about Hinton's book and the characters in it, he displayed a weary suspicion more normal in a man two or three times his age. Janice wondered if the resort's guests, women especially, chose him as a guide for that reason, out of sympathy more than intrigue.

No doubt Leo was smart, even literate, and she agreed to let him take her the next evening to one of the smaller islands where the migratory sea turtles laid their eggs after dark. She'd later wonder if she hired him only because the psychiatrist in her was intrigued. Or was it because she was alone for the first time in twenty years and wanted to do something new, something her husband wouldn't expect her to do.

"Just so you know," Janice said as she shook Leo's hand, "this isn't about sex."

Leo appeared insulted by what she'd said. "That's not what I do," he said. Janice apologized and blamed it on the drinks she'd had. She was relieved that the idea of sex was put out of the way so easily. Still, if she were honest, she'd admit being disappointed that the young man had agreed to her request so quickly.

Leo preferred it that way. Most of the women he escorted were excited by the possibility of sex, not sex itself. For them it was like being strapped into an amusement park ride, one that makes you afraid of falling off, but you won't and you know all along that you won't. Still, you scream. And people like to scream.

Some of the women he got paid to escort thought Leo was gay. He said nothing to correct them. He'd worked for husbands and wives, too, but never for a man alone. An older gentleman on his own once offered to hire him, but Leo turned him down. The man understood. Groups of women who came down for "girls' weekends" were his most frequent employers. They teased one another about seducing the young man, but never did. Or even tried.

The resort's rooms were all large suites and Leo charged the women less for his guide services if they let him sleep on the pull-out sofa in their living rooms. Eventually many let him sleep in their suites for free. It played into their maternal instincts and they were happy to think they were taking care of the distant, but polite, young man.

But that first night Janice Heller agreed to hire him, Leo walked back to his apartment in the village.

The next evening Janice met Leo at the dock and he paddled her in a kayak to one of the smaller islands where the migratory turtles laid their eggs. On the way there, they talked more about their favorite books. They both liked Flannery O'Connor.

"A sickly, Catholic woman in the deep south," Leo said. "There's an outsider."

"You know something about outsiders, don't you?"

Leo shrugged. "Some."

Listening to what Leo said or, more telling, what he didn't say, Janice couldn't help diagnosing him. She'd worked at a half-way house in Los Angeles for juvenile defendants. No one called them "delinquents" anymore, but like many of the young men she'd counseled, Leo exhibited symptoms of "emotional detachment" or "depersonalization disorder", a lack of trust in—and in some cases a pathological fear of—emotional contact with others. Leo kept his distance from Janice, like those boys did. When she asked him about his family, Leo's answers were polite, but brief and without detail. He looked at her the way a dog might, reading her face and body for clues more than listening to, or trusting, anything she said.

On the small island, they watched the huge, leathery sea turtles bury their eggs in the sand and slowly waddle back to the water. Janice enjoyed it. Leo always liked seeing this, too. When they returned to the resort she asked Leo to have a drink with her in her room. The way she asked him, he knew it wasn't a come-on.

In her suite, Leo asked Janice about her thirteen-year-old daughter that she'd mentioned several times. She showed him a photo of her.

"She's beautiful," Leo said even though the girl wasn't, not especially.

"Oh, please, let her be anything but beautiful," Janice said. "She'll spend the first twenty-five years of her life lording it over everyone else for something she had nothing to do with and the next thirty years desperately trying to hang onto it." Then she said something few had before. "I don't want to talk about me, Leo. I want to talk about you."

Leo grinned warily.

"People don't ask you about yourself, do they?" she said.

Leo shook his head.

"And when they do, you never answer them, do you?"

She was right. Leo had a look that kept others at a distance, a look he'd perfected as far back as he could remember. The few times he told people anything about his life it was because he was obliged to—things like job interviews—but even then he made up most of what he said. When he did that he mimicked how characters in movies he'd seen had talked. He could almost hear a film's score playing behind him.

But it didn't matter because, like people everywhere, the guests at La Cachette preferred to talk about themselves. But every so often they'd ask Leo a question about his life, hoping he'd tell them a story they could bring home like the photo of a fish they'd caught. He was, after all, a part of their holiday. So to amuse these people he told them lies ranging from one about his parents having been rodeo clowns to another about being raised in a California religious cult. He got the details from books he'd read and usually the more interesting the lies he told, the larger his tips would be. To the guests, Leo's stories were the same as foreign money, useful for a moment, but worthless and forgotten like the coins they'd eventually stick unused in a dresser drawer.

Janice Heller was different. She didn't give up. "I dare you to tell me about yourself," she said.

This surprised Leo. The woman was a psychiatrist. Was this how she got her young patients to open up to her? Play a game of truth or dare with them? Why would she even have to? No one vomits themselves so willingly into a room like a teenager does.

Normally, Leo would have done what he always did and lied to her. So why on this night did he break his own rule and tell her the truth? Maybe shrinks like her had a secret trick for getting people to open up like the mentalist at a carnival does. The alcohol they'd both had didn't hurt, either. And maybe if he broke down and told her parts of his past, she'd give him a larger tip.

Whatever his reason, Leo told Janice Heller the truth about his parents being killed in a gas station robbery in Oklahoma when he was three years old. He'd watched them both die.

Janice's reaction was immediate. "My God," she said. "That's not even psychological. It's neurological. People will try to convince you that you can talk your way out of that. But they're wrong. Something like that is printed in your brain." Janice put down her drink. "I'm sorry," she said. "I've had too much to drink. I never should have said that."

Anyone else might have been offended and told her nothing more about themselves, but Janice's blunt reaction was different from that of any caseworker Leo had been forced to speak to. Instead of being put off by her reaction, Leo liked it. It meant she wasn't going to empathize with him. She wasn't going to hold his hand and wish that bad things had never happened to him. So Leo said, "I don't remember much about them."

But he said he did remember his mother's smile, her unexpected laugh and her warm breath on his neck. A local beauty queen, Carlotta Jane Diminski was as gorgeous as her husband Bobby

Licklighter was handsome. She'd just turned nineteen when she was killed. Bobby was twenty-one.

He told Janice how, after their deaths, he was taken in by his mother's older sister Iris, her abusive husband Jack and their three children in Oklahoma. Leo's cousins hated him being there and they showed it in the cruelest ways they could.

Iris had never liked the more beautiful Carly and she hated the publicity that followed the three-year-old survivor of a notorious crime. But what would people say if she didn't take Leo in? She was a Christian and the boy was family. One afternoon, Iris watched a video she'd found. Leo watched, too. It was of Leo riding on his father's shoulders, the little boy wearing a red cowboy hat and grinning widely. Leo's beautiful mother snatches him off his father's back, plops the cowboy hat on her own head and peppers Leo with kisses while singing The Doors' *Light My Fire.*

Iris mumbled, "Bitch," and shut the video off before it finished. Leo never saw it again. A Cotton Bowl game that the Sooners lost was taped over it. Leo lived there for two more years until Jack was arrested for selling meth the same week Iris gave birth to her second set of twins.

Both those events sent five-year-old Leo into the Oklahoma foster system that included six more families before he was sixteen. Most of those families only took him for the monthly check they got from the state. Those were the best. The ones who wanted to save him with their love were the worst. They hoped Leo, like a rescued shelter puppy, would make up for—or at least distract them from—their own shitty lives.

"I wasn't difficult or violent like a lot of kids who got shuffled around the system," Leo told Janice. And he wasn't. He'd learned from his first day that the smartest choice was not to rock the boat. Be quiet. Shut up. If you're lucky, no one will bother you. They won't even see you. Most of his foster siblings, desperate for attention, broke every rule they could. But why fight city hall? You can't win. And if you're silent, you're safe. A hunter will tell you it's the wounded animal's squeals that attract the predator.

"So why'd you end up in so many homes?" Janice asked.

His caseworkers asked themselves the same thing. If only all their kids could keep out of trouble like this boy did. The words they used among themselves to describe Leo were "solitary" and "dark". But when they'd try to convince a family to take him, they called him "independent".

The families Leo was placed with saw him differently. Far from placating them with his silence, Leo confused them. Anger these people knew. Rage they were comfortable with. Silence not so much. And when a child like Leo refused the love of an eager Evangelical mother it was worse. It couldn't be her fault. Christ wouldn't let it be. Something had to be wrong with the child. Consider how his parents died.

So his foster parents, their own children and the other foster kids imagined the crimes this boy with his dark history was hatching in his silent stare. They told the caseworkers how much the surprisingly pretty boy frightened them. But Leo scored a zero on the PCLR test for psychopathy, lower than most of his foster parents or their own children would have scored. There was nothing wrong with the boy. He simply had nothing to say. And as if proving that was still part of his makeup, Leo stopped speaking. He'd already told Janice too much. "I'm tired," he said.

Janice wasn't surprised. All she said was, "Thank you, Leo. I know that wasn't easy for you." She didn't take his hand or hug him like someone else might have done and he was relieved when she didn't.

Because she was leaving La Cachette early the next morning and knew that Leo would swim at dawn, she offered the pullout sofa in her suite's main room for him to sleep on. He thanked her for her generosity.

Janice went into her bedroom and closed the door. It didn't bother Leo when he heard her lock it.

5

Janice had already checked out by the time Leo got back from his swim and he asked the housekeeper to give him what Dr. Heller left for him. That's what led to the argument with the concierge and, finally, to Leo meeting Taylor Hoffman.

Once Leo got his things back from Taylor and agreed with him that they looked alike, he left La Cachette and walked the dirt road to his small apartment in Saint-Esprit. Five minutes later, he heard a golf cart puttering behind him. Taylor was at the wheel.

"Where you going, bro?" Taylor asked as he drove alongside Leo who kept walking.

"Home."

"You wanna stay with me?"

"No."

"You don't talk much, do you?" Taylor asked and, as if to prove him right, Leo didn't answer.

"Wait," Taylor said, "it's not like that, bro. I'm not a faggot or anything. My parents rented me this humungous suite and now the assholes aren't even gonna show. So what the fuck? I got all this room and you know the place, right? You can show me what's up."

Leo considered the offer. He didn't like this guy. But if he didn't take the offer he'd have to go back to the grimy apartment he shared with three men who worked the day fishing boats for tourists. The place was filthy and, worse, noisy. The tenants yelled at each other all day and night and, when they weren't fighting, they played loud music. Like most people, their greatest fear was the one thing Leo cherished: silence. On top of that, if he roomed with Hoffman it'd piss the concierge off. It'd be worth it for that alone.

"No strings?" Leo asked.

"Only thing you gotta do is help me spend my parents' money."

Leo returned to the resort with him.

Taylor Hoffman's suite made the others Leo had seen at La Cachette look like rooms in a highway motel. It had two large bedrooms, three bathrooms, a full kitchen, an exercise room full of equipment and closets bigger than the trailers the Chickasaw families lived in. There was an ocean view from each of its two balconies and the main room had not one but two big screen TVs in it. It didn't have a minibar; it had a real bar. It must have cost a fortune. To blow it off and let your kid stay in it by himself meant these people had real money.

Taylor took two beers out of the bar's refrigerator and he and Leo sat on the patio overlooking the sea. Leo asked him what his father did for work.

"My mother's Irma Stowell."

Leo recognized her name, but wasn't sure why. Taylor filled him in. Irma Stowell was the all-American girl-next-door model of the 1980s who'd had her fifteen minutes of fame depending on which rock star or movie star she was sleeping with. She was on the cover of every magazine and guest-starred in countless sitcoms and variety shows. When she got too old for the runways, she married her manager George Merton who was then accused of stealing from his other, less famous, clients. He'd married Irma so that technically he wasn't stealing from her.

George and Irma spent their honeymoon in rehab. When they came out, they created their own line of cosmetics. Irma Stowell Cosmetics was an instant success, starting out in classier shops like Bloomingdales and Saks. Then, following the great American scheme to make the middle class feel more privileged than they really are, Irma Stowell Cosmetics made its way into stores like Target and Walmart. The masses spent money they didn't have on products they didn't need. Leo remembered seeing Irma Stowell products in the bathrooms of his foster mothers, downtrodden women that nothing short of divine intervention would help make look or feel better. But Stowell Cosmetics was eventually pushed off the shelves by the same Chinese-made crap with another, younger, prettier star's face on the jar. Accusations of tax fraud, carcinogenic ingredients and other improprieties were leveled against the company. George Merton was convicted of tax evasion and spent three years in a federal prison in Danbury, Connecticut.

"What's your mother like?" Leo asked.

Taylor shrugged. "I never met her," he said.

George Merton had gotten his client Irma Stowell pregnant when she was too old to find modeling work, print or otherwise, and her reputation was waning. She couldn't make up her mind whether she wanted to keep the baby or not, and by the time she decided that she didn't, it was too late to do anything other than give birth to it. The child's adoption was arranged before he was born. Lawyers for the Hoffmans, a prominent New York family, met George and Irma's lawyers in a trailer in the New York hospital's parking lot. Irma was handed a certified check for $50,000 and the newborn boy was transferred to them like a pedigreed puppy.

"The family who adopted me was rich so who cared?" Taylor said. "They didn't really want a kid, either, so I spent all my time with the nannies. They weren't even the usual spics or Black bitches most New York kids get. At least they don't give a shit what the kids do. My nannies were Austrians. Fucking Nazis."

"You ever talk to your real parents when you were growing up?" Leo asked him.

"I didn't know who they were."

"How'd you find out Irma Stowell was your mother?"

"A few months ago they called me out of the blue. First time I ever spoke to them."

"What'd they say?"

"My mother was all weepy like in some TV movie. My father, he's the same loser all salesmen are, always trying to sell you something. Everything's so big and so special and so exciting. He was like, 'My son, my son.' Truth is, my mother's a legendary cunt. She hates kids. She even admitted it once. I saw this clip of her on

TV. She was selling some of her shit on QVC and they asked how she kept herself looking so young. She said the trick was not to have children. That caused a big uproar with conservatives so they boycotted her products and she had to apologize and say she was joking. But she wasn't. The bitch sold me."

Taylor said that the only reason his mother wanted to meet him now was because she was sick. "She's dying and wants to make it all good before she fades away. Relieve her guilt. So they set it up for us all to meet down here. The three of us, a family. Big hugs, make amends. Then the assholes cancel."

"Maybe she's too sick to come."

Taylor shrugged. "Whatever." He picked up an envelope from the table. "When I get here this morning I find an airplane ticket to LA waiting for me so that we can have the big reunion back there now."

"Are you going?"

"Wouldn't you? I want to watch them squirm. But first I want to spend some of their money here."

Leo pitied this man-child who spoke like a petulant boy. He and Taylor had things in common, but Leo said nothing about his own experiences. And Taylor never asked him. Why would he? Taylor was the one onstage here. The audience was expected to keep quiet.

"As long as they're paying for this place," Taylor said, "I'm gonna enjoy it before I split. Come on, man, show me around. Earn your keep."

6

When Leo came to again, the van wasn't moving and the two cops weren't there with him. Aside from Taylor's body that still lay inches from him, the van was empty and its back doors were shut. It wasn't an official police van, so the doors had handles on the inside. The two policemen might be far enough away that if Leo managed to get the tape off his wrists and ankles he could open the doors and make a run for it. He'd die if he did nothing.

There was a piece of slivered metal ribbing on the van's back door. He shimmied to it and sat up against it. Hearing nothing from outside, he rubbed the duct tape on his wrists against the door's rusty ribbing. He slipped once and cut himself. Eventually, the tape started to fray. But even if he got himself free where would he go? The island was small. Everyone knew everyone else. The police planned to get rid of his and Taylor's bodies so no one would find them. Still, George Merton and Irma Stowell would demand to know what happened to their son, wouldn't they? And after a "thorough investigation" by the island's police—the same people who killed him—it would be determined that their son most likely drowned after having too much to drink, his body eaten by a shark or chopped up in the propellers of a luxury yacht. End of story.

No one would look for Leo. No one would even know he was missing and the police chief counted on that. So Leo had to free himself now. He finally sliced through the tape on his wrists. His hands now free, he tore at the tape around his ankles. He caught his breath. What now? His only hope to stay alive was to get off the island. If he stayed, he was as good as dead. He grabbed the van's door handle just as it was being opened from the outside. A bright flashlight blinded him and a sharp blow on the side of his head sent him back to unconsciousness.

7

Leo's first night in Taylor's suite, he took him to Piro's, a bar in a poorer section of the island where Taylor joined in a craps game. Run by Jean-Paul Monat, a sergeant in the island's police force and its de facto head in this neighborhood, the game was held nightly in the courtyard of the small bar. Like most men, Taylor considered himself a skilled gambler and like most men he was fooling himself. At first he won. At first tourists always won.

Sergeant Monat was chubby in both face and frame and he dressed stylishly to compensate for that. He was a thug who made his income from payola and payoffs. Tourists pulled over for a traffic violation or drinking in public happily paid the bribes that sent Jean-Paul and his men on their way, a small price to experience the corruption of a third world culture. It was part of the island's charm.

Taylor was up a couple of hundred dollars. "Come on, give me a five, that's all I'm asking for," he said and rolled the dice against the building's wall. A three and a two came up. "Yes!" he shouted and he kissed a pretty tourist girl on the mouth, causing her fat father in a loud shirt to pull his daughter behind himself.

"Now let's play for some real money," Taylor said. He peeled off three fifty dollar bills and dropped them on the ground.

"That's too much," Leo said.

"I'm on a streak, dude," Taylor said. He won again on the next roll and everyone cheered. The sergeant threw up his hands in mock surrender and pocketed the dice. "You are too good tonight, my friend," he said.

Leo looked at Jean-Paul and nodded his silent thanks. It was time to take Taylor home. But Taylor grabbed the sergeant's arm. "Don't be a pussy. You can't quit now."

Jean-Paul removed his arm from Taylor's grasp. "Have it your way, my friend," he said with a smile and handed the dice back to Taylor. Leo knew this was where the game would change. And it did. Taylor lost the next two rolls and, as Leo feared, he didn't take it well. The tourists peeled away. No one wants to watch a man lose his money. "This sucks, dude," Taylor said, his winnings now gone. On his next toss he rolled another loser and pointed to Jean-Paul. "You switched the dice," he said.

Jean-Paul was perplexed. "*Je ne comprends pa, mon ami.*"

"Don't spout your fucking French," Taylor said, "I know when I'm being cheated."

The sergeant's men tensed. One pulled his shirt open to expose a large pistol stuck in his belt. The sergeant held up his hand and smiled. The few remaining tourists left.

Jean-Paul smiled again. "This is a friendly game, Mr. Taylor. That is how it goes: sometimes you win, sometimes you lose."

"You mean you win, I lose."

Leo made eye contact with the sergeant and grabbed Taylor's arm. "Let's go."

Taylor yanked his arm away from Leo and walked away. As he did, he turned and shouted at Jean-Paul, "You're gonna be sorry, dude."

"Relax," Leo said and Taylor seemed to do that, until passing a vendor's cart filled with fruit, he grabbed a peeled mango, spun, and tossed it at Jean-Paul. It was a surprisingly good, hard throw. The sergeant turned away, but the fruit hit him squarely in the back, its juice dripping like yellow fingers down his pale linen shirt. Jean-Paul swore and two of his men took off after Taylor, but he was already running down the street. They wouldn't catch him. Leo stayed behind.

"*Assez*," Jean-Paul called to his men and they came back with Leo.

Leo told Jean-Paul about Taylor's mother being sick and how they didn't show up as planned. Jean-Paul took off his stained shirt, exposing his round belly. "My mother made this shirt for me," he said.

"He'll buy you a new one," Leo said.

"A new mother?"

"A new shirt. He'll buy you three of them."

Jean-Paul tossed the shirt to one of his men. "Do not bring him here again, Leo. I see his face, I mess it up."

Several days later as he lay tied up in the van, Leo would regret not letting Jean-Paul rough Taylor up that first night. If they'd caught Taylor and scared him, things might have turned out differently.

But Leo did calm Jean-Paul down that first night and he walked back to the hotel where he planned to persuade Taylor to give the sergeant money for a new shirt. Hoffman was too much trouble. Leo would leave him in his suite at La Cachette and go back to his apartment in town.

Leo found Taylor at the resort's beachfront bar sharing a pitcher of margaritas with three young ladies. Penny and her older sister Julie had come to La Cachette from Los Angeles to celebrate Penny's engagement. Rich kids from Beverly Hills, you could see what they were going to be like in twenty years and no one, especially them, would be happy about it.

Leo had noticed the third girl the day before. She was small, almost waifish in size and very pretty. She was Asian, but maybe not entirely. Was she Korean? Vietnamese? Her brown hair was short like a crew cut that had grown out. It was far too short for most women, but her head was beautifully shaped and her face so perfectly balanced that she didn't need longer hair to compensate for anything. When he saw her at the table where they all sat, Leo told himself to keep walking. But he didn't. He approached the table and Taylor introduced her to Leo as Ki Scott.

"Oh my God, he does look like you," Penny said when she saw Leo.

"Didn't I tell you?" Taylor said.

"You're like twins," Julie said. "You should go cut your beard off. Right now."

But Ki shook her head. "I can tell the difference."

"Thanks," Leo said. She smiled at him with a grin that was slightly off-kilter.

Taylor poured Leo a drink from the pitcher. "Sit down, bro. We're celebrating Penny's upcoming nuptials."

Leo took a seat at the table and toasted her. "Congratulations."

Penny said Leo didn't sound too happy about it. "What's the matter?" Julie asked him. "Don't you like marriage?"

"In theory," Leo said and Ki laughed. Was what he'd said funny? He didn't mean it to be. But it gave him a chance to look at Ki again. He hoped she'd speak more so that he could look at her without seeming to stare.

But Penny did all the talking. She was going to marry a lawyer at the Beverly Hills Hotel and they were going to live in a house in Brentwood in which she was going to raise their five kids. Meanwhile, Taylor was hitting on Julie who was more receptive than usual because she was pissed off that her younger sister was going to get married before she did. Leo had seen how a sister's wedding, especially a younger one, could throw a family into chaos.

Julie asked Leo if Taylor had really thrown a mango at the cop.

"He did," Leo said, "and if he doesn't apologize and buy him a new shirt then I suggest he doesn't leave the hotel grounds."

"Why's that?"

"Because that's how it works in a place like this," Ki said. "The cop's the boss here." She was more worldly than the other two girls.

"I hate authority," Taylor said.

Leo grinned. How many times had he heard the men and boys in his foster homes say that? I hate authority. It was like a mantra or a grace at the dinner table that men felt obliged to say: "In the name of the Father, the Son and the Holy Spirit, I hate authority." Any sign of authority—it could be a cop sitting roadside in his cruiser or even something as simple as a sign that asked you not to smoke or feed the ducks—infuriated these men. But none of them were smart enough to realize their small lives were owned by what they hated.

Taylor bragged. "The fat asshole was cheating me. So what do I have to apologize for?" He ordered another pitcher of margaritas.

Ki said she'd already had too much to drink. She asked Leo where a good place to walk at night was. He offered to take her there.

She carried her wide-brimmed hat on the dark, quiet beach, a hat that Leo would remember three days later as being the same color as the burlap bag that covered Taylor Hoffman's face in the van.

Her skin was fragile, almost paper-like, unlike the skin of the many resort guests who lay for hours in the sun like sweaters drying. Who was it, Leo wondered, that convinced white women they look more beautiful when their skin is the color of a hot dog?

Ki said she didn't like Leo's friend.

"Taylor's not my friend," Leo said and he explained how they became roommates. He left out the part about Janice Heller from Santa Barbara. "Your friends aren't exactly riveting either," he said.

Ki laughed. "They're not, are they? But they're paying for my trip. Or their parents are anyway."

"You're not rich?"

"Me? My father was from Scotland. He died when I was in high school. Daddy was the American Dream. He turned one dry cleaning store in Culver City into a small chain of them. He never made much money, but it wouldn't have mattered if he did because he could never have enjoyed it the way rich people do. My mother, she's frugal in the way only Koreans can be. She got remarried and moved with the guy to New York. But my grandmother's still in LA. She lives in a nursing home."

Ki had grown up middle class and, apart from her father's death, her childhood was uneventful. "Are you gonna go back to LA and marry a lawyer, too?" Leo asked her.

"I am a lawyer," she said.

This surprised Leo. The only lawyers he'd known were the small town crooks his foster families hired to get themselves bail or to sue someone. Then there were the lawyers, both men and women, who came to La Cachette, parodies of the self-important characters on TV shows. Ki wasn't like either kind.

"What kind of law do you do?" Leo asked her.

"Copyright. It's big now with the Internet and all the digital stuff," she said. "Not to mention a generation of kids who think that they should be able to download whatever they want for free."

"Are you married?" Leo asked her.

She shook her head. "You're not, either, are you?"

Leo said he wasn't. When she asked where he grew up, Leo told her. "Oklahoma," he said. He surprised himself, more than her, by telling Ki right away that his mother and father had been killed during a robbery when he was a boy and that he was raised in foster homes. She asked him if that was difficult. He said sometimes it was.

"Did you hate your foster parents?"

If, as one psychologist wrote, Leo had a limited ability to feel attachment to people, then the good side of that was that he was less likely to feel hatred or bitterness either. He wasn't angry at the people who took him in. His foster families had no control over who they were. They were as helpless as he was, miscast in roles they tried their best to play. But all he said to Ki was, "I learned to disappear."

"Is that why you're so quiet?"

"Maybe."

Ki was jet lagged and needed to sleep.

Leo told her that he swam in the ocean each morning and she asked if he'd like some company. They agreed to meet on the beach. After she left, Leo decided he'd stay in Taylor's suite instead of walking back to his apartment.

8

The morning beach was deserted. The water was calm. When Leo got there, Ki was watching the long-legged birds being comically chased by the waves as they picked for food in the soggy sand. She greeted Leo with a friendly kiss on his cheek.

Leo and Ki agreed they'd swim to one of the nearby, smaller islands, the same one he took Janice Heller to. They could have breakfast at the café there that a friend of Leo's owned.

Ki was a good swimmer, but she wasn't in Leo's class. He would speed ahead of her and then circle back to join her. When they finally reached the tiny island, she lay down on the beach, spent. Leo, barely out of breath, sat next to her.

"Show off," Ki said. "Where'd you learn to swim like that?"

"When I was living with my sixth foster family," Leo said. He told Ki how Dan Prescott owned a Ford dealership outside of Tulsa so he didn't need the money they'd get for taking Leo in. What Dan Prescott needed instead was a boy in his home to compensate for his wife and their three daughters. Bringing a boy into a house with three girls close to the boy's age would normally not be allowed. But Loretta Prescott's sister was married to a state senator and Loretta, being a Christian, was happy to help those less fortunate than herself, especially a boy who'd finally shut her goddamned husband up. When Dan Prescott first saw Leo he was disappointed that the boy wasn't any bigger. How did a kid Leo's size survive in the system? He must be tough.

Prescott Ford was a sponsor of the Maywood Christian Academy football team, the Crusaders, and Dan Prescott wasted no time taking Leo to meet with the football coach and his assistants to figure out what position his foster son could play. Leo wouldn't be a lineman or a running back; he wasn't big enough. But he could be a wide receiver or, if worse came to worst, a punt returner. God forbid he'd be a place kicker. He'd rather the kid played baseball with the Mexicans.

The athletic director shook Leo's hand and asked the boy if he had any preferences when it came to sports.

Leo waited for a moment before he said, "I don't like to be touched."

"I guess that rules out football," the athletic director said and everyone in the room except Dan Prescott burst out laughing. No one had ever heard a boy, especially one from Oklahoma, say anything like that and Leo's answer became a running joke. His foster sisters teased him mercilessly and the salesmen at Dan's dealership used the phrase "I don't like to be touched" to mock one another. Dan Prescott laughed with them because he had no choice.

Any hopes he had for the boy disappeared when Leo joined the swimming club. The coach, Joan Halbert, a middle-aged woman with huge shoulders and paw-like hands, heard what Leo had said about being touched. This was a boy she could understand.

Leo took to the water immediately. He found a refuge in it, a silent world where he could be alone. In the water no one speaks. No one asks questions. Swimming became a meditation that Leo practiced every day. He quickly got better and joined the swim team because it was the only way he could use the pool at any hour day or night. Coach Halbert impressed upon Leo that it was when a swimmer's body was out of the water, skimming over the top of it, that it picked up speed. Even so, Leo preferred to be in the water, submersed in it, a world far away from his many homes and the people who lived in them.

Leo attended all the team's medal ceremonies and went to the parties, but never befriended his teammates. He was the reason they won, so they never bullied him. Like everyone else, they left him alone. Even though Leo and his team won dozens of ribbons and prizes, Loretta Prescott never convinced her husband to come to a single meet with her. Dan Prescott thought swimming was a sissy sport. He and his daughters called Leo "the mermaid".

"The coach, she wanted me to go to a swimming academy in Colorado," Leo told Ki. "So I could train for the Olympics. She was even gonna pay for it herself, but I got sent to another family."

"How come?"

Leo hesitated. Had he told her too much already?

"Tell me," Ki said.

Leo did. "I went into the bathroom one night when Sally, the oldest girl, and the plainest, was there. I knocked on the door a bunch of times and when no one answered I walked in. Sally was naked. The policewoman asked Sally why she didn't say anything when I knocked and she said she was in the shower and couldn't hear me. But she was lying."

"How do you know?"

"Because she was dry. She told them that instead of leaving right away I stood there and stared at her."

"Did you?"

"I was thirteen. She was sixteen. She just stood there. She wasn't even holding a towel or anything. She dared me to look at her. Then she screamed and ran out before I could leave. I told that to the caseworkers."

"That was your mistake: admitting that you looked at her," Ki said, sounding for the first time like a lawyer.

The Prescotts didn't say anything about it publicly. It would have been bad for the dealership and Dan wanted to be rid of Leo anyway. Sally gave them the chance they needed. Best of all, they could blame what happened on Leo. He went back into the system.

"Everything worked out okay," Leo said. "I learned how to swim and the next family I went to was the best and the last."

"Who were they?"

"He was a literature professor at the university in Norman. Albert Malone. His wife, Marianne, was an ex-actress. She'd been on Broadway a long time before. They were already like fifty years old," Leo said. "They had money, too, so that didn't figure into why they took me. Marianne took a liking to me. She taught me things."

"Like what?"

"Like how to dress and how to eat. How to speak correctly. And what kind of books to read. Their house was like a library. I read everything I could. Marianne taught me how to dance, too, because she said a gentleman has to know how to dance."

He didn't tell Ki that for the longest time Leo and Marianne practiced dancing without touching one another because touching people frightened him. Marianne understood. She'd been told by the caseworker that Leo was molested by the mother of the fourth family he was placed with. So they started their dancing lessons without touching one another. She gave Leo time. And eventually, while teaching him a simple box step, he let her hold him, but only by his hands. "You could put a Bible in between us," Marianne joked. Even Leo smiled.

"Let's see you dance then," Ki said, standing up.

Leo got up, too, took her in his arms and did a simple waltz step on the sand. Ki moved in closely to him. Leo didn't move away from her.

"You are good," Ki said.

"Marianne said the trick to dancing is to look like you're sure of where you're going."

"Are you?" Ki asked him. "Sure of where you're going?"

Leo shrugged. "For my eighteenth birthday, the Malones officially adopted me. That's how I got their name."

Ki told him that when Leo talked about the Malones his whole body relaxed. "How often do you see them?" she asked, still dancing with him on the sand.

"They died in a car wreck when I was in college."

Ki stopped dancing. "I'm sorry," she said and pulled away. Leo noticed that she was the one who let go of him, not the other way around.

They kayaked back to the main island. As he paddled, Leo thought how strange it was that in the same week two different women had asked him about himself. Even stranger was that he told them. Maybe Janice Heller was wrong. Maybe he could change.

It was dark by the time Leo and Ki got back to the resort. Leo walked Ki to her room and when she said goodnight to him at the door he put his hands on her shoulders and turned her to himself. At first she seemed ready for his kiss. But she turned away.

"Good night," she said. She went into her room and closed the door.

9

The van was moving again. When Leo regained consciousness he saw that the two policemen had re-taped his arms and legs, this time more tightly, making his chance to escape even less likely than before. There was tape over his mouth, too.

Leo thought about Ki and how he lay that night on his bed in Taylor's suite, regretting that he'd tried to kiss her. He should never have told her the story about Sally Prescott in the bathroom. Ki had done the smart thing by refusing to kiss him. Had she seen in him that afternoon the same thing Janice Heller and all his case-workers had?

He heard a knock on his bedroom door. Taylor was drunk again and confused about which door was which. Leo got out of bed and opened it.

It was Ki. She kissed him hard on the mouth, pushed him back into the room and shut the door behind her.

10

Leo and Ki spent the next two days together. They swam and kay-aked. They watched the turtles lay their eggs. They ate at cafés where the chefs made special dishes for them. He took her to Sister Helena's English class. The children had never seen anyone who looked like Ki. The girls rubbed her crew-cutted head and giggled.

Lying on the bed after sex, Leo would watch Ki in the bath-room. He liked that she didn't apologize for her boyish body or small breasts like other girls might. He also liked her slight over-bite and the goofy way she laughed.

He'd always had natural sexual urges, even if he had none of the emotions that are expected, and usually demanded, to go along with them. So he slept with young women who'd come to the island on holiday. He'd meet them at a club or on the beach. They were perfect partners for him. He treated them well, but he didn't need to lie about his feelings for them like other men did because all these girls wanted was a fling on their short vacation and nothing more.

But Ki was different. Should he follow her back to Los Angeles? Or would it be better if their relationship ended here? She had a job in LA. She probably had a boyfriend. She was beautiful; how could she not? Was the time she spent with Leo a fling?

She sat on the edge of the bed painting her toenails a crazy shade of orange that he'd bought for her in the lobby gift shop. Leo leafed through a Bible he'd found in a bedside table drawer.

"Good story?" Ki asked when she saw the Bible in his hand.

"I studied divinity," Leo said.

Surprised, Ki looked up from her nails. "What made you do that?"

Most of Leo's foster families took him to church on Sundays. He liked the silence there. In church no one yelled at him; no one hit or threatened him. Divinity college was the same. When people argued, it was about ideas, not about who slept with the cashier at Walmart or which kid stole drug money from their mother's underwear drawer. If he couldn't be in the water, then divinity college was the next best place to be. "It was quiet," Leo said.

"So does that mean you believe in God?"

Leo didn't know if he did or not. He liked to pray, not to the furious Old Testament God but to whatever power there might be. Humanity couldn't be the top of the pyramid. He liked what the Buddhists said. He liked what Pascal said, too. Why not believe in God? It's a comfort to think there's a God and, if there isn't, then it won't matter anyway, will it? Either way, it wasn't a subject that came up on the island. People who came to La Cachette didn't need faith. They were rich. They had money. Their god was stuff.

Ki finished painting her toenails and waved them in the air to dry. "Every woman you meet wants to save you, don't they?" she said.

"From what?"

"From yourself."

Ki's bedside phone rang before he could say anything. It was the concierge who told her it was important that he speak to Leo. She handed Leo the phone and the concierge said that he'd just gotten a call from Sergeant Jean-Paul. Taylor was in trouble.

"Where is he?" Leo asked.

"Piro's."

Taylor had gone back to Jean-Paul's craps game. The concierge was afraid that if something happened to the boy his parents would blame the resort and, by extension, him. He said, "I know we do not see eye to eye, Mr. Malone. But I need your help with this."

Leo hung up and sat up on the edge of the bed. The last thing he wanted to do was go save Taylor Hoffman but, if he did, the concierge would owe him. Big time.

Ki touched Leo's back. "What's happening?"

Leo stood up and put on his jeans. "It's Taylor." He finished dressing. "Wait for me," he said. He kissed her and left.

When Leo got to Piro's the place was closed and he was taken to the back room where Taylor sat on the stone floor, gagged and surrounded by three policemen. Jean-Paul greeted Leo as if nothing were out of the ordinary. "Mr. Hoffman has graced us with his presence," he said.

"What do you want?" Leo asked the sergeant.

"I politely asked the gentleman to repay me for my shirt."

"How much?"

"Twenty-five hundred dollars."

Taylor yelled something into his gag when Jean-Paul said this. A short policeman kicked Taylor in the ribs, silencing him.

"That sounds fair," Leo said and Taylor protested again by stamping his feet. "But we have to get back to the hotel so we can get you the money."

"What if we never see you again?" Jean-Paul said.

Leo grinned. "Where am I gonna go, Sergeant?"

"Good point."

Leo had just made himself collateral for Taylor's debt. The sergeant pointed to Taylor. "Untie him."

Jean-Paul's men untied Taylor's feet and hands, leaving the gag in until last. But once it was out of his mouth, Taylor said, "I'm not paying you a cent, dude!"

"Shut up," Leo said and grabbed Taylor by the arm and pulled him toward the door.

"Don't let me see him again," Jean-Paul said as he turned away.

"Your momma dresses you like a homo," Taylor said.

Jean-Paul spun around. "Be careful what you say, rich boy."

"What are you gonna do about it, you fat fuck?" Taylor shouted and grabbed a long gaffing hook leaning against the wall. He swung it wildly in the direction of Jean-Paul.

What happened next, happened fast. One of Jean-Paul's crew grabbed Taylor's shoulder, but Taylor swung the hook and cut the man's arm. Another policeman grabbed the gaffing hook and yanked it from Taylor's hand. It clattered to the floor.

Taylor dared Jean-Paul. "Come get me, asshole." But a third man grabbed Taylor and held him from behind. Jean-Paul approached Taylor with a knife in his hand.

"Jean-Paul, don't," Leo said.

The next thing Leo felt was a blow to the back of his head that sent him to the floor. Everything that followed happened in slow motion as he saw Taylor struggle with the men. Groggy, Leo said "no" over and over. But it was too late. He watched as Jean-Paul, with a single, swift motion, dragged his knife across Taylor's throat that turned dark red.

Taylor fell to the ground and looked almost amused when he saw his own blood spreading quickly on the stone floor.

Leo was hit a second time on the back of his head and he passed out.

11

Leo thought it was the van moving again that caused the swaying motion he felt. But then he heard waves and when he opened his eyes he could see stars in the night sky above. He was in a small wooden boat and the stench of the countless fish that had been gutted in it was overpowering.

Taylor's body lay next to Leo's in the boat. The burlap sack still covered Taylor's head and weighted chains were wrapped around his legs. Leo could make out the voices of Jean-Paul and the two cops from the van. One piloted the boat's outboard motor.

The tape used to bind Leo's arms and legs in the van had been removed, but he stayed motionless as if he were still unconscious. Why had they untaped him? Were they going to let him go? If that were true, then why was he still here in the boat next to Taylor's body? Should he speak up now and plead for his life? But killing Leo was still the safest thing Jean-Paul could do. The Sergeant had already killed one man, so killing a witness would add nothing to his sentence in the unlikely event he was caught. And killing Leo would help make sure that Jean-Paul *wouldn't* be caught.

"*Ici*," Jean-Paul said. The two other men lifted Taylor's body and, with some effort, rolled it over the side of the boat. "*Au revoir*," one said laughing. The body made little sound as it entered the water. It sank right away and would be eaten, not dramatically by sharks or crocodiles, but more likely by the millions of other smaller fish and nondescript creatures that call the ocean floor home. Jean-Paul asked his men if Leo was conscious. One of them said he wasn't.

"Kill him."

This gave Leo only seconds to save himself. He saw that the clanking sound on the floor of the boat was made by the knife Jean-Paul had dropped while handing it to his man.

When the cop leaned over to pick the knife up, Leo kicked at him, knocking the man backwards so that he fell into both Jean-Paul and the other cop, causing the small boat to rock wildly. The three men swore at one another and cartoonishly tried to regain their balance. Leo dove into the water. Knowing they'd shoot at him, he swam straight down as far as he dared to go. He could hear the gunshots piercing the water.

Leo didn't head to the shore, but farther out to sea. He guessed that Jean-Paul would never think to look for his trail in the water in the direction away from the island. When he was finally forced to poke his head through the surface for air, Leo saw that he'd guessed right and that the three men were staring at the water between them and the shore. Jean-Paul aimed his pistol at every whitecap, planning to shoot Leo whenever he came up for air.

"Show me your face you piece of shit," Jean-Paul said. "I'll find you. I swear to God I will."

Leo dove again and kept swimming in the other direction out to sea. When he was far enough away from Jean-Paul's boat that he could barely make it out on the ocean's surface, he circled around and headed to the resort's beach on the other side of the island. It wouldn't be safe to land anywhere on the island other than on La Cachette's private waterfront.

It would be a long swim, even for him, and Leo prayed that he'd have the stamina to make it. His head throbbed where he'd been hit, but the cold ocean water helped lessen the pain. He needed fresh water, but there'd be none to drink until he made it to shore. He wouldn't be the first person to die of dehydration in the ocean. And if he didn't die in the water he might still die if Jean-Paul and his men were waiting for him when he got to La Cachette. If he got there.

Like he did when swimming long distances in competition, Leo thought of other, better things. His first thought was of Ki waiting for him in her hotel room. But knowing he would have to leave her saddened him.

Images from his past appeared to Leo. He remembered the last time he saw his mother in Oklahoma. The argument is sudden and loud and it ends only when gunshots are fired and Leo's mother drops him, her three-year-old son, onto the floor of the Shattuck, Oklahoma convenience store. Leo can see his mother through the metal legs of the cigarette machine as she lies on the checkered linoleum across from him, her cheek pressed to the filth that's slowly turning red from her blood. His father is on the floor, motionless behind her. Leo reaches his small hand to his mother, but her own hand doesn't move. He stares at her confused, hoping she'll blow him a kiss or sing the song she sings to him when he's scared. But this time her face is still, her eyes empty and her mouth silent. He hears voices and heavy feet shuffling on the gritty floor, causing an ant carrying a crumb in its tentacles to scurry away. The sirens grow louder and louder until he can hear nothing else. Someone reaches down and picks him up.

He remembered, too, his first meeting with Marianne Malone. Leo sits on a wooden chair in a small room and says nothing for at least five minutes. That whole time Marianne Malone silently returns his stare until she says, "You don't talk much, do you, Leo Licklighter?"

Leo shakes his head. "No, ma'am."

"You're a watcher, aren't you?"

"Yes, ma'am."

When she stands up, Leo figures that she's seen enough. Another prospective parent will be ushered in to stare at Leo like a head of livestock. But, instead, Marianne turns to the caseworker and says, "We'll take the boy home with us."

It took Leo more than three hours to reach the resort's private beach. He stumbled out of the water and collapsed onto the sand next to the deserted lifeguard tower. Jean-Paul and his men were nowhere in sight. Leo lay there sucking in air and gathering his strength. It was dark, but the sun would be up in a few hours. He debated what to do next.

Should he go to the authorities? But which authorities? And who would stand up for him if he did? The staff at La Cachette considered Leo a vagabond who preyed on their guests. The police would say he killed Taylor and they'd produce witnesses who'd support that. The nuns at the school would say nice things about Leo, but no one would listen to them.

Leo had grown up surrounded by criminals so he knew how a man like Jean-Paul Morat thought. The best thing for the sergeant would be if Leo simply disappeared. That meant he had to get off the island as soon as he could.

A plan came into his head. It was a long shot, but what other chance did he have?

Leo walked quickly through the resort's pool area. His clothes and hair were soaking wet and he wore no shoes. His head throbbed where he'd been hit. A dozen middle-aged women, all drunk, were laughing and dancing with each other to loud music. Several of them sat topless in the hot tub.

Leo tried to slip by them unnoticed, but a large woman in a brightly flowered muumuu grabbed him and locked her arms around him. "Look what I got me, girls!" she shrieked and the other women cheered her on. Leo managed a short dance with the woman and pulled away, but she grabbed him again. "Where you going, honey? I ain't even started yet," she said.

His head was pounding. "If my girl wasn't waiting for me upstairs," he said, "I'd stay and party with you all night, doll face." This was enough to satisfy the drunken woman.

"Catch and release," she yelled to her friends and let Leo go. The others shrieked. He walked to the hotel and the women forgot about him before he got there.

The lobby was quiet and the concierge, who normally would have been off duty at that hour, approached Leo anxiously. "Did you find Mr. Hoffman?"

"He was already gone when I got there," Leo said.

"*Merde*," the little man muttered. "At the end of the day it would be most unfortunate if anything untoward happened to him."

"Nothing will happen to him," Leo said. He could feel the concierge's eyes on him as he walked up the stairs.

In the suite, it took Leo no time to find what he needed to carry out his plan: Taylor's airplane ticket, his passport and money. There were several hundred dollars in the desk's drawer, but Leo only took half of it. He wasn't a thief.

He went into the bathroom and stared at himself in the mirror. There was a bruise on his cheekbone and blood from where he'd been hit on the back of his head, but it had stopped bleeding and his hair covered it.

He shaved off his beard and when he finished he looked at himself in the mirror and at the photo in Taylor's passport. He looked even more like Taylor without his beard. The passport was seven years old, so any slight differences between Leo's face and Taylor's photo could be attributed to aging.

No matter what Leo did now—stay or go—there was nothing anyone could do to bring Taylor Hoffman back to life. They'd never find his body or discover what had happened to him. The only crimes Leo would be committing by leaving like this were stealing a plane ticket and some cash and entering the United States under a false identity. Even with the increased security in place a couple of years after 9/11, he thought he could pull it off. Just get yourself into the US and then disappear, he told himself. Once he did that he'd be safe.

Leo stuffed Taylor's clothes into the small carry-on suitcase Taylor had brought to the island. He put on his leather jacket and put Taylor's passport in the pocket. He stuck his own passport into the lining of the jacket where he sometimes hid money. He grabbed Dr. Heller's note and put it in the lining, too. He left the suite and headed to the service stairs so he wouldn't be seen by the concierge or anyone else in the lobby. But as he approached the stairs, he heard Ki's voice.

"Did you find Taylor?" she said.

Leo turned to her. He'd hoped he wouldn't see her before he left, but here she was. "No," he said.

Ki stared at him.

"What?" Leo said. Did she suspect something?

"You shaved your beard."

"Right."

"Why?"

"I was tired of it."

"It makes you look just like Taylor. You could be doubles now." He was relieved when she said this and he hoped she was right. She pointed to the suitcase he was holding. "Where are you going?"

"I can't stay here with that jerk anymore."

"Then stay with me," she said.

"I will. Tomorrow. Right now I've gotta deal with some stuff at my place." He wanted to tell Ki everything that had happened, but he didn't. He couldn't. Anyone else would have blurted it out, but Leo's whole life had been about not telling people things. This was not the time to change that.

"When will I see you again?" she asked.

"I'll come and get you for a swim in the morning,"

"I'd like that."

"Me, too," he said. When they kissed, she put her hand behind his head and pulled him closer. He tensed because she touched him where he'd been hit and it hurt. "I'll see you in the morning," he said and left her there.

He took Taylor's bag to the parking lot behind the kitchens where the dumpsters were. He opened the suitcase and tossed the clothes into two of the dumpsters. He threw the bag into a third. Islanders would pick through the containers and take the clothes and the bag before the sun came up.

He went back into the hotel, down the service stairs and through the cramped and winding staff's quarters. The housekeeper he'd accused of stealing his things a few days earlier was doing laundry in one of the resort's huge, noisy machines. He walked quickly past her, saying nothing.

But she saw him anyway and smiled. "Good evening, Mr. Hoffman," she said.

12

Leo got to the island's small airport. He was relieved that he didn't know the woman behind the ticket counter. He handed her his ticket and she looked at it and then looked back at him.

"You've made a mistake," she said.

Leo froze.

"You're in the wrong line, Mr. Hoffman. This is a first class ticket."

"Right. I forgot," he said. "My parents bought it for me." He apologized to the agent for not calling ahead. "You can bump me down to coach if you need to."

"That won't be necessary, Mr. Hoffman," she said tapping into her computer. "We have several open first class seats."

"Great."

"Are you checking any baggage with us, sir?"

"I sent it," he said. That was what affluent travelers, like those at La Cachette, did. Why carry heavy bags and wait at a luggage carousel like ordinary people when you can pay FedEx to do that for you?

"How was your stay here, Mr. Hoffman?" the clerk asked as she finished the paperwork for his flight.

"It was great, thank you."

She looked more closely at his passport and said, "Oh."

"What?" Leo tensed again. Had she spotted something else that Leo had missed? Something that gave him away?

"You and I, we have the same birthday, Mr. Hoffman. We're both cancers."

Leo smiled. "I guess we are."

The woman handed Leo his boarding pass and his passport. "Have a good flight, Mr. Hoffman. Come back and see us soon."

Leo took his seat on the plane. Once it was airborne all he would have left to deal with was customs in Los Angeles. Still, he was nervous. He'd never done anything like this before. Breaking the law, something that came so naturally to his foster brothers and sisters and the families that took them in, was alien to him.

He reclined the large leather seat and ordered a brandy from the flight attendant. He was exhausted from the swim and everything else he'd gone through that night. From the lining of his jacket, he took out the note that Janice Heller had written to him on the resort's stationery. Distracted by his time with Ki, he'd forgotten about it. When he opened the envelope, Janice's business card fell out. On it was her name and phone number along with an address in Santa Barbara. He stuck the card back into his backpack and read what she'd written him in her note:

Dear Leo, please forgive me for rushing off like this. But the car to the airport is leaving and you're swimming. I'll put your passport, money and this letter in an envelope and give it to the maid.

I want to apologize again for what I said when you told me about how your parents died. I said that you'd never get over it. But I was wrong to say that. You've had a hard life and, as a frightened boy, you built a wall around yourself. But you can get over that wall. It will take work. But with the right person you can do it. You have to remember that not all families are like the ones we see in the movies or read about in books. None are perfect. Many, most in fact, are pieced together unexpectedly and awkwardly. Yours may end up being like that, too, created in a way that you'd never expect it to be. But in whatever way it's put together, I believe you can make a family for yourself that you feel secure in. In the end what else do we have but family?

Janice.

Leo's instinct was to answer the final question in her note asked by saying, "We have a lot of things other than families. Better things." What were families other than genetic accidents? Two of his foster mothers were regularly beaten by their husbands. One would sit at the dinner table opposite his wife, her face bruised and swollen. "Women are like dogs," he'd tell his kids while eating the meal that his battered wife had just cooked for them. "You can beat 'em all you like, but as long as you feed 'em they'll come back." The woman would look down at her plate and say nothing. That's what Leo knew about families.

Still, Leo also understood what Janice meant about the pull of family. He had brief memories of his mother and father before they died. And the Malones were good to him, too. But their unexpected deaths were like a punishment for believing in this myth. Still, how could anyone live in America and not feel the urge to find themselves a family? Everything pushed you in that direction. Movies, songs, books. Even commercials for cars, clothes and food relied on the notion of family to sell you their products. And everything said there was something wrong with you if you didn't go in that direction or at least try to.

He thought about Ki, too. He'd left her the same way he'd left others. Abruptly and with no explanation. This time there were reasons, but Ki would never know that. All she'd know was that he disappeared. But what if Taylor hadn't been killed and forced Leo to run like this? Would his feelings for Ki eventually have disappeared like they had with everyone else? Was he doomed to abandon anyone he felt that way about? Was this what Janice Heller meant when she'd said to him that first night, "You'll never get over it"?

He couldn't look for Ki when he got to Los Angeles. Everything and everyone connected to the island, the resort and Taylor, all of it, had to be left behind as if it never happened. Any connection to those things would tie him to Taylor's death. It'd be best for everyone, Ki especially, that he forget her. And she him. He'd done it before. He'd do it this time.

The flight attendant woke Leo with customs paperwork as the plane began its descent into Los Angeles. The danger of what he was doing hit him again. What if Jean-Paul had screwed up and Taylor's body had surfaced and been identified? Leo would be a prime suspect and what would make him look more guilty than stealing the dead man's plane ticket and passport and using them to sneak back to the States? But it was too late to turn back now.

Leo told himself that Jean-Paul was a professional. He'd make certain that Taylor's body was never found. And if Taylor Hoffman's parents tried to find their son no one would think about looking for him anywhere on Martinique because all records would indicate that he'd left the island, reentered the United States and disappeared. That would be typical behavior for Taylor, wouldn't it? Leo felt better. Once the plane landed in LA and he'd made it through customs he'd be free.

Leo walked towards the bank of customs officers at LAX. What was the best way for him to act? Should he don the international traveler's air of boredom as if this were just one more routine procedure he was forced to endure before getting back to his real life? Or would he rouse suspicions by looking too carefree?

The customs agent signaled him to come forward. Leo handed her Taylor's passport and he took off his dark glasses. She looked at him briefly and then back at the passport. Leo's appearance seemed to pose no problem for her.

The agent leafed through Taylor's passport with long, painted fingernails. She stopped at one page that was covered in stamps and looked over at another agent. From this simple move on her part, the senior agent, a short man with a potbelly and a mustache, came over and took Taylor's passport from her. He looked at the open page and then at Leo.

"Did you have any trouble in Thailand?" he asked.

Leo realized he'd made a mistake by not going through Taylor's passport and checking what countries he'd been to. What if the agent was suspicious of Leo and his question was a test because nothing in Taylor's passport indicated that he'd been to Thailand.

But Leo said, "No trouble at all, sir."

The man seemed satisfied with his answer and after what seemed like forever, the agent nodded and handed Taylor's passport back to Leo. "Welcome home, Mr. Hoffman."

Leo took Taylor's passport from him and said, "Thank you, sir."

His hands shook less as he walked to the doors leading from the gray customs area. To get to the street level you had to walk with your bags up a long ramp. Family and friends waited for the arriving passengers, hanging on the railing of the ramp. Leo's flight was a small one and there weren't many other flights that had landed at the same time. So only a few people were watching the arrivals. Some children sat under the rail, hoping to spot a parent or grandparent.

At the top of the ramp, Leo turned and headed for the doors to the bright street. He walked past half a dozen limo drivers in dark suits and ties who held up cardboard signs with passengers' names printed on them. A couple of the drivers called out the names of their passengers. Leo paid no attention to them. All he wanted was to get into a taxi and get as far away from the airport as fast as he could. He had enough money to find a hotel where he could stay for a day or two while he figured out where to go and what to do next. The terminal's automatic glass door slid open and he stepped toward it. But just before he got to it, someone grabbed him by the arm and spun him back around. It was one of the limo drivers.

"What?" Leo said too loud and too fast, giving away how anxious he was. It'd be so unfair to be stopped here, so close to his freedom.

"Mr. Hoffman?" the driver said. He was older than the other drivers and he held a cardboard sign with the name "Hoffman" written on it. That was the name the driver had been calling out. Hoffman. Leo hadn't reacted to it because it wasn't his name. "I'm here to pick you up, sir."

"You got the wrong guy," was all Leo could think to say as he turned and walked toward the opened glass doors.

"I don't think so," the driver said, following Leo. "At least your parents don't think so."

The driver pointed to a middle-aged couple walking quickly across the lobby toward them, dodging skycaps and passengers with luggage. From the expressions on the couple's faces, Leo could read nothing about their reaction to seeing him instead of Taylor standing there. If what Taylor had told him was true, then they'd never actually met their son face to face. He stood still, watching the dead man's parents coming closer. Why hadn't he considered this possibility? They'd arranged and paid for their son's trip to Los Angeles, hadn't they? And they wanted desperately to see him, so it made no sense that they'd allow him to arrive unmet at the airport. Leo's deadbeat foster parents, the ones who hated authority, would've foreseen this happening.

All Leo could hear above the airport commotion was his own heartbeat and the blood pounding in his head. He spotted two policemen looking in his direction. Did they know? Had customs or someone on the island figured out what had happened and alerted the police? What should he do? Run? Get into a taxi? Where would he go? Should he come up with a story? He could say that

Taylor gave him the ticket. Or he could tell Taylor's parents that it was all a practical joke on their son's part. That seemed believable from what he knew about Taylor. Or did it? But before Leo could decide what to do, Taylor's parents, George and Irma, were standing in front of him, scouring his face with uncertain eyes.

Irma Stowell took Leo's head in her two hands, tears running down her face. "Taylor, my darling, you're finally home," she said and kissed Leo on both cheeks.

PART TWO

Los Angeles

1

Leo is confused. The woman hugging him is Irma Stowell, Taylor Hoffman's mother. Doesn't she realize that Leo's not her son? Surely Taylor's father George Merton, the successful salesman, the ex-con standing next to her, will be less emotionally distracted and recognize that something's not right.

But no. Taylor's father pries his wife off of Leo, pushes her aside and hugs the young man tightly himself. "Welcome home, son," he says with more emotion than his wife just did, his eyes thickened with tears of their own.

Over George's shoulder, Leo makes eye contact with a policeman who watches this scene of a young man and his father hugging. The policeman looks away and disappears into the crowd.

"Let the boy breathe, George," Irma says. Her husband releases Leo from his tight grasp and steps back to stare at him.

"We wanted to surprise you," George says. "We had to pull all kinds of strings to get the passenger list from the airline. They guard those things like Fort Knox now. But you know your mother." George pauses awkwardly when he says this, realizing that in fact his son *doesn't* know his mother. And she doesn't know her son, either. That's the whole point of this reunion, isn't it? For the three of them to finally get to know each other.

George returns to the role of doting parent. "Your mother knows all the right people. She can get anything from anybody when she sets her mind to it, can't you, baby?" he says, shooting a conspiratorial grin at her.

"For God's sake, Taylor, say something," Irma says.

Leo says, "Hi."

"I hope that's not that the best you're gonna do," Irma says in a strong voice, one that's used to being listened to.

George waves her off. "He's surprised is all, honey. Give the kid a break. Look at him. He's exhausted. He looks like shit."

Irma jabs her husband's shoulder. "That's a helluva thing to say to the boy."

"It's true," George says, and Leo laughs with him.

In the pause that follows, the driver asks, "Do you have any bags, sir?"

Leo shakes his head. "No."

"What do you mean you don't have any bags?" Irma asks.

"I had my stuff sent," Leo hears himself say.

George laughs and in his version of a hillbilly accent says, "We got ourselves a rich boy staying with us, mama."

Irma tells George to shut up and grabs Taylor's passport from Leo's hand. "Let me see that," she says looking at the photo in it.

Leo watches her closely. Irma looks twice from the photo of Taylor in the passport to Leo's face. Does she notice a difference? She only shrugs. "Who the hell's ever taken a good passport photo, huh? Tell me that." She hands Taylor's passport back to Leo.

George points to the sliding door. "Let's get the hell out of here."

"This way," the driver says and they follow him to the car through the bright sunlight of the Los Angeles morning.

2

Leo sits squeezed between George and Irma in the back seat of the Lincoln Town Car. Left over from another celebration is the tail end of a deflated red balloon, a yellow ribbon still tied to it. A rack of champagne glasses behind the front seat rattles.

"We should've brought the Dom Perignon," George says.

Irma puts her hand on top of Leo's and keeps it there, loosening and tightening her grip depending on what she says. She points to the bruise on his face. "What happened, darling?"

"I'm not a very good hang glider."

The window between the driver and the back compartment remains open and Leo can see his own reflection in the rear view mirror along with the reflection of the driver's eyes that look back at him. "The freeway's a mess, Mr. Merton," the driver says, "Should we take Lincoln to Sepulveda?"

"You're the boss, Barry." George says.

Irma squeezes Leo's hand. "Are you okay, honey?"

"A bit queasy," Leo says. "I must've eaten something bad."

"We'll be home in no time."

The limousine heads north on Lincoln Boulevard. George and Irma ask their son about his travels, his stay at La Cachette and the trip home. Their questions are simple ones that Leo, or anyone, could answer with a "yes" or "no".

As they talk, Leo wonders: is this all a set up? Have the authorities found Taylor's body and think Leo is his killer? Are George and Irma playing out this reunited family ruse as a way of gathering more evidence against him, hoping that he'll say something to further incriminate himself? Is the driver not really a driver at all but a policeman?

Or maybe it's not a ruse. Taylor told Leo that his parents hadn't seen him since the day he was born. No one would be able to recognize an infant, not even their own, twenty-four years later, would they? And even if they'd seen any pictures of Taylor, which Taylor told him they hadn't, the two men looked enough alike that people confused them. So it's possible that George and Irma aren't pretending.

But even if that's true and George and Irma believe they're sitting in the back seat of this limo on either side of their prodigal son, it's also possible, probable even, that their confusion and their gullibility won't last forever. Something will happen, something will be said and they'll catch on. The game will be over. The question's not 'if' but 'when'.

Leo's frightened. He's been surrounded by crimes all his life, even though he's never been the one who committed them. Taylor's death wasn't his fault, but lying like he's doing, playing these people's dead son and using his identity to get back into the country, that's a serious crime, isn't it? With George on one side and Irma on the other, Leo already feels as if he's caught like an animal in a trap. "Stop the car," he says.

"What's the matter?" George asks.

"I feel sick."

George tells Barry to pull into the parking lot of a diner they're passing. Leo climbs over Irma and opens the door while the car's still slowing. "I'll be back," Leo says and gets out of the car. What now? He said he was sick, but he can't pretend to throw up in plain sight of everyone. They'd know he was faking. He hurries across the gravel lot through the parked cars and enters the diner.

The diner was built in the 1950s or it's a new one designed to look like that. It's crowded. Old rock and roll music plays. Leo looks for the bathrooms. He sees George come in the door. A hanging electric guitar points the way to the bathrooms and Leo walks down the small corridor. He approaches the men's room, but he's disappointed when he sees that there's no back door or window in the hallway that opens to a back lot or loading dock behind the diner. The men's room door opens and a uniformed policeman walks out of it. He nods hello at Leo and holds the door open for him. Leo looks down as he enters, but the cop has already seen his face.

Leo locks the door of the small bathroom. He turns on the cold water and splashes it on his face. He stares at himself in the mirror. There's no window in the room he can crawl out of. Even if there were, what is he thinking? He can't escape like he's in some gangster movie. Where would he go? He curses his stupidity. Panicking like he already did only calls attention to himself and might raise questions in George and Irma who, until he jumped out of the limo, seemed to have no doubts about him. Barry's a driver; he's not a cop. The lowlifes in Leo's foster families would have seen all this immediately. They'd have known to sit quietly and wait it out until an opportunity to escape showed itself. To make it worse, the man who held open the bathroom door for Leo was a cop. Did he get a good enough look at Leo to remember him?

Leo wipes his face with the stiff paper towels he pulls from the dispenser. He'll tell George and Irma that he threw up in the diner's bathroom. Given the trip and the emotional effect of seeing his parents for the first time in his life, that would be believable, wouldn't it?

Once he gets back in the limo he'll string George and Irma along until they get to wherever it is that they're taking him. He won't rush things. He'll take his time to figure the best way out of all this. He steps out of the bathroom and walks into the main room of the diner where George is waiting for him. "Everything okay, son?"

Leo nods. "Must've been some bad food or something."

George buys what Leo says. "The whole day's been pretty damn overwhelming, kid," he says.

As they walk to the door they pass the two policemen.

"This is him," George says proudly to the cops, "the prodigal son." Both cops smile and wish George and Leo luck. How much has George told them? He was a talker, but the cops will probably forget whatever George said by the time he and Leo walk out of the diner.

Irma's standing outside the limo as they approach. "You okay, sweetheart?"

"The kid threw up," George says.

Irma reaches into her bag. "Have a Tic Tac," she says and offers Leo a few of the tiny white candies.

They climb back into the limo and Barry drives them north on Sepulveda. Like before, Leo sits sandwiched between George and

Irma. He's still anxious, but not as much as before stopping in the diner and thinking things through.

It helps that George and Irma are nervous, too, as they speak over one another in the frigid air of the limousine. They bicker, but it's a friendly kind, not the harsh, accusatory sarcasm that was the sound track of Leo's youth. The return of their son is too important for George and Irma to ruin it with any kind of discord. Leo's happy to let them do the talking. During the ride to their home, Leo's silence will be his ally, like it's been all his life.

Leo can see in Irma Stowell the extraordinary beauty she once was. Discovered by a talent scout in her small Wisconsin town, she became the all-American cover girl next door, freckled and smiling. She was unlike the stringy runways models. She looked healthy; she looked American. She was probably in her late fifties now and slightly overweight which did her the favor of smoothing her wrinkles, making her look younger than she was. It was the skinniest women at La Cachette who looked the oldest. She doesn't look as if she's sick. Maybe she's beaten the cancer or whatever disease it was that Taylor blamed their reunion on.

George Merton is a handsome man who'd be cast as the tennis-playing father or bicycling grandfather in a television ad for a sensible car or an erectile dysfunction drug. His face is lined like someone who's spent too much time in the sun and there are bags under his eyes, but his energy compensates for his age or at least distracts you from it. Is he sixty yet? Sixty-five? It's hard to tell. He's an anxious, fidgety man. Is this because he's a salesman or because he spent three years in prison?

As the limo makes its way up Sunset Boulevard, George and Irma regale their son with their recent history. They talk as if the last time they saw him was three days earlier, not twenty-four years before in a hospital parking lot.

"We moved to LA five years ago," George says, fiddling with the tin ashtray in the car's door. "We love it. Absolutely love it."

Irma waves this idea away with her hand, a gesture she uses constantly. "It's a parking lot with taxes."

"Don't listen to her. Your mother loves it, too. We have a place in Bel Air that you're gonna love. It's a home for a family. A real family." George is a salesman. And like all salesmen, he loves everything. At least until he sells it to you. As they talk over one another, Leo decides the two of them couldn't be acting all this. It's too real.

At a stoplight on Sunset, Irma looks at Leo. "How much do you weigh?"

"Who gives a shit how much he weighs?" George says and pokes Leo in the ribs. "Women and their goddamn weight fixation, right? Let's get him home. We got plenty there for him to eat if he wants."

"You're right, sweetie," Irma says.

Leo agrees. "That sounds like a good idea."

Irma turns to him. "That's the first real thing you've said since you got here, Taylor. Aren't you happy to see us?"

Before Leo can answer, George interrupts again. "Of course he's happy to see us. He's overwhelmed is all, babe. I'm overwhelmed. Look at me, I'm crying for Chrissake."

Irma rolls her eyes. "You cry at dog food commercials."

"She's right. I do. Hell, I cry at laxative commercials," George says.

Irma squeezes Leo's hand. "Do you feel any better, sweetheart?"

"Much."

"Then say something nice to us, darling. I want to hear your voice."

Leo turns from one to the other and says to Irma, "It's good to be home." After a beat, he adds the three words, "mom and dad." He says this as if he were testing his proficiency in a foreign language. George and Irma smile broadly, but the driver looks at Leo in the rear view mirror with an expression that implies he's not buying it.

"That says it all," George says, playfully punching Leo's shoulder. "This is gonna be great."

Irma tightens her grip on Leo's hand.

3

George and Irma's Bel Air house was built in the 1950s which makes it an antique by Southern California standards. One story and set away from its neighbors by a mass of tropical plants and shrubbery that surrounds it, the house's design is a hodge-podge, part mid-century modern, part sixties anti-establishment. Lots of glass and stone and a myriad of doors blur the line between interior and exterior, desperate to remind you that the best part of living in California, in fact the whole reason you came here in the first place and the only thing that keeps you here, is the weather.

The driver helps Irma out of the car. "Thank you, Barry," she says. George slips him some cash when they shake hands. Barry nods at Leo, gets back into his limo and leaves.

George gestures to the house. "This is it, Taylor. Home sweet home. Like it?"

"Of course he likes it."

"I asked Taylor."

"I like it," Leo says.

"See?" George says to Irma. "He likes it. Come on in."

The interior of the house is spacious and its walls are mostly windows that look onto a small lawn and more trees. The floors are tiled and its furnishings are as eclectic as its design. On a large table in the living room are a dozen framed photographs. They show George and Irma with celebrities including Bill and Hillary Clinton, Jack Nicholson and Tony Bennett. There's even one of George with O.J. Simpson in which they both hold golf clubs.

Leo's relieved when he sees no photos of Taylor. The only pictures of Taylor they might have would be ones he'd have sent them since they'd reconnected over the phone in the past year. But there are none. Leo's not surprised. The Taylor he met on the island wasn't someone who'd bother to send photos of himself to his estranged parents. Leo looks away from the photos when a dog cautiously approaches and sniffs his shoes. "This is Fina," Irma says.

Leo bends down and lets the dog sniff his open hand. It's a friendly, mid-sized mutt with the ears and markings of a beagle. "Good to meet you, Fina," Leo says, scratching the dog behind its large ears.

"*This* is Fina," Irma says pointing to their housekeeper, a short Filipino woman in an apron. "And in case you're wondering, the difference between Fina and the dog is that the dog does what I tell him to," Irma says and winks at Fina who reacts as if she hasn't heard what her employer just said.

"Nice to meet you, Fina," Leo says and shakes the woman's hand which is hard and wet like a vegetable someone's just washed.

"I'm happy you home, Mr. Taylor," Fina says, staring at Leo with a cold expression not unlike the limo driver's. Does she sense that something's wrong? She has no emotional stake in Taylor's being home, so that might make her judgment clearer than George and Irma's.

"Thank you, Fina. It's nice to be here." Leo returns his attention to the dog, grateful for it being there.

"This one here's name is Percy," George says and Percy rolls over and lets George rub its belly. "Named after Percy Sledge, aren't you, buddy?" George grabs Irma from behind and begins to sing *When A Man Loves A Woman.*

Irma pulls away from him. "Do you have to do that every goddamn time you tell someone his name? Fina will fix you something to eat, Taylor."

Leo shakes his head. "I can't eat right now. I'm too tired." He has to get out of there so he can be alone and think what to do next. "I couldn't sleep on the plane. I was too nervous."

"Of course you were," says George. "I hardly slept a wink myself last night."

Irma takes Leo's hand and pulls him toward a side door. "We set you up in the guesthouse."

"We figured you wouldn't want to be thrown into the circus of the main house here," George says.

They lead Leo out the door to the guesthouse via a stone path. The greenery is overwhelming, colorful and lush, the opposite of the arid foliage Leo had grown up surrounded by.

"What are your neighbors like?" Leo asks. He can't see any other homes through the thick trees.

"No idea," George says. "We've never met them." That means if Leo takes off in the night, it's possible that none of their neighbors will see him.

When they get to the back part of the driveway, George stands over a restored MG-A. It's in perfect condition, painted a deep British racing green with shiny brown leather seats.

"Gorgeous, huh?" George says. "I had her restored top to bottom." He rubs his hand along its smooth fenders and frog-like headlamps. Leo agrees that the car is beautiful and he's not lying.

"She's yours," George says and hands Leo a key.

"For Chrissake, George, if you want to buy the boy's affection why don't you just write him a goddamn check?"

"I'm not buying his affection. He's my son." George puts an arm around Leo's shoulder and says, "The car's all yours, son. No strings attached other than that you have to promise to love and revere me unconditionally until the day I die." Irma waves her hand in disgust and George laughs. "Deal?"

Leo smiles. "Deal," he says and puts the car's key into his pocket.

There's a large swimming pool between the main house and the guesthouse. Pools were everywhere in LA. Even as the airplane had approached LAX over less affluent neighborhoods, Leo saw pools crammed into the cluttered back yards like giant blue and white Easter eggs.

As he looks into the pool's sparkling blue water, Leo thinks of his swim that had started by dodging Jean-Paul's bullets in the cold ocean the night before. It continues here with him standing over this manicured pool in Bel Air.

"This is your new home," Irma says as she opens the door of the guesthouse that consists of a large room with tall windows and a bathroom. On a small table, there's a vase of freshly cut flowers and a large basket of fruit, not unlike what the management of La Cachette has waiting for its guests in their rooms when they arrive. A new computer sits on a desk. A flat screen TV hangs on a wall and under it is connected a video player with a selection of DVDs that haven't been opened yet. Among them are *The Godfather, Parts One and Two*, and several Alfred Hitchcock movies including *Psycho*.

"Make yourself at home, Taylor," Irma says, squeezing Leo's hand again.

George swings open the closet's doors. It's full of clothes. "You said on the phone that you were a size 42 regular, right?"

"I did," Leo says. Luckily, he and Taylor are—or were—the same size.

"We thought we'd get you some California clothes," Irma says as she runs her hand across several pairs of slacks, some shirts and jackets on hangers. "Not that stuffy New York crap."

"New life, new clothes," George says, poking Leo in the arm.

Irma adjusts a red shirt on its hangar. "We'll get you some other things to wear when you've been here a while and you figure out what you need."

Leo nods his thanks. "Right."

"Let the boy get some rest," Irma says to George and she leaves.

When she's gone, George takes a wad of bills out of his pocket and shoves it into Leo's hand. It's a lot of money, maybe as much as a couple of thousand. "Don't tell your mother," he says in an exaggerated whisper.

Leo says, "Thanks." Then he adds "dad" and, when he does, George smiles broadly.

4

Leo locks the guesthouse door after they leave. He puts Taylor Hoffman's passport in the top drawer of the dresser. He puts his own driver's license and passport in a pocket deep in his backpack, the same place he's put Dr. Heller's note. He sits on the edge of the bed and looks around the room. How did he get here? What's he doing sitting in this room full of flowers and gifts and clothes? Every minute he stays here puts him in more danger. On the way from the airport he'd wondered if George and Irma were playing some kind of game to catch him. Now he doesn't think they are. These two people believe that he's their son Taylor. So that means Leo's the one playing a game, the one lying. What matters now is how to get out of here without anyone catching on to who he is and what he's done.

It's dark outside and a person on foot in this neighborhood might attract the attention of private security services or the police. So he'll wait until the next morning to leave. Having supper with George and Irma tonight is the safest thing he can do. The most normal. If he feels like the meal's going badly, he can say he's feeling sick again and leave the table. He'll be fine once he gets through this first evening here, *if* he gets through it.

He'll be sure to remove all traces of himself when he leaves in the morning. If George and Irma still believe he's Taylor—and why shouldn't they?—they'll think their son took off and hit the road, something that shouldn't surprise them, given what Leo knows about Taylor. And because Taylor's dead and Leo will disappear, they'll never hear anything from or about their son again. They'll wait for him to return, their hopes diminishing each day, each month, each year. But at least they'll remember with fondness the day they picked their son up at the airport and took him home and had a meal with him before he disappeared from their lives again. George and Irma will each remember the day differently, but they'll cherish it and argue about it long after he disappears. Looking at it this way, Leo's giving these people a gift, a day with their son that they never would have had if he Leo hadn't stolen his passport and airplane ticket and used them to come home.

Leo opens the closet door. It's full of clothes they bought for Taylor. He takes a deep red shirt off a hangar, puts it on and looks at himself in the mirror that hangs inside the closet's door. The shirt's linen and it must have cost a lot. It fits him perfectly. He's never worn a piece of clothing as expensive as this before. Leo takes the shirt off and lies down on the bed. Exhausted by everything that's happened over the last twenty-four hours, he falls asleep. As he often does, he dreams of his parents' death.

In his dream, Leo's parents, Bobby and Carly Licklighter, are a handsome couple in their early twenties with a small child that Carly holds lovingly. They could be the young couple in a magazine ad, but they're not. Instead, they're robbing a gas station and, as they've always done during their crimes, Carly holds Leo directly in front of her, not so much as a shield, but as a deterrent. She's not the monster the media has made her out to be. After all, what kind of crazy-ass clerk would risk killing an innocent little boy just to save giving away, at most, a couple of hundred bucks, a carton or two of Marlboros and a six pack of Bud? As he always does, her husband Bobby stands directly behind Carly holding his .38 pistol. It's not loaded, but no one knows that. In the eleven robberies the Baby Bandits—as they're called in the newspapers and on the TV—have pulled off so far, it's worked like a charm.

This time they're in a convenience store in Shattuck, Oklahoma and, because the clerk behind the counter is a woman, Carly thinks that'll make this score even easier. But when Carly asks for the money and the cigarettes, the clerk reaches under the cash register, pulls out a .45 pistol and aims it straight at Leo's mother.

Carly's shocked. "What's the matter with you, lady?" she says. "Can't you see I got a baby in my hands?"

"Can't you see I got a gun in mine?" the clerk answers. The clerk might be fifty years old. Or she might be twenty and looks fifty. It confuses Carly that the clerk's not nervous and the way the woman holds her pistol suggests that she's held a lot of guns in her twenty or fifty years.

Bobby sees the clerk's pistol and he tells her how pissed off he is that a woman would endanger his child like she's doing. There are no other customers in the store and over the next few minutes voices are raised and threats are yelled. The clerk, who wears a dirty apron with bright yellow flowers on it, is not about to give in. Leo sees the two guns, the clerk's that points at him and his father's aimed at the clerk and held just below Leo's bare right foot. Leo can feel the cold steel of his father's pistol rub against his shin. In the August Oklahoma heat, the gun's barrel feels good. It makes Leo laugh.

"Go on," Bobby Licklighter says to the clerk, "shoot. I dare you, bitch!"

The clerk takes his dare. She fires instantly and kills Bobby with a single shot that finds the center of Bobby's forehead. He crumples to the ground.

Stunned, Carly drops Leo onto the filthy floor, forcing the child to decide whether to cry or not. Realizing what she's done, Carly bends down to pick Leo up but, thinking she's going for Bobby's pistol which lies next to the boy, the clerk shoots Carly twice, once in the shoulder and the second time in throat, causing blood to gush over the black and white linoleum squares covering the floor.

This is the image Leo dreams of the most often: his mother's pretty face on the floor as blood pours from her throat, soaking her shiny blond hair.

5

Fina cooks the meal in the main house. It's far too much for three people, but Missus Merton told her to "go whole hog" to celebrate their son's return. Fina doesn't care one way or the other. Whatever they don't eat, she'll take back home with her.

Irma finishes her second—or is it her third?—martini and rearranges the food on the dining table as soon as Fina puts it down. George sits on the sofa across the room and watches a black and white episode of *My Three Sons* on the TV. In the episode, Fred MacMurray admonishes his youngest son for something the boy did. MacMurray's father is stern but kind as he questions the teenager. "This guy is good," George says and Fina can hear him mimicking the actor, trying to get his intonation right.

"I liked him better in *Double Indemnity*", Irma says. "He's more like a man in that one: playing a game way out of his league."

"You trying to tell me something?"

Irma shrugs. "Sweetheart, I gave up trying to tell you shit a long time ago."

The sitcom episode ends predictably with its theme music reassuring the audience everything will be fine until the next bump in the TV family's dynamic.

George turns off the TV. "So what do you think?" he asks Irma.

"About the show?"

"About Taylor. You think he's happy he's back?"

"What are you asking me for?" Irma says. "I don't know if *I'm* happy, so how the hell am I supposed to know if *he's* happy?"

"It's a normal question, baby."

"He just got here," Irma says. "Give him some time. Give me some time."

Fina isn't surprised that the Missus doesn't sound as positive about all this as when they'd arrived earlier with the boy. The woman's moods change without warning, especially when she drinks.

Irma turns to Fina. "He's handsome, don't you think?"

Fina nods. "He is, Missus. He look like you."

This makes Irma smile. "Do you think so?"

Fina nods again.

"He reminds me of myself at that age," George says.

Irma scoffs. "You wish."

"I don't mean his looks. I'm talking about the intangibles."

Irma finishes her drink and heads to the counter where the liquor's kept. "I don't know about this."

"You getting cold feet now?" George asks.

"There's something odd about him."

"Like what?"

"He stares at you funny," Irma says. "Like he's sizing you up."

"Wouldn't you under the circumstances?" George stands up and stretches. "Do you think I came on too strong?" he asks.

"You're a salesman. What do you expect?"

"I don't want to scare the boy off."

"You did fine. A little desperate maybe, but fine."

"You think I was desperate?" George says. "I don't want come across as desperate."

"Relax, for Chrissakes. I'll fix you a drink."

"Maybe you shouldn't drink so much tonight, babe."

"Kiss my ass," Irma says as she grabs the oversized bottle of gin. She turns to Fina, mixing a first martini for George and a third—or is it a fourth?—for herself. "You have children, don't you, Fina?"

The whole time Fina's worked for them, Irma has never once asked about her children before, not their names, not their ages, nothing.

"Yes, Missus. Three. They big now." She could tell Irma that her teenaged twin daughters and her ten-year-old son had green, scaly heads with one eye because the Missus never listens to a word Fina says.

But Fina saw changes in Missus Merton after she told her that their son would be coming home. It's usually Mister Merton who's the more friendly and talky one and Missus Merton the touchy one who never says much. But when she found out that her son was coming, the Missus changed. She got excited by things like the flowers in the garden and the old English car in the driveway. She laughs at things that used to make her angry. She even asked Fina's opinion about the clothes they bought for the boy and told her all the things they planned to do with him when he got here.

Of course Missus Merton doesn't tell Fina everything. She gives no explanation of why they never spent any time with their child before now. Like all domestics, Fina is forced to piece the story together herself from what she overhears while the Mister and Missus think she can't hear them.

Fina isn't shocked that they gave the boy away when he was born. Children in her village were often given to other families to raise. The welfare of the village came first in her culture and no child was allowed to harm the community. But in America, rich white America especially, giving up your child is a cause of great shame. And guilt.

Fina has no idea that Leo isn't really George and Irma's son but, even so, she believed from the first time Miss Merton told her about Taylor coming home that nothing good would come of this plan. Fina has heard ghost stories about changelings and the troubles they bring with them. And now that the young man's here something has changed. Something is not right. Fina is sure of that much.

"Then you know, Fina," Irma says, "that being a mother is the most difficult thing in the world, isn't it?"

"It is, Missus." Fina says, noting that the Missus has been a mother for less than three hours.

"I want so much to do this right," Irma says to both Fina and George.

George pats her on the arm. "You're doing great, honey."

"He is good looking, though, isn't he?" Irma says.

"Jesus, Irma," George says.

"What?"

"He's your son."

"I'm just saying he's attractive. What do you think I am?" Irma grabs her drink and heads out the door.

"Don't say anything crazy to him, Irma," George tells his wife as she walks across the lawn. "Remember what we said. You know how you can get."

"Up yours."

Fina puts a tray of dinner rolls on the table.

6

Leo's startled when he wakes from the dream of his parents' deaths and sees Irma in the bedside chair staring at him. How long has she been sitting here? Has he said anything in his sleep that would give him away?

Irma stares at Leo expressionless before saying, "Who are we? I mean seriously, who the hell is anyone?"

Before he can decide how to answer her, Leo realizes that she's not staring at him, but at the wall over his bed where a photo of herself hangs. Leo looks at the photo. Irma's very young in it. Her smile's wide and assured, and her breasts look eager to find their way out of her blouse. The girl in the photo knows she's beautiful and she knows that everyone's looking at her with either envy or lust or both.

"I was so goddamn dumb," she says.

"Were you?" Leo says, relieved they're talking about her and not him. Hoping to keep the conversation about her, Leo asks, "Why?"

Irma finishes her drink and sucks on one of its ice cubes. "Who the hell knows? We were all dumb. Like you are now."

Obviously, the drink in her hand is not her first of the night. Most of the women Leo had been fostered by were either drug addicts or drunks. Sometimes both. Is alcoholism the disease that Irma was forced to recover from? And obviously hasn't? Leo sits up and theatrically shakes the sleep from his head. "I was really tired."

"You were talking a lot just now, honey."

Leo smiles to hide his anxiety at hearing this. "Did I say anything interesting?"

"Who does?" Irma stares directly at Leo as if she's looking for anything that'll tell her who this young man is. But why wouldn't she? This is her son whom she's never met before, someone who'll be playing a huge part in her life from here on. Or so she thinks.

"I'm sick," she says.

"I know."

"Are you gonna leave me before I die?"

"No," Leo says. What else can he say?

After a pause, Irma says, "Tell me you're gonna stay, Taylor."

"Of course I am," Leo says.

"Even if it's a lie."

"It's not a lie."

"You promise?"

Leo nods yes and Irma's expression relaxes as she cracks the last piece of the martini's ice in her teeth.

"Dinner's ready," she says, standing up. She picks up the red linen shirt that Leo tried on. "Put this on. The color will look good on you." She tosses him the shirt and without saying anything else leaves the room.

Leo relaxes in the shower, relieved that he's not said or done anything to give himself away. Irma's short visit to his guesthouse makes it clearer than ever that she believes he's her son. And it tells him how much their son's return home means to her. It saddens him.

Leo dries himself and, in a drawer, he finds new boxer briefs and socks still in their packages. He puts them on. The briefs are gray and the socks striped. He puts on the red linen shirt and in the closet he finds a pair of cuffed khaki trousers. He wears his own shoes. He combs his hair and stares at himself in the mirror. He likes what he looks like in these clothes. He heads to the main house.

Leo's nervous as he stands at the front door. George and Irma will expect him to tell them about his life. Can he do that? Taylor was an easy talker; he never shut up. But Leo has never been good at small talk. Or talk of any size. Other than the Malones, none of his foster families included him in their conversations except to interrogate or blame him. So he decides to imitate the conversations he'd heard the wealthy families at La Cachette have among themselves. Maybe he'll even use some of the conversations between characters in books he's read. He hopes, too, that like they were in the limo, George and Irma will be so wrapped up in themselves that it won't matter what he says.

George sees Leo waiting at the door. "What are you doing standing there like a Jehovah's Witness?" George hugs Leo. "Get in here. This is your house now, too."

"Your father's a hugger," Irma says. "Get used to it." She holds a new drink in her hand.

Leo's always disliked people touching him. There's something desperate about people who constantly hug you, like they're compensating for something. The tightest hugs Leo's foster parents ever gave him were when they were handing him back to caseworkers. But he's playing a role here, so he hugs George back and, when he finishes doing that, he walks up to Irma and hugs her, too.

"Hell, child," Irma says, returning Leo's hug and stepping back. "Now that we've finished our foreplay, what do you say we get ourselves something to eat?"

Seeing the food on the dining room table, chicken and fish, bowls of vegetables and rice, Leo realizes how hungry he is.

The three of them sit. But before they touch any food, George holds up a bottle of champagne. "Here's to our boy being home again!" he says. Leo notes the inaccuracy of the word "again" as George opens the bottle with comic ceremony, causing the cork to pop and a lather of bubbles to run down his wrists and arms onto the table.

"Hear! Hear! The gang's all here." Irma says and the three of them clink their glasses. They fill their plates with food as Fina wipes the spilled champagne from the tabletop.

Leo's happy that he's stayed for the meal. There's no downside in sitting here eating George and Irma's food. Still, he can't let his guard down.

"Now that you're home, son, what are you gonna do with yourself?" George asks, sounding like Fred MacMurray in the TV show.

But George's rehearsed question is hijacked by Irma. "For crying out loud, let the boy catch his breath before you give him the third degree."

"It was a simple question."

"I don't have any plans yet," Leo says.

"Good," says George, "take your time. There's no rush. Your mother and I agreed that you don't have to tell us anything you don't want to, where you've been, your love children, your sordid criminal past, all that." George laughs. "Everything's a clean slate. Tabula rasa, as they say." Leo's relieved when he hears this, certain now that Taylor had told his parents virtually nothing about himself.

"How's the business?" Leo asks, steering the focus away from himself.

"Stowell Cosmetics is in the toilet," Irma says. "We sold it to the Chinese and now it's history."

"You must've got a lot for it," Leo says.

Irma waves her hand at the thought. "You wish."

"I gotta be honest," says George. "Financially things aren't so good for us right now, son."

"He doesn't want to hear that shit the first night he's here," Irma says.

But Leo wants to keep them talking about themselves. "I do."

So George picks up where he'd left off. "I'm thinking about starting a new concern."

"Concern is your father's word for 'racket,'" Irma says, her voice made deeper by her drinking.

George ignores her. "I'm a great salesman, son." Irma reluctantly agrees with him. "Your mother's her usual skeptical self, but I'm very excited about it. There might be something in it for you, too, son. All we need now is a little startup capital."

"Enough already," Irma says.

George looks at her. "I'm only telling the boy we're looking for investors. I'm not asking him for any of his money. Of course there's a position in the business if he's interested." He turns to Leo. "You think you might be?"

Leo's touched by George's offer, but before he can answer his father's—Taylor's father's—offer, Irma slams the champagne bottle hard enough onto the table to cause the plates to jump and food to spill over the edge of several of the serving dishes.

"Enough of this bullshit," she says, "let's put everything on the table. The whole truth and nothing but the truth. Right here. Right now."

Leo freezes. Has George mentioning the money opened a new door? Has Leo said something or reacted in a way that gave himself away? He curses himself for not leaving as soon as he woke up from his nap. For not jumping out of the limousine on the drive from the airport. For coming to Los Angeles in the first place.

"Christ, Irma, look what you did," George says as he helps Fina mop up some spilled sauce with his napkin.

"No worry. I get it, Mister," Fina says.

"Here's the situation, Taylor," Irma says. Leo relaxes when she called him Taylor. Her outburst wasn't because she doesn't believe that Leo isn't her son. "Your father and I want to make a fresh start." Irma pours herself the last of the champagne. "And making a fresh start demands that we all take appropriate blame for our sins."

"Amen," says George.

"I was a terrible mother. End of story."

"Not so fast," George says. "I was a terrible father."

"I was a worse mother than you were a father," Irma says with both pride and shame.

"Bullshit you were." George says.

"I was the mother of all mothers!"

The dog, worried that the pounding of the champagne bottle and the yelling is directed at him, has already gone into another room.

Irma points to Leo and yells at George. "You see that guy sitting right there? That's my baby. I sold my baby to a stranger before he was even born."

"And who let you do that, huh? Tell me," asks George. "I DID. ME."

After a beat, Leo stands up and says, "You both sucked at being parents, all right? So let's all shut up, sit down and finish eating."

This is the longest sentence their son has spoken since he got home. And the loudest. Fina turns from the sink to look at Leo who sits down and calmly begins to eat again.

"We just got over the hump," George proclaims, standing up and holding his champagne glass to toast. "More champagne, Fina!"

"Give us a chance, darling," Irma says to Leo as she and George sit down again. "That's all we ask. A chance."

The rest of the meal is filled with small talk, the kind Leo has sometimes heard but rarely takes part in. Any silences are filled by George and Irma. On the island, Leo learned that salesmen like George are terrified of silence. And, like most wives, Irma is allergic to her husband's opinions. They're drunk and Leo lets them go on. When she asks, Leo tells Irma about his latest girlfriend that he bases on Ki. But instead of making her a lawyer in LA, he says that she runs a restaurant in New York. This is a mistake because Irma asks him about New York, a place Leo has never been.

"I hate New York," Leo says. "I never want to go back there. Ever."

"Amen," Irma says, lifting her wine glass. "I feel the exact same way."

Leo's relieved that his lie about New York doesn't cause him trouble. And to distract them with something he does know about, he tells them that he's a competitive swimmer. George gets up, runs out of the room and comes back with a swimsuit of his own. He tosses it to Leo and tells him he can use the pool any time he wants, day or night. It's heated.

Leo turns down a second helping of Fina's dessert, a dense chocolate cake, saying that he's full. And tired. George hugs Leo again and Irma follows him to the door.

"Remember what I said about staying here?" she asks.

"Of course."

"We don't want you sneaking off in the middle of the night."

"That's not gonna happen, mom," Leo says and walks to the guesthouse.

After Fina turns on the dishwasher, Irma tells her she can go home. Fina's been working for the Mertons since they came back to California, but Missus Merton has no idea where Fina lives other than that she has to take several buses to get to Bel Air when Fina's husband is forced to use their sixteen-year-old Isuzu, its faded color called, ironically, "mink".

"What do you think of Taylor?" Irma asks her.

Fina tells Irma what she wants to hear. "I think he nice, Missus."

Irma nods. "Me, too."

Leo collapses on the bed in his room. The meal with George and Irma, the whole day, has exhausted him. But he couldn't have hoped that it'd go any better than it did. If this were a set-up by the police like he first thought it might be, Leo would have supplied enough evidence for them to arrest him by now. But he's sure that's not going to happen. He can spend the night here in Bel Air without any fear.

George and Irma's need for Taylor to forgive them for giving him away is sad. It's desperate. But maybe their eagerness to reconnect with Taylor is prompted by the money problems George talked about. Do they think Taylor has access to money that can help them out of the financial fix they're in? On the island, Taylor told Leo he had nothing to do with his wealthy adoptive family, the Hoffmans, anymore. But how would George and Irma know that?

Leo reproaches himself for thinking this is about the money. Not all families have to be as conniving as those he'd grown up with, do they? Couldn't two parents like George and Irma simply be happy to see their son?

What surprises Leo most is that his fear of being discovered is being replaced by an affection for this odd, almost pathetic, couple. Earlier, Irma asked him to stay. She used the phrase "until I die". Did she mean it in a practical sense? Or a theoretical one? Every mother wants to have her children in their lives until they die, don't they?

And what would his leaving in the morning do to her, to both of them? But he's got no choice. He can't stay. He convinces himself that this single night with their son is a gift to the two guilt-ridden parents.

George lies on the bed and watches Irma at the bathroom sink rubbing moisturizing cream on her face. It's an Irma Stowell Cosmetics product, one of thousands of jars of the stuff now taking up space in a public storage unit in El Segundo.

"You think he's comfortable?" George asks.

"He's still here, isn't he?" She rubs the cream on her cheeks, careful not to get any in her eyes because it burns like hell when that happens, an effect that helps explain the product's—and its company's—demise.

"He's different than I expected," George says.

"What did you expect?"

"He's gentler than I thought he'd be."

"What do you mean 'gentler'?"

"Quieter. More reserved."

"He looks at you funny," Irma says.

"At me?" George asks.

"At everyone."

"He's nervous. Wouldn't you be?"

"I guess." Irma screws the top back onto the cosmetics jar.

"I want him to feel at home, that's all," George says.

"Then stop talking about money so much."

"Did I do that?" he asks.

"You should've heard yourself."

"That's how men talk. You don't understand because you're a woman."

"I understand fine," she says.

"You gotta be careful, too."

"Of what?"

"Of your attitude."

"What's that mean?" Irma asks.

"You said you were gonna be nicer when he got here."

"I am being nice."

"You keep falling back into your pissed-off character. He's your son, remember?"

Irma slams the product jar on the table. "Kiss my ass."

"I rest my case."

"Fine then," Irma says, "I'll be sweetness and light as long as you promise to stop talking about money."

7

Leo wakes early the next morning and packs up his things. He doesn't know if George and Irma are up yet, but he's decided that he'll leave after having breakfast with them. He puts on the swimming suit George gave him and jumps into the pool. He has plans to make and he does his best thinking in the water. He feels safe once he gets in the pool where the water is cool.

Percy circles the pool, confused and concerned by whatever it is that Leo's doing in it. Most of the families Leo had grown up with were hunters and they had hound dogs like Percy, only bigger. Hounds don't trust water because in it they lose whatever scent they've been tracking.

"Is that why I've always spent so much time in water?" Leo wonders. Has his love of swimming been a means to cover his tracks, a way to keep others from finding out who he really is? Is it a way to keep George and Irma from sniffing out the truth about him?

As he swims, Leo rehearses what he'll say to George and Irma at breakfast. He'll tell them he's taking the MG for a ride. What young man wouldn't want to take his car, that car especially, for a ride on a beautiful California day like this one? That'll give him until late at night or maybe even the next morning before they become worried and call the police. By then Leo Malone will be far away and Taylor Hoffman will be no more.

Leo will take nothing with him other than the clothes he wore here and his passport. He'll take Taylor's passport with him, too, and destroy it, leaving open the possibility for George and Irma that their son could have gone anywhere in the world and disappeared. It'll be painful for them to accept this second loss of their son, but at least they can have hope that their son is still alive.

Leo climbs out of the pool and dresses in the guesthouse. He hears George and Fina's voices, both raised. Leo sees George running out of the main house toward the guesthouse. Percy follows him, baying.

"Taylor, come quick," George says, "it's your mother."

Leo follows him back into the main house where Irma's laying on the floor next to the dining room table. George bends over her, telling her that everything's going to be all right. The dog circles, unsure what's going on. Irma slurs her words. George wipes foam from the corner of her mouth. "You're gonna be okay, baby. You're gonna be okay," he says over and over.

"What happened?" Leo asks, joining George over Irma, whose eyelids flutter.

"We have to get her to the hospital."

Fina holds the phone in her hand. "I call 911."

"They'll take too long to get here like the last time," George says. "Taylor, you and me, we gotta take her."

Leo and George gently lift Irma off the stone floor and carry her to their dark brown 1980's Mercedes sedan in the driveway. She moans incoherently as they put her on the back seat where she slumps over. George sits her upright again and says that he'll drive if Leo will stay in the back with Irma and do whatever he can to keep her from lapsing into unconsciousness again. George drives wildly down the driveway, scraping the passenger side doors on branches. Leo's emotions are torn. One part of him is concerned about Irma. The other regrets not having left in the night.

"Talk to her, Taylor," George says. "Keep her conscious."

Leo uses phrases he's read in books or heard in movies, promising her that everything will be fine and that, once they get to the hospital, the doctor will fix whatever's wrong with her. He tells her how happy he is to finally be home and how much he likes the pool and the clothes they'd bought for him, especially the red shirt.

Irma squeezes his hand and says, "It looks so good on you, darling." George makes eye contact with Leo in the rear view mirror like the limo driver did when coming home from the airport.

At the Santa Monica hospital's emergency entrance, two male nurses help Irma from the car, put her into a wheelchair and push her into the building. George tosses an insurance card at Leo and follows his wife and the nurses down the hospital hallway, yelling to Leo to take care of the details.

Leo stands at the admitting desk where a nurse takes Irma's card and processes it. Two policemen stand at one side of the desk speaking to a doctor about someone they'd just brought in. One of the policemen looks familiar. He's not the cop from yesterday in the diner, is he? No, he's just a cop in an emergency room. Leo tells himself not to overreact.

"What's your relation to the patient?" the nurse asks Leo who's thinking about the cop. "Sir. Your relation to the patient?" the nurse repeats. The policeman turns to Leo.

"I'm her son," Leo says and the policeman looks away. Leo takes a seat in the waiting room. All this turmoil might have made it a good time to leave, but in the confusion of getting Irma to the hospital, Leo didn't take his passport or his license or anything else with him. He left those things along with Dr. Heller's note to him in his backpack at the house where anyone can find them.

A well-dressed woman sits across from Leo. A girl maybe five years old sits on her lap. Who are they waiting to hear news about? A father? A husband? A brother? The mother turns the pages of a picture book for the disinterested girl.

Leo's spent a lot of time in emergency rooms, occasionally as a patient, but mostly as baggage, dragged along while an adult or another child was pieced back together. Those emergency rooms were full of victims of car wrecks and fights. The people who waited for them were usually exhausted women and frightened children.

George comes back into the waiting room and sits next to Leo. He puts his hand on Leo's knee. "Your mother's okay. She mixed up her meds. She's done it before. I didn't tell them how much she drank last night. Or every night," he says shaking his head. "They gave her a shot of something. Perked her right up. We can take her home."

Two nurses help a groggy Irma out of her wheelchair and into the back seat of the Mercedes. George pushes Leo into the back seat next to Irma "just to keep an eye on her," he whispers.

Irma apologizes the whole trip back to Bel Air. "I'm such an idiot," she says. "I'm so sorry."

"There's nothing to be sorry about," Leo tells her.

"What a way to greet my boy after all this time," she says and grips Leo's arm. "I'm so happy you were here. It gave me something to live for."

"What about me?" George says from the front seat.

Irma waves off George's question. "Who the hell are you?"

George laughs at his wife's response. Leo's surprised at how relieved he is to see that she's back to normal.

Irma spends the rest of the day "recovering", her medication made up in large part of gin and tonic. George finds Turner Classic Movies and the three of them watch TV together.

"Perfect," Irma says, stretched out on the sofa. "Let's watch movies with dead people in them." They spend the afternoon doing that, during which George and Leo laugh at Irma's constant criticism of the story, the acting or, most frequently, the actresses' make-up and costumes. George and Irma even laugh at some things Leo says.

But George and Irma still haven't asked their son anything about his past. Is this odd? Wouldn't a parent want to know what their son had done with himself over the past twenty-five years? What he's interested in? What he likes? Or doesn't? Maybe they're intimidated by their son's other life, afraid of not measuring up to what the rich family in New York City was able to give their boy. But like he did before, Leo blames George and Irma's seeming lack of interest in Taylor on the fact that they're so self-involved.

In that way, they're not any different from the foster parents Leo grew up with.

8

In the guesthouse that night Leo reminds himself that he's pushing his luck if he stays here any longer. Everything he's learned in his life so far tells him to get out now.

On the other hand, what if his concern is exaggerated? Foolish even? He's stumbled into a paradise. George and Irma, keepers of that paradise, have welcomed him with open arms. Any fears Leo had about being caught or any guilt he originally felt about taking advantage of George and Irma's good intentions have been replaced by something he never expected to feel: a belief that maybe someone or something owes him this and he deserves whatever George and Irma are willing to give him. The food, the money, the car, the clothes and, above all, the attention. In her note, Dr. Heller said that families can be put together in unusual ways. Is this an example of that? And, if so, why shouldn't he stay and take advantage of it? Considering the families he'd been forced to grow up with, anything he got from George and Irma could be seen as a form of payback from God or the universe.

But this feeling of entitlement doesn't stay in Leo's head for long. Besides being dangerous to be here, it's wrong. On top of that, he imagines the pain George and Irma will feel when they find their son gone from their lives once again.

Confused by the argument going on in his head, Leo calls Sister Gregory who runs the Choctaw Mission where he worked before going to Martinique. She's honest and she's always listened to him. He picks up his cell and dials. Sister Gregory answers in her gravelly voice.

"This is Sister Gregory," she says. Leo hesitates. Was it a mistake to call her? "Hello?" she repeats impatiently.

"It's Leo, Sister."

She pauses before saying, "We all took bets on whether any of us would hear from Leo Malone again. Your call means I lost." Leo can tell that she's smiling when she says this. "The kids here miss you like crazy."

"Did anybody ask about me recently?"

When Leo asks this, Sister Gregory's tone changes. "What would they want to know?"

Leo doesn't answer her question. Instead he says, "I might want to come back and work there for a while."

"What's stopping you?"

"It's hard to explain."

"You want me to convince you?"

"Maybe."

"Where are you?" Sister Gregory asks him.

"Los Angeles."

"Are you in trouble?"

"No."

"Don't lie to me, Leo," she says. "I work with kids. I got the world's best truth meter."

Leo gets up from the bed and walks in circles around his small room. He tells her, "I'm staying with a family."

"What kind of family?"

"Rich people."

"Good for you," Sister Gregory says. He can hear her sarcasm. "How'd you end up with them?"

"I knew their son. He died."

"You have anything to do with his dying?"

"Not really."

" 'Not really?' "

"It's complicated."

"Even worse."

"The thing is: it's like I've taken their son's place in their minds. In their lives."

"I've seen that happen," Sister Gregory says.

"Not like this."

"Someone like you has to be careful."

"Why?" Leo asks her.

Sister Gregory doesn't answer him. Instead, she asks, "Are you lying to them?"

"Not on purpose."

"A slippery answer."

"They're using me. And I'm letting them," Leo says.

"You can't control what other people choose to do."

"Do you believe in karma, Sister?"

"You're asking a nun who works on a reservation if she believes in karma? Yeah, Leo, I believe in karma."

Leo finally asks her what he's wanted to all along, "What if I deserve this?"

"What is it that you think you deserve?"

He looks at his room and all the things in it. "All this."

"All what?"

"I had a shitty life."

"No one's denying that."

"What if God or fate put me in this situation? On the island I met a shrink who told me that families get put together in all kinds of ways. Who's this hurting? And maybe they owe me."

"Who owes you what?" Sister Gregory asks him.

"The people I had to live with. The people who made me afraid to go near anyone. They owe me. Somebody owes me."

"The people in LA aren't the ones who did that to you."

"But why shouldn't I take what they're giving me? At least for a while."

"You don't need me to tell you what to do, Leo."

Of course he knows it. "I should leave them, shouldn't I?"

"You know the answer to that question."

Leo pauses. "You never said if I could come back to the mission."

"Clean up what you have to there first," Sister Gregory says. "You can come back here after that."

"Thank you, Sister."

Sister Gregory says, "Do what's right, Leo," before she hangs up.

Leo's glad that he called Sister Gregory. She cut through all the bullshit like she always does. He lies on the bed. It's Tuesday. He'll leave on Wednesday. Or Thursday. Definitely by Thursday. He'll go back to the Mission. The pay there is shitty and the work hard, but it'll be a good place to hide out for a while. Best of all, there's no chance that George and Irma or anyone will look for him in a place like that.

9

Early the next morning Leo swims laps in the pool, the repetition like meditation. It calms him and he feels safe in the water. He'll miss these morning swims when he leaves Thursday. Or maybe he could stay until Friday. Who would that hurt? He decides that Friday will be the perfect day to leave.

On the breakfast table in the main house sits the usual cornucopia of muffins and scones surrounded by pots of jams and jellies. Irma comes into the room and, before sitting down, she bends over and kisses Leo on the cheek, apparently recovered from whatever it was that sent her to the hospital the day before. "Good morning, sweetheart," she says.

Leo says aloud what he practiced in the pool. "I might take the MG for a spin after breakfast." As soon as these words come out of his mouth he regrets saying them. Who says they're "taking a car for a spin" anymore? It sounds rehearsed, like a line from one of the old movies they'd watched the night before.

But Irma nods disinterestedly as she butters her scone. "You can do that another time, sweetheart," she says. "Because this morning your father and me, we're taking you to someone who wants to meet you."

"Who's that?" Leo asks, trying to sound more curious than concerned.

At least a dozen times on the way to their appointment with Dr. Roberta Frank, a psychiatrist who specializes in ex-convicts and addicts, Irma reminds Leo that this is his father's idea, not hers.

"It began as a condition of my parole," George says, "but it's helped me a lot over the last couple of years."

Irma scoffs. "Not that I can tell." Irma's from rural Wisconsin where analysis holds no more sway than it did in Oklahoma. But Leo's touched when Irma admits to him that she's willing to try anything—"even bull-shit like this"—to repair the damage she's done to their family. She turns her face to the car's window to hide what look like tears.

Dr. Frank is a thin woman in her early forties with short, curly hair. She's got a tattoo on her left wrist written in what looks like Latin. Leo tries reading it, but her sleeve covers most of it. Some part of her is always moving—her hand, a leg, her mouth. Psychiatrists were the least animated people Leo ever had to meet with, but he's never seen one who moves as much as Dr. Frank.

She asks Leo if he's ever had counseling before. Of course he has. In the foster system, he'd endured countless hours of state-mandated therapy that searched for the right home to place him in. He's been dragged through Freudian analysis, Jungian therapy, cognitive therapy and even things as far out as scream therapy—an unlikely choice for a boy about whom the main complaint was his silence.

But Leo reminds himself that he's not in Dr. Frank's office as Leo Malone. He's here as Taylor Hoffman, adopted and raised by a wealthy family on the East Coast. So he says, yes, of course, he's been in therapy. Every rich kid from New York he met at La Cachette had been in therapy. Every adult, too.

"Then you won't be intimidated," Dr. Frank says. She has a habit of laughing slightly whenever she says anything. It makes her seem insecure.

Dr. Frank lowers the room's lights and asks them all to close their eyes. "I don't practice hypnotism," she says, "but I do like my clients"—George already warned them that she never uses the word 'patient' which she considers demeaning—"to allow their emotions to freely travel in time and place. Like an emotional LSD trip." Leo would never have allowed himself to be hypnotized for fear of his saying something that gave himself away. But he'll go along with this and play the role of the aggrieved child. He'll be Taylor Hoffman in this room. Leo never liked the guy, but because he was with him the night he died, he feels an obligation to speak for the dead boy. Taylor would be the last to admit it, but he and Leo have a lot in common.

Dr. Frank asks Leo how he feels so far about coming home. "Be completely honest, Leo," Dr. Frank says. "Nothing you say today will upset anyone."

"I don't know about that," Irma says. Dr. Frank ignores her.

Trying to make his reaction seem more like Taylor's might be, Leo says, "I'm pissed off."

"About what?" the doctor asks.

"Being abandoned."

Irma reacts. "The word 'abandoned' is a little strong. It's not like we left you in the woods."

"You said it yourself last night, Irma," George says.

"Don't tell me what I said."

Leo speaks up. "You did say that, mom."

"I had a lot to drink, okay?" Irma says and, having lost this round, she folds her arms and sits back in her chair.

"Forget about your parents for now, Taylor. They don't matter. They're not even here. Tell me, tell them whatever you have to."

Leo recalls how angry Taylor was when he spoke about his parents. "You gave me away," Leo says. "You sold me."

"I was messed up on drugs," Irma says. "So was your father. Everyone was back then. And those other people, they wanted you so much."

"This is good, everyone," Dr. Frank says. "I want you to visualize it, Taylor. Close your eyes. See it."

Later that night Leo will remember that it was at this moment he began to confuse Taylor's childhood with his own. He'd told the many state psychologists the details of what happened to him, but never what he really felt about those events or how they affected him. That didn't surprise his counselors. The boy had been diagnosed with emotional detachment disorder and, besides, when he told them nothing about himself it meant they had less work to do.

But here in Dr. Frank's office, Leo feels an urge to speak. He knows it's dangerous, but in this room, surrounded by these people, something makes him want to speak. Maybe it's his anxiety or fatigue or confusion. Whatever the cause, when Leo closes his eyes, what he sees is not some imaginary version of Taylor, but himself at three years old and his mother lying dead on the floor of the convenience store. An Oklahoma State Trooper, a tall woman, speaks to him. "Come with me, sweetheart, and don't look back," the trooper says, but Leo doesn't hear anything else as she takes his tiny hand in her large one and leads him out of the store to the police car. The squad cars' lights flash brightly and Leo's excited about getting into one of them and away from all these faces staring at him.

Dr. Frank interrupts this memory. "What are you seeing, Taylor?" she asks. "Tell us."

"The lights, the faces, all of it," Leo says and suddenly a thousand other memories of Leo's childhood flood into his mind. As much as he wants to, he can't tell the people in this room about his own parents' death. Or the beatings by drunken foster fathers or the times he was molested by his foster siblings and once by his foster mother.

He tells them instead an experience from his childhood that any child, rich or poor, might be able to tell. In it he's six years old and sitting in the back of Clarence Buell's Pontiac station wagon. It's summer and cotton candy-like stuffing pokes through cracks in the car's hot, vinyl seats. The other kids tease the silent Leo mercilessly. Kaye Buell, who's driving, yells over her shoulder, "Shut the hell up or I'll whack you hard, you little shits."

"The other kids, they tortured me," is all Leo says in Dr. Frank's office.

"What other kids?" Irma asks.

"Don't interrupt," Dr. Frank says and Irma sits back in her chair again.

"We were driving somewhere," Leo says, "and I got sick in the car. But she said that if I got sick again, she'd return me the same way she returned the toaster oven to Sears."

George and Irma look at each other, confused by what Leo's saying.

Leo stands up and paces Dr. Frank's small office, pounding his fist into the palm of his hand. "I did get sick, but I couldn't let anyone see me get sick because I was afraid that they'd toss me out of the car and leave me there. So I kept the vomit in my mouth and I swallowed it." He pauses. "I SWALLOWED MY OWN VOMIT." Leo breathes heavily as he remembers the acidic taste of the vomit in his throat. His memory has nothing to do with anyone in the room, but he feels good telling someone about this for the first time. It's a relief to accuse someone, anyone. Unlike what happened in the car that sweltering Oklahoma day, Leo finally lets the vomit spew out of his mouth.

George reaches over and puts his hand on Leo's shoulder, but Leo pushes it away.

Dr. Frank asks Leo, "Would you like a glass of water, Taylor?"

He shakes his head. But Dr. Frank's question breaks Leo away from his memory and reminds him where he is and what the cost of saying something else—something that might incriminate him—would be. What he's told them is true. But it isn't George and Irma he wants to tell that story to. It's his own parents, all of them, biological and foster.

The room is silent for another few moments and Leo wonders if he's said too much. Episodes like this are why he can't stay with George and Irma much longer. Eventually something will be said.

It's Irma who finally speaks. "I told you last night I wasn't the world's greatest mother, okay. I did it. I'm guilty. I'm sorry. But I didn't come here so I could be accused of child abuse."

Leo's grateful for Irma's remark because it takes the focus off him. It also gives Dr. Frank the opening she's been waiting for.

"You have a lot of guilt, don't you, Irma?" the doctor asks her. This is the first time she uses Irma's first name.

"Everyone's guilty of something, sweetheart," Irma says.

Dr. Frank's session ends and on the way to the El Cantino where they plan to have lunch, George says to Leo, "Your mother's a piece of work." There's more than a little pride mixed in with his annoyance of her.

"Look who's talking," Irma says.

Leo's happy that Irma reacted like she did and stormed out of the session. It was the perfect antidote to his emotional outpouring that he now realizes was a mistake. He should never have said what he did about himself. What if he'd lost all control and said something that gave himself away? But Irma had upstaged him. Thanks to her, no one in that room would remember what he said.

They enter the Mexican restaurant, blinded by how dark it is inside. While Irma goes to find a table, George takes Leo by the arm and pulls him aside. "I gotta say something first."

Leo might've been nervous if George had said this to him a day or two before. But now nothing other than a blatant misstep on Leo's part will alert them that anything's wrong. It's crazy, but the longer Leo stays with them the more he becomes the standard against which anyone claiming to be Taylor will be judged. If the real Taylor Hoffman were to walk into El Cantino now, Taylor would be the one suspected of being the phony, proof of how slippery and self-serving the whole notion of the family is.

"Your mother can't apologize," George says to Leo. "She never could. Not for anything. But I can. And I will. Right now." George holds Leo by both shoulders and stares into his face. "I'm sorry for what we did to you, son. What I did to you. I'll make it up to you. I promise."

"That's okay," Leo says and turns to enter the bar's main room.

But George holds him there. "Do you forgive me?"

"Of course."

"I want to hear you say it. Please, son. Say you forgive me."

"I forgive you."

"Dad. Say 'dad.' "

"I forgive you, dad," Leo says.

"I love you, son," George says and he hugs Leo tightly.

At a small table in the nearly empty bar, the three of them laugh when Irma does an imitation of Dr. Frank, the way she spoke and the way she moved. George laughs so hard he pounds the table and sends the chips flying out of the bowl. Leo laughs, too, both at Irma and at the way George and Irma make each other laugh. Leo can't remember laughing like this before and whenever he'd seen people do it he always thought they were faking it.

Two margaritas later, Leo's nearly as high as Irma. In the men's room he splashes water in his face and tells himself to be careful. He can't slip and say something.

When they leave the bar, Leo sees two men standing next to George's car in the parking lot. Both men wear suits that make them look like police. Leo stops short in the restaurant's dark doorway. His heart pounds as he recalls that there's a back door to the restaurant next to the men's room. He can claim that he's left something in the bathroom and go back there and slip out the door. He learned a lesson when he was taken unexpectedly to the hospital with Irma, so now he keeps his passport and drivers license in the lining of his jacket at all times.

But before Leo can make a decision, it's Irma who reacts to the two men. "Sonofabitch. It's them. They found us," she says.

George tells her to relax. But it's Leo who relaxes now because he knows the men are here because of George and Irma, and not him.

The smaller and older of the two men has slicked back hair. He stands next to George's Mercedes while the younger man, who wears a Nike tee shirt shirt under his suit jacket, leans over the front tire. The men aren't wearing tropical shirts, but they're no different than Jean-Paul or his henchmen who sliced Taylor's throat on the island and tried to kill Leo before he escaped.

"Looks like you're low on tire pressure, George," the older man says when George approaches.

"Thanks, Pete, I'll have that checked."

The younger man takes a large knife, his, out of the tire that's already deflated.

"Sonofabitch," Irma says to George.

"Relax, honey."

"Mr. Weathers is anxious to talk to you, George," Pete says.

"Who are these guys?" Leo asks George.

Pete turns to Leo. "Was I talking to you, sonny?"

"Be quiet, Taylor," George says to Leo.

Pete and his partner walk away, but not before Pete says, "Mr. Weathers will be in touch."

George, Irma and Leo watch the men get into their own car and leave the lot. No one says anything until Irma does. "The sonofabitch is coming for us."

"Don't overreact, honey," George says.

"He's waited long enough and now he wants his money."

"Who are they?" Leo asks.

George plays it down. "Skeletons from our closet, that's all."

"What are we gonna do about the tire?" Irma wants to know.

"I'll fix it," Leo says. "You guys wait over there." He points to a bench where customers sit while the valets retrieve their cars when the place is busy at night.

George and Irma argue as Leo changes the tire. From what Leo can hear, George and Irma owe money to someone Pete works for, a man called Weathers, the man they hoped wouldn't come after them. But now he has. One way or another, people you owe money to always do. Leo's foster families were experts in debt, both owing and collecting. Debts were what caused most of the violence in their families. Debts were first, sex was second. Often both.

Leo tightens the final lug nut and waves George and Irma over to the car.

"Where'd you learn how to change a tire, son?" George asks him.

"On the road," Leo says. He reminds himself to be more careful about what he does in front of them. Rich kids from New York, especially Taylor, probably have no idea how to change a tire.

George drives home. Irma sits silently as they pass a park full of people in white rolling balls on the grass trying to hit smaller balls.

George tells Leo that Weathers has bought or "factored" a debt from a group of investors George owes money to. Now George owes Weathers that money. He never says how much it is and Leo doesn't ask, but he knows that people who factor a loan never settle for a part of the debt like investors do. They want all of it and they usually have ways of getting it.

Leo figures that money was probably part of the reason George and Irma have reconnected so eagerly with their son. But he doesn't hold that against them. He's their son and Leo's touched by what George said to him an hour earlier in the Mexican bar. And isn't that what families are supposed to do: help one another?

But the encounter with Pete removes any lingering doubts Leo had about leaving Irma and George. He doesn't have the money to help them and, more importantly, what if another meeting with Weathers' thugs escalates into a something that involves the police? Leo could be identified. He has to leave before anything like that happens.

Fina has lunch ready by the time they get home. Percy greets them enthusiastically, but only Leo takes time to play with him. Irma isn't hungry. George is distracted.

George and Irma look at each other when the phone rings. "Don't answer it," Irma yells at Fina. "It's probably some retard selling garbage bags." Irma goes into the kitchen and pours herself a large glass of wine. They both listen to hear if the caller leaves a message on the answering machine. The caller doesn't.

"I put mail on the table," Fina says to Irma who picks up the dozen or so letters and riffles through them disinterestedly. When she tosses the letters back onto the table several fell onto the floor. Leo sees the return address of one of them. It's from La Cachette. He has to get this letter before George or Irma do.

When Fina bends down to pick up the letters, Leo grabs an orange from the bowl of fruit on the table and purposefully drops it. The orange hits the floor with a thud and rolls under a chair. Percy chases it down and works to get it from beneath the chair. Fina calls the dog off and, as she bends to recover the piece of fruit, Leo picks up the resort's letter and slips it into his pocket. Fina sees him do this. And Leo sees that she sees him do it. But Fina says nothing and hands him the orange. "Thanks," Leo says and he can feel her stare trained on him as he heads to the guesthouse.

Once inside his room he shuts the door, sits on the bed and opens the letter. Following a perfunctory greeting it reads:

A week ago Taylor Hoffman left the resort here without checking out. Please advise where to send his personal belongings. A bill for the room and incidentals will be mailed to you shortly.

In his haste to leave the Island, Leo hadn't gotten all of his Taylor's things out of the hotel room. Leo decides he'll write to the concierge as Taylor and tell him to have the items sent to his parents' address in Los Angeles, but not for a week's time. That way they'll be sure to get there only after Leo leaves. He stuffs the concierge's letter into his jacket next to his own passport.

Both George and Irma's problems with Weathers and now the letter from La Cachette remind Leo that it's time to leave the fantasy world he's created here and go back to the Mission.

10

Leo puts the few things he's going to take with him into his backpack. He puts the red linen shirt in it, too. He changes into his swimsuit and swims laps in the pool where he finalizes his plans. He'll tell George and Irma that he's going to put the top down on the MG and go for a midnight ride along the shore. Instead, he'll drive to LAX and park in a Long Term Parking lot. He'll get on a flight to Tulsa, land there in a few hours and get to the mission by the next morning.

On his sixty-fifth lap he sees George and Irma standing on the edge of the pool, watching him as he swims. Their expressions are solemn. When he climbs out of the water, Irma approaches him with a towel. She wraps it tightly around him. Leo sees Fina watching the three of them from the kitchen window of the house.

"Did you think we wouldn't know?" Irma says as she squeezes Leo's torso tightly under the towel.

Leo says nothing.

"Your mother was the one who figured it out," George says. "And I just checked. As usual the lady's right."

"About what?" Leo asks.

" 'About what?' " George says, mimicking Leo. Then he smiles. "It's your goddamn birthday, kiddo."

Leo breathes deeply. "Oh, right."

George mocks Leo's reply. " 'Oh, right.' Listen to how cool this kid is. 'Oh, right'. He's just like his old man."

Irma slaps George with the damp end of towel. "You wish."

George and Irma take Leo to an upscale restaurant in Santa Monica to celebrate Taylor's twenty-fifth birthday. The place has a Michelin star and its patrons are affluent and well-dressed. This will be Leo's last meal with George and Irma before he leaves them later that night.

George and Irma drink a lot. Leo hardly drinks at all, afraid of what effect alcohol might have on him. He's still upset for having said so much in Dr. Frank's office. As usual, George and Irma do most of the talking, bickering about how they plan to market a new line of Irma Stowell Cosmetics for the Mature Woman. Irma rolls her eyes at what George says about her still being beautiful, but it's a false modesty. She's flattered.

After their desserts, Irma slides a small jewelry box across the table to Leo. "We've been saving this for you, sweetheart," she says.

"Go on, open it," George says. Leo does and in the box is an antique Gruen wristwatch, made of rose gold with a brown snakeskin band. Leo doesn't know much about watches. It's small compared to watches like Rolexes that sit on your wrist like salad plates and scream their worth at everyone, but it's a beautiful piece. It's restrained; it doesn't try too hard.

"It was my father's," Irma says.

"Do you like it?" George asks.

"What do you think?" Leo says, not lying. He's touched by this gesture. He'll take the watch with him when he leaves later that night. He hopes that George and Irma will be happy knowing that their son is wearing it. Wherever he might be.

"I don't know what to say," Leo says.

"You don't have to say anything," says George, "but I'd like to."

"Oh, for Chrissake, George," Irma says. "Please, not here."

"No, no, I want to do this." And prompted by too much alcohol, George stands up and claps his hands. When the surrounding tables finally silence, George addresses them. "I'm sorry to interrupt your meals, everyone." The other diners stare at him. "But I have something to say."

Leo tenses. George making a public statement that garners attention isn't a good thing.

Irma covers her face with her hands. "For shit's sake, George."

George ignores her. "I can see that many of you are families and, as we all know, family is the cornerstone of our society and our lives," he says to the other patrons, all watching him now. Even the waiters stop serving to see what the man at table nine will say next.

"My wife and I are celebrating the return of our son who we lost many years ago," George says, pointing to Leo. "I sincerely hope none of you go through the pain of losing a child like we did. But I want to share with you, a roomful of strangers, how grateful we are that our son has returned to his family and that we're complete again." George wipes a tear from his eye. "I have nothing else to say except that I'm not going to pay for your dinners." Several of the customers laugh.

"The prodigal," George says, leaning over and kissing Leo theatrically on the forehead. George sits down and some of those at the other tables applaud lightly. A man at a neighboring table says, "*Mazel tov*," and turns back to his meal.

Leo's moved by George's maudlin speech. It's the perfect sendoff for Leo, or Taylor. "Thanks, dad," he says.

"You are such a geek," Irma says to George, but her eyes are full of tears, too.

The Maitre d' approaches the table. "The establishment would like to offer you a cordial of your choice, Mr. Merton," he says, handing George a small after-dinner drink menu.

"I should make a speech more often," George says and he smiles at the Maitre d'. George points to an expensive brandy on the menu and orders one for him and one for Irma. Leo declines the offer.

Leo feels a hand on his shoulder. He expects it's the Maitre d' insisting again that he select his complimentary drink. Instead, Leo hears his name spoken.

"Leo?" a woman asks.

Leo looks up to see Ki from La Cachette standing over him.

PART THREE

Los Angeles

11

Leo stands up, ready to deflect whatever Ki might say to George and Irma about him or Taylor. His mind races with possibilities, all of them bad.

"I wouldn't have noticed you except for that speech," Ki says. Turning to George she says, "It was very sweet."

"See? The young lady liked it," George says to Irma who shrugs, but stares at Ki who wears a tight black dress that accentuates her boyish figure.

Leo introduces Ki before she can say anything else. "Ki, hi. These are my parents, George and Irma. Mom, dad, this is Ki Scott. We met at La Cachette."

Surprised, Ki looks at Leo. "These are your parents?"

"That's right."

"Who the hell is Leo?" Irma asks.

Leo forces a laugh. "That's a nickname I use sometimes."

"Why 'Leo'?" George asks.

"It's a long story. But Taylor's my real name," Leo says to Ki and gives her a look that begs her not to question anything he's saying. The expression on her face tells him that she's confused, but understands enough to say nothing else about his name or that she was just introduced to an orphan's parents.

"Where do you know each other from?" Irma asks Ki.

Leo answer s for her. "La Cachette."

"Right," Irma says, "you said that."

Leo grabs the watch from the table and uses it to steer the conversation away from himself. "See this? It was my grandfather's. My parents just gave it to me."

"It's his birthday," George says.

"It's beautiful," Ki says. "Happy birthday, Taylor." She says, stressing the name 'Taylor' as she looks directly at Leo.

"Have a seat," George says to Ki.

Ki shakes her head. "Thanks, but we were just leaving."

George insists. "Sit down, sweetheart. I'll get you a chair. Have a drink with the birthday boy."

Leo prays that she'll refuse. "She said she was leaving."

Salesman that he is, George says, "I insist."

For Chrissake, Leo thinks, shut up and let the girl go home.

"That's very sweet of you," Ki says to George. "But my husband's getting our car."

When she says 'my husband' Ki turns to Leo to gauge his reaction. Their eyes meet for a second before Leo looks at the simple gold band on her ring finger, a ring she wasn't wearing at La Cachette.

Another time, Ki's admission that she was married might have been the most surprising thing anyone said in the last few minutes. But here in this restaurant with George and Irma, it doesn't come close. Leo takes Ki's arm. "I'll walk you to your car."

Ki tells George and Irma how nice it was to meet them and that maybe she'll see them again. Leo assures her that she will, and leads her out of the room.

Some of the patrons stare at this young man, the object of his father's maudlin tribute. But most of them look at the striking young woman with the short dark hair. The men scope her out and quickly look at their wine glasses. The women watch her for as long as they can before pushing their unfinished plates of food away.

Leo quickly replays what everyone's just said at the table as he and Ki leave the room. George and Irma seem to have bought everything he said.

Ki stops at the restaurant's door and turns to him. "I thought you were an orphan. Who are you? Were you and Taylor, or whoever that was, playing some kind of game? What?" She's angry. "I thought on the island that we had—" she begins to say.

"I can explain everything."

"I don't want to hear it."

Leo grabs her wrist. "I want to tell you. I have to."

"You're hurting me," she says.

Leo lets go of her wrist. "You told me you weren't married."

Before she can say anything, a man dressed more casually than anyone else in the restaurant approaches them. "I was waiting with the car," he says to Ki. This is her husband and he's annoyed.

"I ran into an old friend," Ki tells him. "Carl, this is—"

"Taylor," Leo says and shakes her husband's hand. His grip is weak, uninterested. "It's good to meet you, Carl," Leo says.

"You ready?" Carl asks Ki, ignoring Leo and walking out the door.

Ki kisses Leo on the cheek and hands him a business card. "Call me," she says and gets into Carl's BMW. The parking valet shuts the door behind her. She doesn't look back at Leo as they drive away from the restaurant.

Leo goes to the men's room. Ki's card says that she works at a law firm in West LA. Leo splashes his face with cold water and looks at himself in the mirror. That was much too close.

When he gets back to the table, George says, "That was one beautiful girl."

"She looks like a boy with that hair," Irma says. "And what is she anyway? Chinese?"

On the drive home, Leo answers Irma's pointed questions about Ki in few words. She and George argue whether the restaurant's food and service has gone downhill. Irma thinks it has.

Once home, Leo changes into his swimming trunks and jumps into the pool to swim laps. He goes over what happened at the restaurant. Nothing disastrous, he decides. It was a simple, chance meeting with a girl he'd met at the resort, and George and Irma suspect nothing more. Why should they?

But seeing Ki changes things for Leo. He didn't forget about her when he arrived in LA and moved in with George and Irma.

There were times when he thought about looking her up. But he'd quickly nixed that idea. He has to leave LA. So what would be the point?

But when he saw her at the restaurant, Leo realized how much he still wants her. His attraction confuses him. He swims his laps faster and faster. He tries to convince himself that the smartest thing to do is to throw her business card away and leave for Oklahoma in the morning like he plans to. But now that he's seen her, he has to speak to her again. He needs to tell someone what's happened, what's been happening. And who better than her?

In the main house, Fina prepares to leave for the night. "Anything else tonight, Missus?" she asks Irma who stands at the living room window holding back the curtain so she can watch Leo swimming.

"No," Irma says. "The kid's like a goddamn seal. He's in the water more than he's out of it."

George sits on the sofa with Percy watching a rerun of the first season of *The Sopranos*.

Irma looks at George. "So you think everything's going okay?"

"We're doing the best we can, babe," he says. "He's still here, isn't he? You saw how much he liked the watch we gave him."

"What kind of a name is Taylor anyway?" she asks no one. "It sounds like a job. Taylor. Butcher. Plumber. It's so damned WASPy. Why did they have to call him that for Chrissakes?"

Irma's birth name was Gertrude, a name she's always hated. When she was fourteen she read a magazine article about a French actress called Irma something and decided to call herself that the first chance she got. It was sophisticated. Her first commercial agent, Marty Weisenberg in Chicago, agreed, and so seventeen-year-old Gertrude Rose Stowell became Irma Stowell.

"The name was their choice, not ours," George says. "If we'd kept him we could have called him whatever we wanted."

She hates when George reminds her that they gave their son away. "You think I don't know that? But 'Taylor'. Christ."

"It's going well," George says. "Let's not rock the boat."

Fina opens the front door. "Good night, Missus," she says and leaves the house, carrying in her bag food that will go bad before George and Irma ever eat it.

George watches the show, surprised how much the actor playing Tony Soprano has changed over the run of the series. His voice and mannerisms have become exaggerated, almost caricatures of what they were the first season. George mentions this to Irma, making a point about how playing a role can change the people playing it, either on TV or in real life. He wonders if the two of them playing parents for the first time has changed them into parents. "Do you feel different?" he asks.

"About what?"

"They say that you feel sadder when you cry," George says. "And that you can make yourself happy if you smile, not necessarily the other way around."

"Who says that? Dr. Phil?"

"Real scientists. I read it in Danbury."

"You having second thoughts about all this?" Irma asks him.

"I'm saying the opposite of that. I'm saying I'm starting to feel … paternal."

Irma ignores him and watches Leo who finally stops swimming. She looks at her own reflection in the window before she asks, "Do you think that girl was pretty?"

"The one at the restaurant? Jesus, she's what? Twenty-two, twenty-three years old? Who isn't pretty at that age?"

"She's not gonna age well. The Chinese are like the Russians. They're beautiful when they're young. Then they drop off a cliff. Like with those gymnasts."

"For Chrissake, Irma, be careful," George says, "it's happening again."

"What's happening? What are you talking about?"

"You promised you were gonna change when he got here."

"I did. I am."

"You're starting to slip."

Through the living room window, Irma watches Leo get out of the pool and walk to the guesthouse, passing Fina who heads down the driveway in her small car.

Irma shuts the curtain. "You think he fucked her?"

"That girl?" George asks. "For his sake, I hope so,"

"Kiss my ass."

12

Leo calls Ki's office the next morning. Her assistant, who asks that Leo call her Maria, tells him that Ms. Scott will meet him at her office at one o'clock.

The law firm is on Olympic Boulevard in a building that looks more like a factory than an office, hip camouflage for lawyers and MBAs. The firm Ki works for, Canter, Herman and Phillips, is on the ninth floor, its design sleek and modern, all steel, glass and cement.

Leo approaches the receptionist. "I'm meeting Ms. Scott," he tells her, but before the receptionist can reply, he hears Ki's voice.

"Taylor, hi," she calls to him as she walks down the hallway towards Leo. She greets Leo in front of the elevators with a polite kiss on the cheek. A man getting off the elevator smiles at Ki and she smiles back to him. "I just spoke with Brian and it's all set," she yells to the man as he disappears down the hallway and, holding the elevator door open, she says to the receptionist, "If Mr. Herman asks, tell him I'll be back for the two o'clock." It's obvious that Ki wants to get Leo out of her office as quickly as she can. She steps onto the elevator and stares at him. "So who am I having lunch with today? Taylor or Leo?"

"Leo," he says.

Another couple, a man and a woman, get on the elevator before its door closes and Ki says nothing else. Leo looks at her reflection in the elevator's mirrored door. He'd forgotten how beautiful she is. She wears a little make-up; she doesn't need it.

When they get off the elevator, Ki walks through the lobby and into the coffee shop. Leo hurries to keep up with her. Ki says hi to the barista over the counter. She orders two coffees, remembering from her time with Leo on the island what he drinks. They sit opposite one another at a table by the window.

Before Leo can say anything, she leans over the table and says to him, "What was last night about?"

Leo's planned all morning how to tell her his story and, as he sits there, he tries to remember how he rehearsed it. But Ki can't wait. "Tell me," she says, "now."

Leo hasn't had anyone to tell what he's done and what he's been going through since he got to LA. Now that there's someone who wants to know, it floods out of him. He tells Ki everything. He tells her about his last night on the island, from leaving her in her room to look for Taylor, to finding Taylor, to Taylor's death at the hands of Jean-Paul, to his own escape from the island using Taylor's plane ticket and passport.

She's still confused. "But that doesn't explain why last night you were—"

"Wait," Leo says and he tells her what happened when he arrived in LA, how he was met and welcomed by George and Irma and how he's been living with them ever since then as Taylor.

Her chair scrapes the floor as she sits back from the table. "You're telling me that Taylor's parents actually think that you're him, Taylor, their own son."

Leo nods. "They do."

"So that wasn't some bullshit act you were all playing last night?"

"No."

"How is it possible that they think you're him?"

"They haven't seen him since the day he was born," Leo says. "And people believe what they want to. You know that."

"Why didn't you tell them the truth?"

"How could I? Think about it. Everything that happened on the island makes me look guilty. Jean-Paul would say I am. The concierge, too. I was scared. So I split. I figured I'd get to LA and disappear. It never occurred to me that I'd see his parents. But there they were at the airport waiting for me—for Taylor. What was I supposed to do? What could I say? I was trapped. I was gonna leave that night. Or the next day. And every day since. But I didn't. I haven't. Not yet."

"Why not?"

"I don't know," he says. And it's true. He doesn't know why.

Ki's silent as the barista brings them their coffees. When he leaves, she says, "This is crazy, Leo. It's insane."

"I know, but it's what happened. What's still happening."

She reaches across the table and takes his hand. At first he does what he always does when someone tries to touch him. He tenses and pulls his hand back. But she reaches for it again and he lets her take it. "Relax," she says.

The feel of his hand in hers calms him. He's glad he came to see her. She says that he looks nervous, the same way he did the last night she saw him on the island, in the hallway of the resort, just after he shaved, making him look so much like Taylor. His fear was obvious to her then, but she didn't know what caused it. She thought it was because he was running away from her.

"I *was* running away," he says, "but not from you. I couldn't let Jean-Paul find me."

"I waited three days for you. I kept asking everyone, anyone if they'd seen you."

Leo feels bad about this, but he needs to know what the other people on the island thought. "What did they say?"

"What could they say? That you disappeared. They said people like you always did that. I felt like such an idiot."

"What did they say about Taylor?"

"The concierge was upset. He kept asking Penny and Julie and me about him, but we couldn't tell him anything, so he must've figured he just split."

Leo's happy to hear this. It means that no one found Taylor's body.

Ki squeezes Leo's hand. "You're not thinking of telling Taylor's parents the truth, what really happened, are you?"

"How can I? The only thing I can do is leave them."

Ki nods in agreement. "You're right. When?"

"Soon."

"When is 'soon'?"

"Soon," Leo says again and he repeats it as if to encourage himself. "Very soon."

"You realize you're living a lie, don't you?" she asks him.

"Look who's talking," he says, pointing to her wedding ring.

"I lied about not being married on my vacation so I could sleep with someone other than my shitty husband. Someone I liked. That's not a crime. It's not even close to what you did. What you're doing." Ki plays absentmindedly with sugar that's spilled on the tabletop. "And what are you doing it for anyway? Their money?"

"George and Irma have no money. They want money from Taylor."

"Then why are you still there, Leo?"

"I started to leave a hundred times, but didn't," he says. "It's like they've got this hold on me."

"What kind of hold?"

"I feel safe there."

"That's the last place in the world you should feel safe."

"But it's like what happens in a real family, isn't it? I've seen it a million times. You stay there even though everything tells you it makes no sense and that you should leave. But you can't." He tells her that in all of the homes he's lived in he's always been considered an outsider. Now for the first time he's wanted. George and Irma feel like a family to him.

"That's not how a family works, Leo."

"Then how does it work?"

"By genetics," Ki says, "by...blood."

"That's all chance. Isn't it better to create your own family than to live with the one that was handed to you by your DNA?"

Ki says nothing.

"The way I see it," Leo says, "God or fate or whatever took my family away from me when I was three years old. I spent the next fifteen years in strangers' homes being treated like a dog that snuck in at dinner time."

"And you think this is God's way of paying you back?"

"Maybe. Maybe this is how He evens things out." When he says this, even he can hear how crazy it sounds.

"Putting aside God's plans for a minute, let me speak to you like a lawyer. What you're doing looks bad, Leo. And what if Taylor's body turns up?"

"It won't."

"You can't be sure of that. These people's son is missing. He's dead. You took his money and his passport and now you're living with them pretending to be him."

Leo becomes defensive. "They took me in," he says. "They want me."

"It doesn't matter. You're conning them."

As much as Leo hates that word, Ki is right. Still looking for some justification or rationale for what he's doing, he asks her, "But aren't all families a kind of con?"

"Not like this."

"George and Irma are good people," Leo says.

"They could be saints, but—"

"I don't want to hurt them."

"You already have."

"They feel guilty about abandoning their son," Leo says.

"Their son is an asshole…*was* an asshole."

"They don't know that," Leo says. "I'm their son now. And they love me. George said that meeting him—meeting me—after all these years was the best thing that ever happened to him."

"Listen to yourself, Leo. This is psycho. It's crazy."

She's right. It is crazy.

"Aren't you scared?" Ki asks.

"Of them?"

"Of yourself. These people are not your family." Leo wishes she'd stop saying that. "And you're not their son."

He quotes what Janice Heller wrote to him in her note. "No family is perfect."

When Leo says this, Ki shakes her head and they both laugh. It's as crazy as the last line in the old Marilyn Monroe movie they'd watched together at La Cachette. Nobody's perfect.

Ki stops laughing first. She makes a heart with her finger in the spilled sugar on the tabletop. "You're all I've thought about since I got back here. I thought we had something, you and me."

"We did. We do." Leo wants to say more, but he holds back.

"Did you ever think about looking me up when you got to LA?"

"At first," Leo says. "But I couldn't. I didn't want to involve you in all this."

"What changed your mind?"

"Seeing you last night." Seeing her enthralls him. It confuses him. But he doesn't tell her that. He's told her enough already.

"I have to get back," she says, standing up. She leaves a dollar bill under her cup and Leo follows her out of the café. Is she angry? Does she regret meeting him?

Outside the café he asks her, "If I need it, would you help me? Legally?"

"Technically, I'm not a lawyer yet."

"But you won't tell anyone what I told you?"

"You asked me for advice, so I can't."

"I'm sorry," he says. "I never should have told you all this."

He turns to go but, as he does, she reaches for his hand and pulls him into the quiet hallway that leads to a garage. She pushes him against the wall. She puts her hands behind his head and kisses him hard on the mouth. She closes her eyes like she did when she kissed him on the island.

Ki pulls away from him. "Something brought us together again, Leo," she says. "Maybe it's so I can protect you."

13

Leo doesn't leave Bel Air. He meets with Ki as many times as he can that week and the week after. She's happy to ditch the upscale restaurants where her lawyer colleagues lunch and, instead, takes Leo to places like Pinks' Hot Dogs on La Brea or her favorite pho restaurant in a Venice shopping mall. But she refuses to come to George and Irma's place with him.

"It's a crime scene," she says. "You only want me to go there so I can validate it for you. So I can touch it and tell you it's real. But it's not real, Leo."

Leo knows she's right. He does want someone—especially her—to tell him it's real. But it's not.

Over those two weeks they meet at hotels, several times at a small one in Culver City and once at a fancier one in Beverly Hills. Her husband Carl often goes to New York on business so they spend some nights together at the hotels.

Normally, Leo wouldn't sleep with a married woman, but his feelings for Ki are more than sex. For the first time in his life, he's met someone whom he's comfortable being with and who likes him for who he is. Ki tells him the same thing.

He learns about her past. She went to USC law school. Her husband Carl is an agent for sports stars who, thanks to endorsements, now make more money than movie stars do. Why did she marry him? Good question. Maybe it's because her father had just died. Or because she wanted to prove to her mother that she was grown up. Whatever the reasons, it was a mistake. She and Carl share nothing. His life is sports and betting, statistics and athletes who, when you meet them, seem like they belong to another species. She can name at least three women Carl's slept with since they married. She doesn't care. She doesn't understand why he won't leave her. But Leo knows. It's because she's less annoying to Carl than she is beautiful. It's an uncertain balance, but that will change. Carl will eventually dislike her more than he wants her. Ki's beauty will no longer compensate for the distance between them. Leo's watched it happen to other men.

Leo and Ki spend part of their afternoons in bed eating food they order from take-out or room service. For such a small lady, Ki eats a huge amount and Leo loves that she never apologizes for that like the women on the island always did. He teases her for taking the leftovers home with her and accuses her of having a secret family she's feeding.

They laugh at the daytime shows they watch on TV. Ki does perfect imitations of the ESPN announcers and their guests, some of whom are Carl's clients. "Oh, look," she says, "over-the-hill athletes and the nerds they used to beat the shit out of in school, all desperate to be right about a game that hasn't happened yet." She laughs when she says this, but her contempt for Carl is obvious.

She tells Leo that one of the reasons she loves these afternoons with him so much is because he doesn't talk endlessly like her colleagues do. "It's like what they say about sharks," she says, "if they stop moving they die. With lawyers, if they stop talking they die."

Sometimes her office or Carl calls and she takes her cell into the bathroom so Leo doesn't have to hear. He still thinks what he did when he first met her at La Cachette: that she's too nice to be a lawyer. He can't see her arguing in a court with crude men and women in cheap suits. But maybe her shyness is her weapon. Maybe it lures people into letting their guard down before she pounces on them.

On a Saturday afternoon Ki takes him to visit her grandmother in a nursing home in Arcadia. It's a private facility, antiseptic and painted in calming pastels. Most of its "residents" are Asian and on the weekend the place is filled with visitors. The patients' spouses and adult children amble sadly in and out of the rooms while younger children run through the hallways until they're corralled by their parents.

Ki's grandmother has dementia and lives in a private room. She can't be much older than seventy, but she looks like she's a thousand. Ki introduces Leo to her and when he takes her hand it feels like the tail of a kite. The fragile old woman looks up at him as if she sees nothing. "She's forgotten everything," Ki says, "and now her body will forget, too. Her lungs will forget to breathe. And eventually her heart will forget to beat. That's how she'll die."

Ki whispers something to her grandmother in Korean as they leave and she kisses her softly on the cheek so not to frighten her. Leo's moved by Ki's loyalty. He's always been told that one finds this kind of love only in a family. But he never believed it because he's never seen it until now. Ki speaks to an orderly in the hallway and hands her some cash before they leave. She tells Leo the staff takes better care of patients when you do that.

The second afternoon they spend in the Culver City hotel Ki drives Leo back to George and Irma's place. But she won't drive her car up the driveway and says what she always does. "It's a crime scene." She asks Leo how much longer he plans to stay there. He tells her he's going to leave Monday, five days away. But she says what she always does: "I think you should go now."

"I'll go Monday."

She says she's beginning to wonder if Leo is lying to her about ever leaving George and Irma's.

"I'm not."

"Prove it."

"Now you sound like a lawyer," Leo says.

She doesn't laugh. "Then tell me when you're leaving."

"Monday," he says again.

"If you don't then I can't see you anymore. It's too dangerous. Something bad's gonna happen."

"A few more days," Leo says. "I promise."

She leaves Leo at the end of George and Irma's driveway and drives off.

14

Oh, the weather outside is frightful.
But the fire is so delightful!
And since we've no place to go,
let it snow, let it snow, let it snow!

The Christmas standard blares from a CD player in the Merton's yard as Leo and Ki hang gaudy holiday decorations on a short palm tree. George wears a red Santa hat as he circles a juniper bush with a string of electric lights in one hand and a drink in the other. "And since we've no place to go," he belts out, "let it snow, let it snow, let it snow!" His voice isn't half bad, and Leo and Ki sing the final few lyrics of the song, too. Percy howls along with them as they do.

Ki's finally given in to Leo and she's agreed to come to the Merton's house. But she'll still only park on the main road.

George appears less worried about Neil Weathers. He and Irma are planning a business trip to Palm Springs to meet with investors for their new venture: Irma Stowell for the Mature Woman. George is going to re-label all the old products that are currently sitting in the El Segundo public storage unit and sell them under their new name.

"Is that legal?" Leo asks him.

George shrugs. "Is anything?"

Leo hopes George raises enough money to get them out from under Weathers' thumb. He'd like it to happen before he leaves them. A success like that might distract from the sorrow they'll feel when their son disappears. But this July afternoon Leo puts all that out of his mind.

Nothing ever made him feel more like an outsider in his foster families than Christmas did with its tawdry, hand-me-down gifts that no one else wanted and the family rituals that everybody except Leo knew by heart. But here at George and Irma's home, Leo's helping create a tradition. He hopes his role in this Christmas-in-July celebration will be something for George and Irma to remember with fondness after he leaves them.

Irma sits poolside with a drink. She wanted nothing to do with this stupid celebration, but George convinced her it's important they do it, so she wears a red Santa hat, too. "This damn thing is hot as hell," she says to nobody in particular.

"It's a Hallmark Christmas!" George says, looking for an electrical outlet to plug the light strand into. Not finding one, he solicits Fina's help. The housekeeper, who wears an elf hat, climbs through the shrubbery with the extension cord in her hand. She swears under her breath in Tagalog as the evergreen's sharp needles jab her. All this is more than foolish to her. It's sacrilegious. She finally finds the outlet, plugs in the cord and the string of lights goes on.

"Look at that, will you?" George exclaims.

"Breathtaking," Irma mumbles without looking up from her magazine. She sneaks a look at Ki over the edge of her magazine. Irma had once been as beautiful as this girl. More beautiful. And famous, too. She was on the cover of *TV Guide*, but that doesn't lessen her annoyance at having to see this pretty gook (Isn't that what they used to call them when she was a kid in Wisconsin? Gooks?) drinking her liquor in their backyard. Ki's only saving grace is that she has no tits. The girl has to have some flaw. Otherwise it wouldn't be fair at all.

Ki stands back and admires the lights. "It's gonna look incredible at night."

"What do you want to hear next?" George asks.

"How about a little *Silent Night*?" Irma says.

Ki's had enough to drink that Irma's remark makes her laugh. She's fascinated by Taylor's mother, peppering her with questions about various creams and ointments. She's careful not to call Leo 'Leo'. She makes that mistake once, but all it does is to make the others laugh at what a stupid nickname it is.

The Little Drummer Boy begins to play and Ki says, "Oh, my God, this is my all time favorite."

But after the song's first few notes, Fina shuts the CD player off. "Two men here to see you, Mister," she tells George.

Leo looks at Ki. But she doesn't show any concern. She hasn't heard Fina.

George masks his own apprehension with a joke. "On Christmas Day?"

Irma tenses and sits up. "Who is it?" she asks Fina, never as good as George at hiding her anxiety.

"They not say, Missus."

"Nobody move. I'll take care of it. It's probably Santa Claus. Or his lawyer," says George who turns the CD player back on and increases the volume. He hands a string of lights to Leo and Ki. "You guys finish putting these up."

George goes to meet his visitors while Leo stands on a stepladder holding the lights over the juniper bush. From here he can see two men waiting for George in the driveway. One of them is Pete from El Cantino's parking lot. He doesn't recognize the other man, but he's well dressed. George joins them and the new man walks straight up to him. Their conversation becomes animated.

The Little Drummer Boy on the CD drowns out whatever George and two men are saying. *Come they told me, pa rum pum pum pum*. Ki asks Irma's advice about the hair dye in a magazine ad because she's thinking of coloring her hair. "What hair?" Irma wants to say but, like Leo, she's distracted by what George is doing.

Leo sees the well-dressed man push George who falls out of Leo's line of sight. *I am a poor boy, too, pa rum pum pum pum*. Leo drops the string of lights, climbs off the ladder and hurries over to George who's brushing the driveway's dirt off himself. "What's going on?" Leo asks.

"I tripped over that damn thing." George says pointing to a rake on the ground.

The new man looks at Leo. "Who the fuck are you?"

"That's my son," George says.

"Since when do you have a son?"

"Since he came home. Taylor, this is Neil Weathers. Neil, Taylor."

Neil Weathers has finally made an appearance. He's tightening the noose. Leo shakes hands with Weathers. "What's up?" Leo asks.

"That's between your father and me."

Leo stands his ground. "It's between the three of us now."

Pete laughs. "Go back inside, little boy."

Leo sees that George's hand is bleeding. "Are you okay?" he asks him.

"I cut myself on some of this crap," he says, pointing to the cart full of rusty garden equipment. "Leave Taylor out of this, Neil," George tells him.

Leo says, "I want to know what the problem is."

"You father owes me money. That's what the problem is."

"How much?"

"Two million three," George says.

Neil corrects him. "Two million five as of this morning."

George shrugs. "It's a long story."

"It's a short story, sonny. It's a fucking haiku," Weathers says as he walks to his car. "And don't try to hide from me, Merton, because I'll find you."

"No one's hiding from you, Neil," George says with a forced laugh.

Pete's already in the car so that by the time Weathers gets in and shuts the door it's half way down the driveway.

George, clearly shaken by Weathers' unexpected visit, says to Leo, "That was brave what you did for me, son."

Leo points to George's hand. "You're bleeding."

George waves it off. "I always bleed there."

"You don't have the money he wants, do you?" Leo asks.

"Not right now, no, but I'm gonna make it right. Don't you worry."

Irma and Ki arrive at the scene. Ki hasn't seen the two men or their argument with George, so she doesn't think what's happened is anything more than an accident.

Irma points to George's hand. "You're bleeding."

"I fell on these damn things," George picks up and waves a pair of rusted garden clippers. He hands them to Irma who holds them at arm's length, "I hate the sight of blood."

"How do you think I feel?" George says.

Irma gives the clippers to Leo who tosses them back into the cart. Ki takes George's arm in her hand. "Let me see."

"Did I cut an artery?"

"Not even close. But you might need a couple of stitches."

"Get in the car," Leo said, "I'll take you to the hospital."

"No hospitals."

"When did you get your last tetanus shot?" Ki asks George as Irma opens the door of the Mercedes and pushes him into it. Some of his blood rubs off onto the back of the front seat.

George gets out of the car. "I told you I'm not going to any hospital."

"Jesus, George, you got your blood on the leather," Irma says and tries rubbing it off the seat, but only makes it worse.

Ki tells George to hold his arm up. "We need something to wrap your hand with. Use your shirt," Ki tells Leo. Leo takes off his polo shirt and Ki ties it around George's forearm to stem the blood.

"You some kind of a nurse or something?" George asks her.

"Girl Scout."

"Look what they did to your shirt, Taylor," Irma says. "That's a real Polo."

"I'll buy the kid a new one," George says. "The girl's a magician. The bleeding's already stopped."

"Let me see," Ki says and gives Leo his shirt that she used as a bandage. She looks at George's wound. "It's not so bad."

"So I don't have to go to the hospital?"

"Not if you disinfect it and keep it wrapped up you don't."

Fina brings out a bandage. "Go get me some Lysol or something," George says to her.

"You don't put Lysol on a cut," Irma says. "Even I know that. I'll get you something. And give me that thing." Irma grabs Leo's shirt from him. "I'll soak it before the blood sets in."

Irma and Ki go into the house to look for disinfectant, leaving George and Leo alone on the driveway. The CD keeps playing *The Little Drummer Boy* while George watches Leo pick up a small spade, a worn gardening glove and a bag of Miracle-Gro that's fallen out of the cart.

George is staring at Leo with a smile on his face. "What?" Leo asks him.

"Nothing at all," George says.

I played my best for him, pa rum pum pum pum.

15

Leo sees Fina putting two of Irma's Louis Vuitton suitcases into the Mercedes when he climbs out of the pool the next morning.

"Let me help you," he says and picks up the larger of the two suitcases and puts it into the trunk.

"Thank you, Mr. Taylor."

George comes out of the main house and hands Fina another bag. He greets Leo garrulously for so early in the morning. "Want a drink, old boy?" It's not ten o'clock yet, but George holds a bloody Mary, his first Leo hopes. "Of course you don't. Here's the deal, son, your mother and I are going to Palm Springs."

Irma comes out of the house holding her own bloody Mary. "We're meeting the investors for our new line," she says.

George leans in to Leo. "But before we get to Palm Springs we're meeting with Weathers."

Leo's surprised. "Why?"

"I called him last night and said that I have a deal I want to talk with him about. I'm gonna offer him a piece of our new venture, Irma Stowell for the Mature Woman. A big piece of it. A very big piece."

Leo looks from George to Irma and back again. "You think he'll take it?"

"Your guess is as good as anybody's," Irma says, checking her bags to make sure Fina hasn't forgotten one.

"What choice does he have?" George says. "Other than to kill us?"

Irma rattles the ice in her drink. "Kill *you*, you mean."

"Kill *me*," George says, winking at Leo. "We're meeting with him this afternoon and then heading to Palm Springs to line up the money for the deal. You have our cell number in case you need us?"

"What's he gonna need us for?" Irma asks. "He's a grown man for Chrissake. He can take care of himself."

"I'm making sure," George says and picks up the last suitcase sitting on the walkway. "We'll be back in a couple of days, son."

Their trip to Palm Springs will make it easier for Leo to leave because George and Irma won't be there when he does. "Good luck," Leo says and kisses Irma on the cheek. He can smell alcohol on her breath. George hugs Leo as tightly as he did when he first met him at the airport and he holds him like that for several seconds. It's almost as if George knows that, by the time they get back, Leo will have left and neither of them will see their son again.

"Let's go, for Chrissake," Irma yells. "Traffic's gonna be hell."

Salesman to the last, George says, "Everything's gonna be fine, son, you'll see. Don't worry about us. We're coming back with great news." But George's optimism sounds forced, even for him.

George starts the car and gives a short honk as he heads down the driveway. The last thing Leo sees, the last thing he'll see of either of them, is George's hand waving goodbye to him through the car's open window.

Leo calls Ki and tells her that George and Irma have left on a trip to Palm Springs. This will be his final night in Bel Air.

Because Carl's in Colorado to watch a client play baseball, Ki says that, to celebrate Leo's leaving, she'll come over to spend her first and only night with him in Bel Air. She whispers into the phone that she wants to fuck Leo in the pool.

"No, you don't," Leo says. "You only want to make sure I'm leaving."

"That, too."

16

Early that evening a call comes into the L.A. West Division reporting that two kids are hanging out in an illegally parked car off the road leading to the horse stables in Will Rogers Park in Pacific Palisades. The woman who makes the call says the kids look too young to drive and have probably stolen the car. It's too fancy for them.

When the two responding officers, Rivera and Fellows, get there the car's empty. The kids are gone. Fellows jokes about them being eaten by P47, a mountain lion that lives in the area.

A few minutes later Detective Louis Ford and Officer Denise Riccio, a recruit Ford works with, drive up the hill to the State Park. Riccio parks their squad car behind the Mercedes in question.

Ford circles the car, a brown 1986 Mercedes 420 SEL. There are some small scratches on the passenger side door but, other than that, it looks well taken care of and its owner isn't likely to have left it there.

Rivera tells Ford that the car hasn't been reported stolen, not yet anyway. Riccio points to a stain on the front passenger seat. "That look like blood to you, Detective?"

Ford looks at the stain. "Good eye," he says to Riccio. He wants the young recruit to feel part of the investigation.

"Think we should have the lab take a look at it?" she asks him.

"Absolutely."

Fellows tells them, "The car's registered to a George Merton on Vestone Way in Bel Air."

"Why does that name sound familiar?" Ford asks him.

Rivera says that Merton's married to Irma Stowell. Ford, Rivera and Fellows all react to the news.

"Should I know who that is?" Riccio asks.

Ford grins. "She was before your time, Officer." He asks the other two cops to call in and have the car towed to the impound lot on South La Brea where Mr. Merton or someone he sends can pick it up.

"What do you think, Officer?" Ford asks Riccio when they get back in their car, "Should we go to Bel Air and tell Irma Stowell that we found her Mercedes?"

17

While Detective Ford decides whether to tell Irma Stowell that her husband's Mercedes has been abandoned in Will Rogers Park, George and Irma sit in a rental car in the empty parking lot of a church off Mulholland Drive. It's almost midnight and the view of the San Fernando Valley below is a flat one of endless lights disappearing into a distant mountain. In the dark you can't see the smog or the hideous shopping mall architecture below. What city isn't beautiful at night? Irma asks herself. Even the goddamn San Fernando Valley.

"There's got to be a better way of doing this," George says as he drums on the steering wheel.

"There isn't." Irma says. "We've been through it a million times and this is the way we're doing it. It's too late to quit now. End of story. And stop pounding on the goddamn wheel like that. You're making me nervous."

George takes his hands off the steering wheel. "Maybe we can wait and see what happens. Neil will cool off."

"In my experience, darling," Irma says, "people don't cool off about money unless you give it to them and, in case you forgot, we don't have any to give him."

"I'm gonna offer him a stake in the new venture. Fifty percent, sixty percent, whatever he wants. Within reason."

"The last thing Weathers wants to hear about is one of your godforsaken ventures."

Irma's right and this annoys George. "How did everything get so goddamn complicated?" he asks.

"It's not complicated. It's simple, as simple as we can make it. Everything will work just fine."

"One mistake and it could all fall apart."

"It doesn't matter. If it falls apart, we've covered our bases. We've done nothing wrong. The alternative is that Weathers hurts us."

"He won't hurt us."

"He might not hurt me," Irma says, "but he'll have no problem hurting you, sweetie-pie. You're the one who was in prison. You should know about that shit better than anyone."

The truth of what she says quiets George. Irma was in the El Cantino parking lot when Neil Weathers' two goons threatened them and she was there when Weathers came to the house during their ridiculous Christmas celebration. But George has never told her about the half dozen other times Weathers' men followed him into a store or "accidentally" spilled a coffee on his sleeve in a Starbucks, signs that Weathers' patience is coming to an end.

Finally, a car pulls slowly into the lot from Mulholland, and George and Irma sit up and stare at it. "Is this him?" George asks.

"How the hell should I know?"

"Look at me," George says. "I'm shaking. Why did we agree to do this?"

"Stop asking me that for Chrissake."

They both look at the car as it moves slowly toward them. They can hear the loose gravel beneath its tires.

"It's him," Irma says.

"How do you know?"

"Because I do."

George and Irma watch as the car comes to a stop facing them, its headlights shining brightly into their own car, forcing Irma to shield her eyes. "Why doesn't he turn off his goddamn lights?" George says nothing as his fingers beat out a rhythm on the steering wheel. "And stop that, will you?" Irma says. "You're driving me nuts."

George stops his tapping as the other car's door opens.

"It's him," Irma says.

Taylor Hoffman steps out and walks toward them across the unlit parking lot, his figure backlit by his car's headlights.

PART FOUR

Los Angeles

18

Taylor opens the rear door of his parents' car and gets in. "Mom, dad, what a pleasant surprise," he says with as much sarcasm he can muster.

"Where the hell have you been?" Irma asks him. "We've been sitting here for over an hour."

"Where the hell have *I* been? I've been sitting in a fucking backwater listening to the same five chords of reggae for a month waiting to get the go-ahead from you."

"It hasn't been a month and we never gave you the go-ahead," George says.

"I realize that, old man, but I wasn't about to wait any longer."

"We had to let it play out right," George says. "We still do. You shouldn't have come. Things aren't ready yet."

"They're ready when I say they are," Taylor says, staring at his father. This is not the slacker who shared his room with Leo at La Cachette. This young man wears an expensive gray suit with a dark tie and his hair is fashionably cut and gelled. He speaks with an almost too-perfect diction.

"Relax, both of you," Irma says. "Like it or not, George, our boy's here now."

"And it's such a pleasure to see you, too, mother." Taylor leans over the back of the front seat and kisses her on the cheek. "You look good. Are they having a Botox special at Walmart this week?"

"Bite me."

"Seriously mother, you do look good. But lying always makes a woman look younger. Especially you." Taylor punches his father on the shoulder. "How's business, old man?"

George says nothing, so Irma answers. "Weathers has been breathing down our necks day and night, that's how it is. I was afraid he was gonna come out of those bushes over there and stab us."

"No one's coming out of the bushes to stab you, mother, and your need to exaggerate is most annoying." Taylor sits back in his seat. "You can relax now because I'm here. We can finally get this show on track."

Taylor then goes over the plans he made, plans George and Irma agreed to, constantly reminding his parents how clever he is to have come up with them in the first place.

George does not like his son and his regrets for having reconnected with him resurface now, stronger than ever. It was Irma's idea two years ago that they find Taylor who'd soon be twenty-three years old. The guilt they'd had all those years at giving him up was lessened by the wealth and prestige of the family that took him. It wasn't like the kid was suffering. He was privileged in a way most people could only dream of. The many businesses, lawsuits, bankruptcies and prison term that George and Irma went through helped erase any guilt they had about what might be seen as selling him. His life was better than theirs.

But two years before, Irma was diagnosed with a common precursor of cancer, cervical dysplasia, and suddenly the most important thing for her to do before she died was to see her child. George didn't like the idea, but went along for Irma's sake. What could he say? The woman was sick. She might die. And it'd be easy to find the boy. If he wanted to be found. And if they did find him, how much trouble could he be? They might all benefit from a reunion, especially Irma.

George let himself become excited at the idea of reconnecting with his son. He read books and articles about parents who'd reunited with the children they'd given up years before. Without exception, their experiences were nothing short of magical. George imagined all the things that the three of them would do together.

But from the first moment nine months earlier when Taylor took a seat across from them in a Manhattan Beach International House of Pancakes, George knew their reunion wasn't going to be anything like he'd imagined. He wanted to like his son. Hell, he wanted to love the kid. Isn't that what parents are supposed to do? But instead, he immediately recognized in Taylor all the young men he'd crossed paths with in the Danbury prison, a frat house of sociopaths in which Taylor would have fit right in and most likely have ruled.

The way Taylor spoke to people, in this case their overweight IHOP waitress, exposed the boy's cruelty. When the server—her name was Gloria—became confused it was as if Taylor smelled blood. He turned vicious, zeroing in on her stutter that appeared suddenly. Like all bullies, Taylor knew exactly what buttons to push. The poor girl left the table in tears and another waitress finished serving them. The manager picked up their tab.

George shared his doubts with Irma about Taylor after that first meeting, but she accused her husband of overreacting. The boy was still a child; he was nervous, trying to impress them. If George would shut up and wait, he'd see.

But George knew it wasn't the boy's age. Or nerves. As far as he could see, Taylor didn't have any nerves. He was damaged goods. Was it their fault for giving him away like they did? Or were the Hoffmans to blame? Maybe it was the old argument of nature versus nurture? While in prison George had decided it was nature. The men who George shared cells with were like rabid dogs. They had no choice over who they were or what they did. They were doomed from the start. Still, even though it's not the animal's fault, you shoot a rabid dog. That's what George's favorite fictional father, Atticus Finch, did. That scene always made him cry. When George was a kid he'd wanted a father like that. Now that he was older, he wanted a boy like Atticus's son and the young man sitting across from him in the IHOP was not that boy.

To be fair, George included himself among those who committed unsocial, admittedly criminal, acts. He was a salesman, in other words a borderline con man, and people were his targets. But he never hurt anyone, not really, and he'd bet anything that his son couldn't say as much.

Irma saw none of this. All she could see in Taylor was a handsome, well-spoken and tastefully dressed man. George hoped it was Irma's illness that fuelled her affection for Taylor and that, when she recovered, she'd see how dangerous he was. She did recover. The dysplasia didn't result in any kind of cancer. Still, she never saw what a miscreant her boy was.

Taylor was no fool. He recognized George's feelings about him from the first day. He considered the old man a clown. He said nothing, but George knew that Taylor knew what he thought of him, and Taylor knew that George knew Taylor knew. Every family lives in a house of mirrors.

Irma asked Taylor to move in with them in Manhattan Beach, but he refused. He was ashamed of them. George was relieved that Taylor kept his distance. The boy went off for weeks at a time and came back with money from "a deal", cash obviously stolen from a mark. George had friends in "the business" and after making calls to a fence in New York, he learned that his son's cons usually targeted the elderly who'd fall in love with the handsome and well-spoken young man. The victim's relatives would come after Taylor, but he was smart enough to con just enough money to make the legal costs of pursuing him and the ensuing publicity more than they were worth. Taylor brought his mother an expensive gift whenever he came back from one of his "trips".

George asked Irma not to tell Taylor about their own financial troubles, but Taylor eventually got the truth out of his mother, including the debt that was sold by George's ex-partners to Neil Weathers. George played it down, but Taylor saw the situation for what it was. Surely, he told them, their house in Los Angeles must be worth a few million. But George and Irma had borrowed against it many times, making it completely under water. The only reason it hadn't been foreclosed on was that banks in LA don't like the publicity that comes with foreclosing on celebrities.

But where his parents saw a problem, Taylor saw an opportunity. He met with them one night in a bar and told them he'd come up with a plan that would solve their problems. George thanked him, but said they didn't need his help.

Irma quieted her husband. "Shut up, George, and let the boy speak. He's trying to help us."

"That's exactly what I'm doing, dad," he said, staring at his father.

Irma looked at Taylor proudly. "Look at the boy; his eyes are sparkling."

"Because this is what I do," Taylor said. "I love this shit." Irma took a small notebook out of her bag ready to write in it as Taylor spoke.

Taylor reminded his parents that they had two problems. One was Neil Weathers. The other was their lack of money. "I can solve both for you," he said.

"How?" George asked.

The first thing George and Irma had to do was throw out their renters and move back into their Bel Air place.

"I can live with that," Irma said, jotting it down in her tiny notebook.

"And you have to hire a housekeeper," Taylor said.

Irma wrote this down, too. "Even better."

"The next thing you do is take out two insurance policies on both your lives."

The mention of "insurance" raised a red flag for George. Even the most amateur grifter knows that insurers are the last people you want to deal with. They're the hardest to con.

But Irma was eager to hear more. "How much?" she asked.

"Ten million. Each."

"Wow," said Irma, impressed by her own worth. "Once we do that, then what?"

Taylor smiled. "Then we have to find someone to kill you."

"I beg your pardon?" Irma said.

"Weathers?" George asked.

"No," Taylor said dismissively. "That's far too obvious." Taylor told his parents about a young man he'd seen at a resort in Martinique the year before. At the time, Taylor was there escorting a "client".

"What happened to your client?" George asked.

"What difference does that make?" Irma said, poised to take more notes.

"The place is called La Cachette and it's full of nouveau riche assholes. The whole time I was there, people kept confusing me with this American kid who lives on the island and makes money by taking tourists to see animals and waves and more waves. That kind of shit. I even saw him once or twice myself. He's white trash. Not as good looking as me, but he'll do for what we need from him."

"And what is that, dear?" Irma said, still taking notes.

"That would be to kill you, mother," Taylor said.

He told them that this boy, who George later learned was called Leo Malone, would be forced to steal Taylor's ticket and passport "after my own tragic death" he said with a grin. Taylor explained how he'd pay off the local police. "This guy will use my ticket to escape back here. But you'll meet him at the airport and he'll continue to pretend being me. He'll have to. And, if I'm right, he'll play along and keep being me so that he'll get something out of it." What would be best was if they got this guy to come to the Bel Air place where their maid would see him. "And maybe some of your friends, too. Do you have any friends?"

George and Irma answered at the same time. "No."

The friends didn't matter. But if this Malone character actually stayed at the house and pretended to be Taylor that would be the icing on the cake.

A couple of days after Malone appeared, George and Irma would disappear and the evidence would point to Malone having murdered them. The drifter would be convicted. Meanwhile, from one of his underground contacts Taylor would get his parents new identities that they'd use to leave the country. "And in no time, the two of you will be out of the country, waiting for your insurance money," Taylor said. "Of course you'd have to remain incognito until we cashed your checks."

For George the plan relied on so many variables he could barely follow it. But when he questioned it, Irma told him to shut up and took more notes. She'd explain it to him later.

George let Taylor think that he liked his plan. But even if Taylor got this other kid to do what they wanted, George knew that, without his and Irma's bodies, there was no chance they'd see any money. Insurance companies had armies of investigators whose sole job was to find a reason not to pay anyone anything, especially if the circumstances were suspect.

But George didn't care about the insurance payout. Let Taylor delude himself about that. The important thing was for Taylor to get them false identities so they could leave and get into a country where Weathers wouldn't find them, a country that had no extradition treaty with the US like Russia or Cambodia. George might be able to set up a new company in whatever second or third world backwater Taylor got them into. Places like that were always full of billionaires eager to invest their money, especially the old Soviet bloc countries. That would be something to think about later. The first thing was to get themselves safely abroad and away from Weathers and everyone else they owed money to.

George never voiced his doubts about the insurance part of the scheme. But he knew that Taylor was certain that he'd collect the insurance payout because sociopaths think they're smarter than everyone else and can easily work them. It's both the grifter's strength and weakness. So George said nothing. Why not let Taylor try this plan of his? At the very least, they'd get out of the country and he and Irma would end up somewhere safe. Nothing would be lost, apart from the money Taylor would waste on the resort and the cash they'd have to pay the local police on the island for their part in it. Let the boy and his mother have their way. Watching their children learn by the mistakes they made was something the fathers on TV shows like *Father Knows Best* reveled in.

When he finishes reminding them of the plan, Taylor sits back in the rear seat of the car. "So, tell me, mom and dad, is our boy Leo buying your act?"

"So far," Irma says.

"Of course he is," Taylor says. "He's done everything I said he would, hasn't he? Though it's hard to believe he's stayed at your place this long. He's got balls."

George shrugs. He hates to admit it, but so far things *have* played out the way Taylor hoped they might. Even better. The Malone kid was still with them.

But the one thing George didn't foresee was how fond he'd become of this boy they were setting up. He's nothing like Taylor says he is. Sure, the kid might have been lying to them for almost a month, but there's an honesty, a goodness to him. Did they really have to use him like they were planning to?

Taylor continues. "He saw you for a couple of easy marks and he went for it."

"I don't know about that," George says.

Taylor ignores his father. "He's the worst kind of bore. Utterly predictable. And the rest of it will go just as smoothly."

"Maybe," George says.

"What do you mean 'maybe'? He took the bait and ran with it, didn't he? I only hope you didn't fuck him, mother."

Irma turns sharply to her son. "Jesus Christ, Taylor."

"Because that would really complicate things."

"I did not sleep with him."

"What about the girlfriend?" George asks his son.

Taylor looks at his father. "What girlfriend?"

They tell him about Leo reconnecting with a girl called Ki at the restaurant. Taylor remembers her from the island. George points out that this is the kind of unexpected thing that screws up a scheme like Taylor's. But Taylor says that the girl's a gift. If they need her to, she can confirm everything that happened on the island and play the perfect witness to Leo's conning of George and Irma here in LA. "In the long run she's the best thing that could've happened," Taylor says.

Irma waves the thought off. "That crew-cutted tomboy is not his girlfriend. She couldn't be anyone's girlfriend."

"He's sleeping with her, isn't he?" George says.

"So what? I'm sleeping with you, aren't I?"

Taylor laughs. "Touché, mom."

"Did you think he might be a fairy?" Irma asks.

"No one calls them "fairies" anymore, mother."

"It took me twenty years to get her to call them *that*," George says.

Irma's not finished. "And let me tell you something else. Kids always tell their shrinks how bad it is to see their parents screwing. Try watching your children do it."

"He's not your child," George says.

Irma snaps at him. "I'm making a point."

Bored by their bickering, Taylor changes the subject. "When are you leaving on this fictitious business trip of yours?"

"We left this morning," George says.

"Then we have to get this plan going. I rented an apartment for you. I'll take you there now. It's a dive, but the other tenants there are all illegals so they won't ask any questions. They won't know who you are. They don't even know who the president is. I filled the refrigerator with food and booze so you won't have to leave the place while I get your paperwork in order. That's the most important thing. Whatever you do, stay inside. Do not leave. Not for a second. Remember: you're supposed to be dead. If you need anything, tell me and I'll bring it to you, all right?"

Irma says, "Anything to get this show on the road."

"Dad?"

"Fine," George says softly.

"I can't hear you."

"I said fine." Clearly, George is not happy.

"Follow me," Taylor says. "I won't drive too fast for you, old man." He gets out of the car and slams the door shut behind him. George and Irma watch him walk across the dark parking lot.

19

Ki gets to Bel Air later than she expects because a meeting at work dragged on forever. When Leo told her that George and Irma went to Palm Springs for a couple of days, she decided to break her own rule and spend the night there with him. Still, like she usually does, she parks her car on the main road, not in the driveway and she hurries up to the guesthouse on foot. Putting her hand over Leo's mouth before he can say anything, she pushes him onto the bed.

"Don't say a word," she says. "Not a single one. I've heard nothing but words and more words the whole day. All I want you to do is fuck me." She takes off her clothes, but while doing this, she sees the photo of Irma hanging over Leo's bed. She grabs the picture off the wall and, laughing, slaps it face down on the desk. She takes off the rest of her clothes and jumps on top of Leo.

Later, they sit on the lounges that border the pool. The Santa Ana winds have been strong that day, making the night a sultry one. Percy lays next to the pool on the stones, still warm from the day's sun.

Ki remains naked, but Leo puts his cargo shorts back on. He's eager to tell her something he's been planning to all day. He wants to get it right. He sees his chance when Ki puts a towel around herself and sits on the pool's edge, dangling her feet in the water. Leo sits next to her.

"I had an idea today," he tells her.

"Before you say anything," Ki says, "I had one, too." She's excited when she tells it to Leo. "Instead of going to Seattle, we could live in northern California. Like San Francisco or even farther north like near the Oregon border. It's so beautiful up there. That way I could still take the state bar exam, which would be a lot easier for me to do, and you could enroll in one of the public California colleges. And it's still far enough away from here that you'd never run into George or Irma. You'd love it up there. What do you think?"

Still preparing what he's been planning to say, Leo doesn't answer her. Instead, he says, "there might be a different way to go with all this."

"What way is that?"

He looks closely at her because he needs to see her face when he tells her his idea. "From the day I got here there have only been two options," he says. "Either I stay with them and live as their son Taylor—"

"—which is crazy—"

"—or I could leave them and be my real self somewhere else—"

"—which is what we're doing—"

"—but maybe there's a third option, one we didn't think of before because it's so obvious."

Confused, Ki stands when he says this. "What kind of option?"

"What if I told them the truth?"

"Told who the truth?"

"George and Irma," Leo says.

"What part of the truth?"

"Everything."

"Are you crazy?"

"Think about it. What if, when George and Irma get back from Palm Springs, I sit down and tell them exactly what happened to Taylor on the island."

"About him dying?"

"And how I got here. Who I really am. My name. My past. Everything."

Ki backs away from him. "You're not serious."

Leo ignores her. "I'd tell them how Taylor was killed and how I was set up to take the fall and why I had to escape the island any way I could. I'll tell them that I never meant to deceive them, but that I was scared and confused when they met me at the airport. I was lying to them, sure, but what else could I do? And even though they'll never see Taylor again, maybe I could be a kind of replacement. I could even show them the note Dr. Heller wrote to me about how families are pieced together in all kinds of different ways. I don't know why I didn't think of this before."

"You didn't think of it before, because it's insane," Ki says. "You want to tell two parents, whose son is dead, that you've been pretending to be that son for the last month? The first thing they're gonna think is that you killed him."

"But I didn't kill him."

"But they're gonna think you did."

"How do you know?"

"Because I'm a lawyer. I listen to people all day long. And the first thing everyone thinks is the worst thing they can imagine. The minute someone opens their mouths they start to lie and they think everyone else is lying, too."

Concerned by Ki's tone, Percy gets up and heads to the main house.

Ki walks around the pool's edge. "The past three weeks I've been making plans with you, Leo. I'm ditching my husband for you. I'm leaving my job, my grandmother, my whole life down here and going somewhere with you so we can be together. And once we do, you and I will have a family. A real one. Not like this crazy one here. If you leave here, then when George and Irma get back from Palm Springs they'll realize that their psycho son disappeared. Like he always does. Maybe they'll be sad for a few days or a week, but so what? That's not your fault. You're free. We're free. They're free, too. But what you're saying now makes me think that I've been making a mistake."

"You're not."

"But if you tell them who you really are," Ki says, "you're putting everything at risk. Including me. Sure, there's a chance George and Irma will forgive you and embrace you like a replacement for their long lost son. But there's a better chance they'll go straight to the cops. And they'll be even more pissed off if they were hoping to get any kind of money from you."

"Money has nothing to do with it."

"Money has something to do with everything," she says. "Okay, maybe they don't give a shit about any money, but it's still too risky to tell them what you've done. It's crazy" she says. She turns and walks to the guesthouse. "I'm going."

Leo follows her. "No, wait," he says and, reluctantly, she lets him embrace her, before she pulls back from him and smiles. Leo's confused when she does this.

"What?" he asks her.

"Can't you see what you're doing, Leo?"

"What?"

"You want to become their foster kid."

"No, I—"

"Listen to yourself. If you do what you're saying, then you're becoming the foster kid in another family. This family. This crazy, messed up family. You want to play that role because it's the one you've always played. It's the devil you know. But it's not safe, and you know it's not safe, but that doesn't matter to you because people always return to what they know even if it's no good for them."

Leo considers what she says. It never occurred to him that if they do what he's suggesting, he'd be like George and Irma's foster kid. "You're right," he says. "My idea is crazy. I'm sorry. Being here has affected me. I'm not thinking straight. You see things I don't. We'll leave together in the morning like I said I would."

"You promise?"

"Swear to God."

Ki takes his face in her hands. "You're like a child," she says sweetly. "When we live together, I'm gonna have to get you a babysitter so you don't get yourself into trouble." She smiles at him. "Tomorrow morning, I'm putting all your shit in your bag myself and following you out of here."

They kiss, but as they do, a car pulls into the driveway and Ki looks over Leo's shoulder to see who it is. "Is this them? George and Irma? Are they back already?"

Leo looks at the car, too. But it's not George and Irma's car.

It's a police car.

When Ki sees it, too, she lets go of Leo. "What are they doing here?" she asks as she watches the squad car pull in next to Leo's MG. "You think they're here because of you?" Her voice becomes more tense. "What if they found Taylor's body? Or if they found out who you are? I knew I never should've come here. Shit."

"Relax," Leo says as much to himself as to her. "It's probably nothing."

But this doesn't calm her. "I can't let them see me here."

"Come with me," Leo says and pulls her into the guesthouse. "Where's your car?"

"On the street, thank God."

Leo takes her into the bathroom. "What am I supposed to do in here?" she asks.

"Stay and be quiet," Leo puts the toilet seat lid down. "You'll be fine."

She sits on the toilet lid. "They'll know I'm here."

"They won't."

"Whatever you do, don't tell them who you are."

Leo shuts the bathroom door and scans his room, looking for anything that might implicate him. But implicate him for what? He's a young man living in his parent's guesthouse. That's what it looks like, doesn't it? That's what it is. Why should anyone have a problem with that?

There's a knock on the guesthouse door and he opens it. He's surprised to see Fina. He thought she'd already gone home for the night. Did she hear his argument with Ki at the pool?

Fina ushers a Black man in a dark suit and a younger white woman in a police uniform into the guesthouse. She points to Leo. "This Mr. Taylor."

"Louis Ford," the suited cop says. He sounds bored which makes Leo nervous. He's heard policemen use this tone when they wanted to distract his foster parents before springing an accusation on them.

"Hello, Detective," Leo says, shaking hands with him. "Come in. What brings you here?" Did he sound too carefree? Too much like George sounded that morning? His foster parents always sounded overly casual whenever the police came to their homes. Is Leo's voice like that now?

Ford takes a small notebook out of his pocket and writes in it with a yellow pencil. The uniformed cop offers Leo her hand and he shakes it. "Officer Riccio," she says.

Leo sees Ki's panties on his bed at the same time Riccio sees them. Leo and Riccio make eye contact, but the policewoman says nothing.

"And you are?" Ford asks Leo.

"Taylor Hoffman, the Merton's son," Leo says. Is he overcompensating now by sounding too formal? He tells himself to relax. He hates that he's such a bad liar. Ki says she likes that about him, but she's probably not so happy about it now.

Ford picks up a small, framed photo of George and Irma from Leo's desk. "Your mother is Irma Stowell?"

Leo nods. "That's right, officer."

Ford points to Fina. "This woman told us your parents are away."

"They are," Leo says, trying to determine what's too little to say and what's too much.

The uniformed cop looks at a sheet of paper in her hand. “They drive a car registered to George Merton. A 1986 420 SEL Mercedes.”

“Yes, ma'am, that's dad's baby,” Leo says, smiling. Now he's mimicking James Dean in some movie that he and George and Irma watched when she got back from the hospital. But that's not good because James Dean always looks like he's hiding something. Leo stands up straighter. “Why do you ask, Detective?”

Riccio answers. “We found the car abandoned near Will Rogers Park.”

Leo's upset when he hears this not because he thinks it implicates him in anything. He's worried about George and Irma. Did Weathers refuse their offer and do something to them? But he can't think about that now. He has to deflect anything the cops say from himself. “That's weird,” Leo says. “They took it on their trip this morning.” Leo looks at Fina. “Right?”

The two cops looks at Fina who shrugs weakly at what Leo asks her.

“Did they tell you where they were going?” the detective asks him.

“Palm Springs. On business.”

“What kind of business?” Ford asks.

“My father's raising capital for a new venture,” Leo says, using the same word George did for the project, hoping to make it sound more believable. “Irma Stowell For the Older Woman. No, wait, that's not it. Irma Stowell for the Mature Woman.”

Ford writes this in his notebook. “And they were driving to Palm Springs?”

“I assume so. Or maybe they took the train,” Leo says. “They might have parked the car at the station and someone stole it.”

Riccio agrees with him. “That's possible.”

“Is your father having any trouble with anyone?” the detective asks.

“What kind of trouble?” Why were they asking Leo this?

“Competitors,” Riccio says.

"My father has competitors, sure, but I don't know if I'd say he had 'trouble' with any of them." Leo wants to sound as if he knows what's going on with George and Irma. He's their son, after all. So he says, "Now that you mention it, there was one colleague my father was having some trouble with." By bringing up Neil Weathers without actually naming him, Leo hopes he'll distract them from wondering what Leo's story is. If they're even doing that.

"What kind of trouble?" Ford asks and Leo regrets having said anything about Weathers.

"The usual. Money stuff. My father doesn't tell me much about his business. It's not my thing," Leo says. Is he being too casual now?

The Detective's interested. "Who's this colleague of theirs?"

"A Neil something. I forget his last name." He has to make it sound real, so he turns to Fina and says, "You remember, Fina, don't you? The guy who came here the day we were putting up the decorations?"

Fina shakes her head no.

"She doesn't remember," Ford says as he writes this in his notepad.

Leo's not going to say much more, especially if Fina won't back him up.

"You haven't heard from them since they left this morning?" Ford asks.

Leo shakes his head. "Is there a problem, officer?"

Riccio says, "What concerns us is what looks like a blood stain on the front seat."

"Shit," Leo says. His concern is real until he remembers how the blood got there. "Wait. That was from an accident my father had with the garden shears." He turns to Fina. "Remember? When we were putting up the Christmas decorations last week?"

"In July?" Riccio asks.

Leo smiles at her, hoping it doesn't look forced. "It's a long story, Officer," he says and turns to Fina again. "Remember?" But Fina shakes her head no again.

"She doesn't remember that, either," Riccio says.

"Sure you do," Leo says to Fina. Shit. Why is she being so unhelpful? Has she suspected all along that Leo's not Taylor and is trying to nail him here? At least she's said nothing so far to the police about his having come home like the prodigal son. He's thankful for that.

"You were stringing the lights around that bush," Leo reminds her, "and my father cut himself with the clippers, remember? We were gonna take him to the hospital in the car and that's probably when he got blood on the seat."

"Yes," Fina says, "your girlfriend help him then."

"See? She does remember," Leo tells the detectives.

Ford looks up from his notebook. "Your girlfriend was here, too?"

"She's not really my girlfriend. Just someone I met. I don't even remember her last name." He hopes Ki hears him say this.

The Detective says, "Why don't you try calling your parents while we're here, Mr. Hoffman?"

"Right. I should've thought of that before. I got his number right here." Leo grabs the cell phone from the desk and dials it. The four of them wait silently as it rings. It feels like forever. Leo pictures Ki in the bathroom sitting on the toilet lid. After several rings, George's cell phone answers. "This is George Merton. Tell me something I don't know."

Leo leaves a message. "Hey, dad, it's Taylor," he says, the faces in the room watching him. "The cops found your car and are here to see what happened. I want to know, too. Call me when you get this message."

Leo hangs up and says to the police, "You got me worried now."

"Like you said, the car might've been stolen," Riccio says, "and your parents probably don't even know it yet."

Leo nods at the idea. "If you know my parents, that sounds like the most likely scenario."

Ford hands Leo his card. “If you hear from your parents, tell them to call me. Or you can call me if you think of anything else, Mr. Hoffman.”

“I will, Detective. Thanks for coming by.”

“It’s probably nothing,” Ford says.

Ford and Riccio leave with Fina. Leo waits until he hears their car start up and head down the driveway before opening the bathroom door.

Ki comes out of the bathroom and grabs her panties from the bed. “These were sitting there the whole time. Did they see them?”

“No,” Leo says. This is a lie. He knows that Riccio saw them. Maybe Ford, too. Ki looks at Leo. Could she tell he was lying?

“How can you be sure?”

“Because they would’ve said something,” he says.

Ki rounds up her few things and stuffs them into her bag that she’s hidden under the bed. She sits on the edge of the bed and stares at the floor. She’s shaking. “Shit, shit, shit. You told them my name.”

“I only said Ki.”

“Couldn’t you make something up?”

“I’m a terrible liar.” Leo says and sits next to her.

“I can’t be involved in this.”

“In what?”

“I could get arrested. They’d never let me become a lawyer then.”

“You won’t get arrested.” She looks up and stares at Leo. “What?” he asks.

She pauses before she says, “Tell me you didn’t do it.”

“Do what?”

“Kill them.”

“What are you talking about? ‘Kill them.’ Who said anybody was killed?”

“That’s what that cop was implying.”

“He didn’t say anything like that.”

"He said there was blood."

"From the accident. With the clippers. You were here that day. You were the one who bandaged George up, remember? I explained all that to him."

"They wouldn't have come here if they didn't suspect it was more than that." Ki gets up and moves away from Leo. "I want to hear you say it."

"Say what?"

"That you didn't kill them."

"Are you serious?"

"Say it."

What she asks is less a demand than a plea. Even so, Leo's upset that she thinks it's possible that he'd do something like that. He and Ki are going to leave together and start a family. "That's crazy," he says.

"Why is it crazy? I don't know you. Not really. I met you a month ago on some island. Now look at what you're doing, living here and pretending to be these people's son who's missing. Who's dead. No one else knows that but you. But he is dead. And now you're the sole heir to the Stowell Cosmetics fortune—"

"—there is no fortune—"

"—or at least you're pretending you are."

"There's no fortune."

"It doesn't matter. Try thinking like a policeman, Leo."

She's right. Ki knows how men like the detective think. Leo looks at the card Louis Ford gave him. It'd be natural for Ford to see Leo as the perpetrator. But the perpetrator of what? Nothing has happened. Has it?

"I didn't kill anybody, Ki," he says. "And no one said George and Irma were dead, either. We don't even know if they're missing yet." He grabs her. "They're probably in a hotel in Palm Springs drinking martinis and selling their Irma Stowell shit to some rich Arabs."

Ki relaxes; she smiles. "You're right. I'm sorry. I lost it. I believe you, I do, but you have to understand that I've got a lot on the line here." She pulls away from him. "I can't stay here tonight, Leo. Not now. I never should have come in the first place," she says, hurrying out of the guesthouse. "You've gotta leave, too."

"I will."

"I mean like right now. Tonight. This changes everything. Don't you see? Even if nothing happened to George and Irma, the cops have been here and they've seen you here. It's too dangerous to stay here. Get out of here and we'll go somewhere new and start over like we said. Please." She kisses him hard on the mouth before she walks down the driveway to the road where her car's parked.

Walking back to the guesthouse, Leo crosses paths with Fina who's putting the garbage into a bin. Percy sniffs at the can. "Are you going home now, Fina?" he asks.

"I stay when Mister and Missus away."

What does she think about George's car being found like it was? What does she think of everything since Leo got here? A guest at La Cachette told him that the hired help in their homes are like the chorus in a Greek play. They see everything, usually more than the people who live in the homes do. That's how they can explain the plot so well to the audience. Better than the play's main characters can.

Percy follows Leo into the guesthouse where he'll sleep under Leo's bed.

20

Denise Riccio drives the squad car down the canyon road and Ford looks at the affluent homes they pass, most of them far from the road and hidden behind thick trees and bushes.

Denise Riccio's father Robert was Ford's first partner when Ford graduated from the academy twenty-six years before, so Ford knew her as "Denise" long before he knew her as Officer Riccio. Now that she's in a uniform, she's made it clear that she wants her relationship with Uncle Louis to be completely professional. No family shit. Ford gets that. He doesn't call her Denise, but he can't bring himself to call her Officer Riccio, either. He's been to the girl's First Communion and high school graduation. So he calls her "Riccio" and sometimes "officer", but almost never "Officer Riccio" unless he's driving home a point.

"What do you think, Officer?" Ford asks her.

She makes the turn onto Sunset. "You know there was somebody in the bathroom, don't you?" she says.

Ford saw the panties on the bed, too. But he's waited to say anything, hoping that Riccio had seen them. "What do you think? Boy or girl?"

"Those were girl's panties," she says.

"That doesn't mean much these days."

Riccio gives him a look of impatience that Ford meets with a shrug. Denise is gay. A lot of officers are now. In Ford's early days on the force, a lesbian like Denise would have kept it quiet or been hounded out by the department's Neanderthals. Ford's happy things have changed. Denise's father isn't. She came out while she was still at the Academy and he was furious, more as a cop than a Catholic.

"The panties looked small to me," Ford says. "You don't think he was hiding a kid in there, do you?"

"I don't."

"Why not?"

"I just don't."

Ford's happy to defer to Riccio when it comes to questions about sex. She's usually right about them and Ford hopes she's right about this. He wouldn't forgive himself if it turned out the guy they just questioned at Irma Stowell's place had an under-aged boy or girl locked in his bathroom. "So why would the lady have been hiding?" he asks.

Riccio shrugs. "Married?"

"Maybe." Work a few years as a cop and you find out most questions are easily explained because people are so predictable. They rarely do anything unexpected and they almost never do anything either interesting or original. "He's got a different name than either his father or his mother," Ford says.

"This is LA. Everybody makes up their name."

"Check it out anyway. And see what you can find about his father, George Merton. I remember him being in some kind of business trouble."

"It makes sense what he said about the blood on the seat, right?" Riccio asks. "Like it was an accident. And the maid backed the kid up on it." She calls Hoffman "kid" even though he's not much younger than she is. But she's not wrong. There was something naïve about him, something uncertain. "You think he was lying?" she asks.

Ford agrees that the Hoffman kid seemed nervous. But was he lying to them? Every cop tells you their job makes them experts at knowing when people are lying. But maybe being a cop has nothing to do with it. Maybe just getting older and cynical makes you an expert on lying.

"He might've had dope in the room." Ford calls it "dope" because he's old school. About a lot of things. People tell him he acted like an old man even when he was a kid. His grandmother says that when his mother died he went into his bedroom alone, shut the door and didn't come out for a day. "Twenty-four hours," she said. "You went into that room a seven-year-old boy and you came out an old man."

"You think the media will go crazy with a story like this?" he asks Riccio.

"Not unless something weird happens. They're C-list celebrities."

“Is there really a list?”

“Like everything else,” she says.

“Maybe they should post signs on the front doors of celebrities’ homes with the letter A, B or C. Like they do in restaurants.”

Was that a smile on her face? That’s rare. Ford likes working with the kid and he hopes she likes working with him. He also hopes that she’s right in thinking there’s nothing more to this story than a stolen car, a nervous kid and his girlfriend hiding in the bathroom.

21

Leo wakes up at sunrise and lets Percy out. He puts the cell phone George and Irma gave him into his backpack next to the note from Janice Heller. He sticks Taylor’s and his own passport in the inside pocket of his jacket. He also pockets the letter from La Cachette.

Leo opens the desk drawer and takes some of the cash that George gave him the first day, the same way he’d only taken some of Taylor’s cash before leaving the island. He leaves the antique watch that George and Irma gave him, the one that belonged to her father. He hopes that this will tell George, or whoever finds the money and the watch, that Leo wasn’t a thief, that he didn’t come here only for whatever he could get from them and that, in the end, he wanted to do more good than harm.

He checks the room a last time. He picks up the small, framed photo of George and Irma from the desk. The picture was taken maybe twenty years earlier. The two of them look happy. Leo takes the photo out of the frame and slips it between the pages of his passport.

Percy runs to him as he approaches the MG and Leo tugs playfully on the frayed rope that hangs from the dog’s mouth. “I wish I could take you with me, buddy, but I can’t,” he says.

From the kitchen window, Fina watches Leo playing with the dog. "You need anything at the store?" he yells to her.

Fina shakes her head and Leo gets in the small car. He starts it with a loud burst and heads down the driveway. Percy runs after him for a few yards before he turns around and heads back to the house.

Leo leaves the MG on a side street in Westwood. In a 7/11 he buys a couple of granola bars and a cigarette lighter and he walks to a deserted construction site. It's early so there's hardly anyone on the streets. He stands over an empty metal barrel and takes Taylor's passport out of his pocket. He looks at Taylor's photo a last time. They do—or did—look alike enough to have fooled people. Leo leafs through the passport. Taylor's been to a lot of different places. Leo closes his eyes and says a short prayer as he holds the flame from the lighter to the passport. He swears when the fire singes his hand, but only when he's certain that the passport will burn does he drop it into the barrel. He tosses the letter from La Cachette in after it. This is how Taylor Hoffman's life will officially end: in a rusty barrel on a construction site in West LA.

Leo buys a motorcycle with some of George's cash. It's a beat up seven-year-old Yamaha he finds on Craig's List. The seller, a UCLA student, has no papers for the bike and Leo doesn't ask him for any. It makes the bike cheaper. The kid throws a helmet in with the deal. Leo drives to the Mid-Wilshire district where he gets a room in a motel.

22

Detective Ford is surprised when he gets a phone call from a Mr. Taylor Hoffman. He says that he's just arrived this morning at his parents' home in Bel Air for a much-anticipated reunion only to be told by the housekeeper that they aren't there and that the police were there the night before looking for them. Mr. Hoffman also says the housekeeper is confused about who he is because another man claiming to be Taylor Hoffman has been living there for several weeks.

The man on the phone with Ford is perplexed. None of this makes sense to him, but after putting the pieces together he's figured out what's happened and wants to tell the police. Ford asks the man to wait at the Merton home until he gets there.

It bothers Ford that he'd never asked the young man they questioned the night before for any identification. But why would they? Nothing seemed out of place. The man who said he was Taylor Hoffman reacted as Ford would have expected him to. The housekeeper was cool about everything, too.

When Ford tells Riccio about this second guy's call she grins. "I guess we were wrong, huh?"

Ford and Riccio drive up Stone Canyon Road. Ford looks at the stories she's Xeroxed from old magazine articles about Irma Stowell and her rocky relationship with husband-turned-manager-turned-convicted-felon George Merton. Ford remembers Irma from the popular magazines his grandmother used to read. He hopes Riccio is right when she said they were C-list celebrities that no one will care about. It'll make the investigation easier. Still, the public likes a mystery and one with a celebrity in it, regardless of their alphabetical rating, is even better.

The first thing both Ford and Riccio notice when they get to the Merton home is how much this man who claims to be Taylor Hoffman, the son of George Merton and Irma Stowell, resembles the man they met here the night before.

When Ford asks him for identification he shows them a New York driver's license issued to Taylor Hoffman. Ford gives it to Riccio to check on their car's computer. It's valid.

Before Ford has a chance to ask him anything, this Mr. Hoffman tells them everything that's happened since he arrived at LAX earlier that morning. "The customs officer said that their records indicated that I'd come through LAX a month ago," he says, "and that I hadn't left the country since arriving. I said that was impossible, but they verified that's what was on record." Mr. Hoffman is very exacting, telling his story like a witness on the stand who's been prepped by a lawyer. Ford can't place the man's accent.

While Hoffman's speaking, a dog with long ears approaches him and sniffs at his shoes. Hoffman swiftly kicks at the dog that yelps and hurries back to the housekeeper. Ford turns to her and asks, "What happened to the man we spoke to last night?"

"He leave this morning," she says.

"Let me finish," Mr. Hoffman says sharply to the housekeeper and then he tells Ford and Riccio how he'd met a man named Leo Malone at a resort in Martinique called La Cachette precisely because people mistook them for one another. He thinks Malone is from Oklahoma or somewhere like that. "Even I had to admit the resemblance was uncanny," he says.

Ford notes how different this Mr. Hoffman is from the man they'd met the night before. They look alike, but this one is better dressed and a more polished speaker. The kid last night would never have used the word "uncanny". The one last night was more polite, too, less arrogant. But that might be because he was lying to them.

Hoffman tells them how his passport, airplane ticket and Leo all disappeared the same day. He hadn't made any connection. He assumed that Malone, "a slacker ex-pat American", had simply disappeared and someone else had stolen his documents. It happens all the time in places like that.

"I chastised myself for not placing my passport and airline ticket in the hotel safe," Hoffman says. "You'd think I'd have known better. But I immediately applied to the backwater consulate there to get temporary transit papers done so I could come home and see my parents as planned. There was some snafu with the airline about my ticket having been used, but I was in a hurry to get back here and got myself a new one. Only when I got to LAX did I put it all together: that Malone had stolen my ticket and my passport and has entered the country pretending to be me." He points to Fina. "This one here says my parents met him at the airport and took him home."

When Ford asks him how it was possible that his parents could confuse the two men, Hoffman tells them his history, how his biological parents gave him up for adoption to a New York family the day he was born (which is why his surname is Hoffman). He tells them how they'd tracked him down six months earlier, spoken on the phone and were eager to reconnect with him because his mother is ill.

"After they told me they couldn't make it to Martinique, I thought I'd fly to LA and have our reconciliation here," Hoffman says. "I was very excited to see them, to meet them for the first time really. The best news is that my mother has started to recover. I decided I'd come here this morning and reunite with them without telling them I was coming. I thought it would be a wonderful surprise for them. Now it appears that I'm the one who's been surprised."

"I assume that, at the resort, you told Mr. Malone all these plans about how your parents were waiting to see you, to meet you for the first time really?" Ford says.

"I did indeed."

"And you think he came home before you did, pretending to be you?" Riccio said.

"That's what I just told you, isn't it?" Hoffman says impatiently and points to Fina. "At least that's what she says."

Ford turns to the housekeeper who's said nothing so far. "Are you following what he's saying, ma'am?"

Fina nods to him. It's possible that the woman's here illegally and, even if she isn't undocumented, it's likely that someone in her family is, making her wary of police. Officer Riccio assures her that this is not an ICE matter and the housekeeper tells them that the "other Mr. Taylor" has been staying here almost a month and that the Missus and Mister acted like he was their son. They gave him a car and bought him clothes and took him to eat at fancy restaurants. They even let his girlfriend come to the house. "She here when you come last night," Fina says.

Ford looks at Riccio. She was right. It was a girl.

"Many time I hear the Mister and Missus talking about the man when he not there," Fina says.

Ford asks her, "What did they say about him?"

"They want him to like them."

"Why didn't you tell us this last night?" Ford asks her.

She shrugs. "You didn't ask."

"There you go," Taylor says as if you couldn't expect anything else from a foreign-speaking domestic.

Riccio has trouble wrapping her head around this. "So you're saying that your parents took this guy in thinking he was you? How is that possible?"

"I just told you that my parents hadn't seen me since the day I was born, so it seems very possible," Hoffman says, annoyed by Riccio's question. He points to Fina. "If you don't believe me, ask her."

Ford turns to Fina. "What else did they say about this man?"

"Like he their son."

"But what did you think, Mrs. Incarnacion?" Riccio asks her.

"What do I know?"

Ford smiles at her. "I think you know a lot. Please, tell us. It might help us very much."

"Go on," Taylor says, "tell them. No one will hurt you."

Fina looks from one face to another before saying, "I thought it a bad idea from start."

"That's easy for you to say now," Taylor says.

But Riccio persists. "Why did you think that, ma'am?"

Fina gestures to all of them. "You here now, no?" meaning the police have come because of the boy, proving that it was a bad idea.

"But did you think he was their son, Mrs. Incarnacion?" Ford asks.

Fina says, “No matter what I think.”

“It matters to me,” he says.

Hoffman’s impatient. “For God’s sake, tell them.”

Fina looks at Taylor and then back to Riccio. “I think nothing of it ever good.”

Ford’s intrigued. Is it possible that today’s Taylor Hoffman and the one from last night are working on some kind of scam together? But to what purpose? To con the parents? How would that work? And what do the parents have that they might want? Are they that rich? Riccio said they’d declared bankruptcy two years before. But rich people do that all the time to protect their money.

“How come this Malone guy didn’t think that you’d come home and ruin his scheme?” Ford asks Taylor.

“That’s a good question, Detective, and at first I couldn’t figure that out. Then I remembered reading somewhere how men like that are good at knowing these things.”

“Men like what?”

“Con men, grifters, whatever you people call them. That’s what they do, isn’t it? That’s their skill. They read people. And who knows? By the time I got here, maybe he would’ve persuaded my parents that I was the phony one.”

“Or maybe they knew he wasn’t you all along,” Ford says, “but they felt sorry for him and played along with him.”

Mr. Hoffman looks genuinely surprised by what Ford says. “That’s even harder to believe than the other story and, besides, that’s not how my parents think.”

“How would you know?” Riccio says. “You’ve never met them,”

Her remark annoys Taylor. “All I know, Officers, is that someone stole my passport, came to LA, moved in with my parents, pretended to be me, has lived off them for a month and now they’re missing. He’s missing, too. I don’t mean to tell you your job, but doesn’t this raise a red flag? Shouldn’t you be doing something?”

“That’s why we’re here,” Riccio says.

Before they leave, Ford tells Taylor what he told the man the night before: not to jump to conclusions. It's likely that his parents are fine. He also tells Taylor that it might be safer if he stays somewhere else until Mr. Malone is tracked down and all this is settled. Taylor thanks the Detective for his advice, but says that he's perfectly able to take care of himself.

Before she even gets behind the wheel of their squad car Denise says, "This is now officially weird."

"You think?" Ford says, but he's not sure how weird it is yet. Denise Riccio will eventually find out that many of the cases she'll slog her way through will start with a domestic problem, usually with one person lying to another. Trying to figure out the 'hows' and 'whys' of a family is like walking through a minefield. It's best to keep your distance and watch the other people blow themselves up while they stumble through their own mess. Still, he has to admit that not many cases start out like this.

"You think those two, the kid last night and this one, are working on something together?" she asks.

"Maybe. But the first thing we gotta do is to find out everything we can about the two of them, this Taylor Hoffman and the other one. What did this guy say the other's name was?"

"Leo Malone. From Oklahoma."

23

Irma hates the apartment in South Hollywood that Taylor found for them. Riddled with bugs the size of mice, the nauseating stench of spices and the endless squeals of little brown children, it's even more of a dump than she feared it'd be. If that weren't enough, it's guilty of the three biggest sins of Los Angeles design: cottage cheese ceilings, green shag carpeting and the *piece de resistance*: a wet bar. "What asshole came up with the idea of a wet bar anyway?" she asks George when she sees it. "Hey, I have an idea. Let's put a sink in the living room ten feet from the one in the kitchen. Genius."

But the worst thing about the place is that George and Irma can't leave it, not even for a second. Taylor's plan relies upon their being missing and never found and if anyone recognizes them, it will ruin everything. Taylor will get them new identities in a few days so they can leave the US—separately, not together, of course—and go to a country like Morocco or Cambodia, one that doesn't have a US extradition treaty. Irma likes the idea of Cambodia. It sounds exotic; she's always wanted to go there.

But the more time they spend in the apartment, the more George's doubts grow. He's never been entirely on board with Taylor's plan from the start. He knows from years of working his own schemes that this one's too complicated. The simpler a scheme, the better. They're never going to see any insurance money no matter what Taylor says and now that they're stuck in this small, shitty apartment, George repeats his doubts to Irma. What if Taylor can't get them believable identities? Things like that are a lot tougher since 9/11. There are lists. And people check them. George's guilt about what will happen to Leo if things do work is growing, too.

Irma's response to George's doubts is simple. He only feels this way because he's never liked their son.

George doesn't disagree with her. "Do you? Like him?"

"The boy is my flesh and blood," she answers.

"That's not what I asked you."

But before Irma can say anything else, Taylor enters the apartment and slams the door behind himself. He grins and says, "I worked that cop like a marionette. He bought every thing I told him."

His mother is anxious and his father doubtful, but Taylor expects that. They're amateurs. Worse, they're old. Their doubts will be magnified by his father's ego and his mother's drinking. When they finish the three bottles of booze he bought for them he's not going to replace them.

Taylor brags, "It's working exactly like I said it would."

"Don't get ahead of yourself, darling," Irma says. "You do that a lot."

"And don't you talk to me like I'm ten years old, mother dear."

Irma waves her hands. She's tired of arguing, but she likes when Taylor calls her 'mother' even if he is being sarcastic.

Taylor looks from his mother to his father in the silence that follows and asks, "What's the problem now?"

"Your father has qualms."

"We both have qualms," George says.

Irma points to George who paces on the shag carpet. "Mostly him."

"This is not the time to get cold feet, old man," Taylor says.

"I don't have cold feet. I have doubts. Serious doubts."

"About what?" Taylor says. "They find Malone's shirt with your blood on it. They find the garden shears with your blood and his prints—all of which you set up. Right?"

"Right," George says in a voice so low Taylor can barely hear him.

"We're aware of the roles we played in this, darling," Irma tells Taylor.

Taylor pours himself a glass of water. "They never find your bodies and I'm forced to accept that you've been brutally murdered by a vicious con man that I introduced you to myself. Oh, the cruel irony of it all. But my sorrow's mitigated by the twenty million dollar life insurance that I'm awarded by Colonial Life. Any questions, class?"

George says nothing. He keeps pacing. "It's not right."

"What's not right?"

"Everything. It's wrong."

"Your father's been saying that a lot today."

"What exactly does that mean, father? 'It's wrong'?"

"What do you think it means? Get a dictionary and look it up. Wrong: Evil. Wicked. Immoral. Take your pick." A spark flies from George's finger when he touches the steel wet bar counter. He swears and rubs his hand. Irma looks out the window at the street traffic while George resumes pacing.

"What am I missing here?" Taylor looks from one parent to the other.

Irma turns and points to George. "He loves him."

"Loves who?" Taylor asks.

"I don't love him," George says to Irma.

Irma shrugs. "You said you did."

"I did not say that," George says. "I said that I've grown fond of him. I'll admit that."

Taylor realizes what his parents are saying. "You're shitting me," he says to George and then turns to his mother. "Tell me he's shitting me."

"He's not."

"He's a good boy," George says.

"Malone? Is he really? This 'good boy' of yours watched me get my throat slit and did nothing other than steal my passport and my plane ticket and then come to LA and pretend to be me."

"We all make bad decisions," George says. What can he possibly say that Taylor will understand? He can't tell him that Leo's the son he wishes he'd had all along. The boy wouldn't understand any part of what George is feeling. Sociopaths like Taylor don't have the first clue.

"So what are we saying here?" Taylor asks.

Irma throws up her hands. "Your father and the boy connected."

"You connected?"

"We connected," George says. "We bonded."

"When exactly was it that you bonded with him, dad? When you were setting him up for a life sentence?"

"If you ask me," Irma says, "it was the day your father and he put up the Christmas decorations,"

"Is that why they're up now in the middle of the summer?"

"Traditions like that have a strong effect on families," Irma says.

George shakes his head. "It started earlier. At Dr. Frank's office."

"Who the fuck is Dr. Frank?" Taylor asks.

Irma points at George. "His shrink. The woman he sees on account of his parole."

"You took Malone to your shrink with you?"

"So what if I did?"

"I didn't say you could do that."

"We don't need your permission for what we do," George says.

Taylor looks at Irma. "You hate shrinks."

"We thought it would help establish that we believed he was you," she says. "In case the police asked her."

Taylor's annoyed, but the logic in their plan is valid. Still, he hates that they did anything without asking him first.

"We had a breakthrough," George says.

"What kind of a breakthrough could you have had? He's not your son."

George frowns as he recalls the session with Dr. Frank. He was moved by Leo's memories. The boy's story about his getting sick in the car was heartbreaking. But all George says to Taylor is, "Things were said. Important things."

"He's a con," Taylor says. "He's working you."

George shakes his head. "I'm a con. I know when people are working me and that boy is not working me."

"That's why I chose him. Because I knew the minute you guys acted like you thought he was me, he'd milk you for everything he could get out of you and that's what he did. The last thing I expected was for you, of all people, to fall for *his* scam."

Irma turns to George. "When he says it like that, dear, it does make sense."

But George is adamant. "He's wrong. It's not a scam. You can't fake that kind of emotion."

"You've been doing it your whole life," says Taylor.

George bangs his fist on the wet bar. "He's the son I never had."

Taylor sneers at his father's melodramatic display. "I'm the son you never had, old man."

"Excuse me," Irma says, "but speaking as the only one in this room sporting a uterine canal, I can assure you both that, after much pain and enough epidural to sedate a goddamned water buffalo, you were most certainly had."

"I can't take any more of this," George says, putting his coat on.

"Where are you going?" Taylor asks him.

"Out."

"Out where?"

"Out there."

"You can't leave here." Taylor stands in front of the door. "I'm not letting you."

"Try and stop me."

Irma puts a hand on George's shoulder. "Taylor's right, dear, someone could see you."

"I don't give a shit."

"I've done too much work to let you blow the whole thing apart now, old man." Taylor grabs the sleeve of George's jacket. But despite their age difference his father is stronger than Taylor. George punches him and even though his punch lands clumsily, not on his son's jaw as he intended but above his ear, it sends Taylor stumbling across the room where he slips and hits his head on the counter of the wet bar.

"Taylor!" Irma runs to him, turning to George as she cradles her son's head. "Look what you did to your son."

"Go to hell," George says as he leaves, slamming the door behind him.

Taylor's dazed and bleeding from a cut high on his forehead. His mother holds him.

"I hate wet bars," Taylor says, making Irma feel proud about this taste that she shares with her boy. Maybe it's genetic. Taylor tries to stand, but he stumbles and sits down on the carpet again. "I'll kill the prick."

"Don't talk like that, darling," she says, grabbing a damp towel and dabbing at the cut on Taylor's forehead. Doing this makes her feel maternal. She and Taylor must look like that famous statue of Mary holding Jesus that she'd once seen in Italy while she was doing a *Cosmopolitan* shoot. Granted, in the statue Jesus is dead, but she wishes someone were here to take a picture of them, this mother and her child. "Despite his flaws," she says, "that man is your father." Taylor's cut has stopped bleeding. "Although, left to his own devices, he'll probably bring us all down."

24

Detective Ford leafs through copies of *Vogue* and *Vanity Fair* while sitting in Dr. Frank's waiting room. He has yet to see anyone in either magazine, especially in the ads, who looks like any human being he's ever known. Dr. Frank's door opens and a thin teenage boy—or maybe it's a girl—shoots Ford an angry look as he or she rushes past him and out of the office.

Ford stands up when the doctor, who's younger than he expected, appears in the doorway. "Detective Ford? I'm Phyllis Frank," she says and they shake hands. He's surprised by the tattoos that start on her left wrist, continue up her arm and disappear under her sleeve.

Ford's unsure where to sit in her office. He sure as hell isn't going to sit on the couch like he's in some cartoon. Dr. Frank saves him by dragging a small chair from against the wall and placing it in front of her own, larger chair. "How can I help you, Detective?"

"George Merton's parole officer tells me that he was assigned to you."

"For a time after his release, he was. But he's chosen to continue working with me." She's proud of this. "We've developed a strong rapport."

Ford hands her an enlarged photocopy of Leo Malone's face from his still-valid Oklahoma driver's license. "Is this the man that came in here with Mr. and Mrs. Merton?"

Dr. Frank looks at Leo's photo. "Yes, that's their son Taylor Hoffman."

"Are you sure?"

"Of course I am."

"Just to be clear, you're saying that when George and Irma Merton were here several weeks ago, they came in here with this man and it appeared to you that they believed this young man was their son Taylor Hoffman."

"Of course they did." She laughs in a way that might be taken by some as a put-down.

Ford ignores her laugh, put-down or not. Doctors annoy him. Doctors and airplane pilots, they know everything. "And you, doctor?" he asks.

The doctor sits up straight in her chair. Ford notes that she answers like an experienced suspect does, never saying yes, never saying no. "I know how parents react to their own children, Detective. And their responses were classic. Is there any reason they wouldn't be?"

Ford gestures to the photo she holds. "Because he's not their son."

She pauses. "What do you mean?"

"That man's name is Leo Malone."

"I don't understand, Detective." Dr. Frank looks at the Xerox'ed photo from Leo's drivers license again. "Who is Leo Malone?"

"That's what I'm trying to find out. Right now all I can say for sure is that he's not Taylor Hoffman. He's an imposter."

This news upsets the doctor. "Are you sure, Detective?"

"Positive."

"I've never had anything like this happen before," she says. "Not even remotely. If, as you say, he was an imposter—*is* an imposter—he's an extraordinarily good one because I can tell you, as a professional, the Mertons believed that he was their son."

"Did they?"

"Absolutely."

"Or maybe they fooled you into thinking that they believed he was their son."

Dr. Frank considers and quickly rejects this more complicated possibility, giving a short laugh in reply. "Oh, no, no, no, they couldn't do that," she says. "I've sat in this chair and listened to felons and addicts for almost thirteen years. There are no better liars in the world. I know their tricks. I'm far too experienced for that to have happened."

Ford stands up and hands her his card. "Will you contact me if you hear from George Merton or Irma Stowell again?"

Dr. Frank looks at the card. "Has anything happened to them?"

"We don't know yet." Ford thanks the doctor and leaves. None of this makes any sense. He's still not ready to indict Malone. He gave Malone his card that first night and he hopes the kid will use it to call him and clear everything up. But the longer this drags on, the more unlikely it is that's going to happen.

25

Leo pays cash for his room at the Mid-Wilshire hotel. He collapses on the single bed and goes over his options. He's destroyed Taylor's passport, but maybe that was the wrong thing to do. Doing that and leaving town will make him look even more guilty than ever.

Maybe he should go to Detective Ford now and explain why and how he'd come to LA. He'll be admitting to a crime, a couple of crimes actually, but what if Weathers has done something even worse to George and Irma? Leo, or whoever the police think Leo is at this point, will be on the hook for that and maybe going to the cops now will make him look less guilty. But guilty of what? Nothing's happened yet, has it? If he just disappears, maybe nothing will happen. He's never run from anything before. He's never had to. He lies on the small bed and decides that going to see Ford is his only option. But first he needs rest.

Having gotten no sleep the night before, Leo is out soon after he closes his eyes. Like he often does, he dreams of his parents' death. But this dream is different from the others because in this one, for the first time, his mother speaks to him. She smiles at her son across the gas station's filthy linoleum floor. There's blood on her cheek, but in this dream it's dried blood, not fresh. "What's the matter, Leo, darling?" she asks him.

"I'm scared, mama. I got myself into trouble and I don't know what to do." In the background, Leo hears the sirens grow louder and louder. "Should I tell George and Irma the truth?"

His mother gives a small shrug of her bloodstained shoulder. "I can't really say, sweetie, but I will tell you never to trust anybody but yourself."

"What should I do now?"

"You should do what your mommy and daddy always did."

"What's that?"

His mother smiles at him like she did in the one video he saw of her. "Run," she says and then breaks into a loud, witch-like laugh. "Run like the devil, my little boy, run, run, run!"

Leo's prepaid cell rings over his mother's laughter, startling him out of his dream. He hopes it's Ki. She can help him decide what to do. Maybe she'll even go with him to Detective Ford. He sits up and answers the phone. "Ki?"

But it's a man's voice on the other end. "It's me." Not recognizing the voice, Leo waits. "It's George, Leo," the voice says. "George Merton. I need to see you."

Leo's relieved to hear George's voice. It means Weathers hasn't done anything to him. And if George is safe, that means Leo's safe, too. He can leave with Ki like he plans.

But George has said something that changes everything and he repeats it—"Did you hear what I said, Leo? I'm fine."

Leo sits up, confused. George has called him by his real name and Leo doesn't understand. "How do you know my name, George?"

"That's what we need to talk about, Leo," he says.

By the time George gets to the diner next to the motel, Leo's sitting in a booth having finished his meal, the hamburger special. He's spent the last half hour trying to figure the different ways that George and Irma could have found out who he really is.

Leo sees George standing at the diner's door and immediately regrets agreeing to meet him. Wouldn't the smartest thing have been for Leo to go to the cops and tell them that George called him? The man's unharmed. But would the police believe him when he says that George called him? And before Leo does anything else, he has to know how George has found out who he really is. And what he and Irma will do now that they know.

"Leo," George says as he slides into the booth opposite him. The old man wears a porkpie hat with an unrecognizable animal on its crest and sunglasses big enough to make him look like the blind man in a comedy sketch. Leo says nothing.

"Aren't you happy to see me alive and kicking?" George asks and sits silently as the waitress hands him a plastic menu the size of an election poster. "A coffee for me, darling," George says to her. He taps his fingers nervously on the Formica tabletop and stares at Leo who says nothing. Finally, George speaks. "Taylor's alive."

This is the last thing Leo expects George to say. How could Taylor have survived his throat being cut and dumped into the ocean with chains around his legs?

George explains. "It was a con, kiddo, a crazy goddamned con." And he lays it all out for Leo, going through each beat of the story, from Taylor reuniting with him and Irma in Huntington Beach the year before, to Weathers' threats, to the insurance scam, to Taylor's feigning his death on the island, to paying off the island cops for playing along, to sitting here in this coffee shop with Leo. Any relief Leo felt at seeing George alive has changed to anger by this time.

At first his anger's directed at George, Irma and Taylor. They'd found Leo's soft spot like all good cons do and zeroed in on it the same way his foster father Dan Prescott did when a prospective buyer walked into his Tulsa showroom looking to buy a car.

But Leo's most angry at himself, furious for letting these people play him like they did. It's happened because he did what he'd learned as a boy never to do: he opened himself up to others. Worst of all, he believed what they said. The foster child who'd been shuttled back and forth from one home to another should never have done what the adult Leo did.

"Say something," George says when he finishes telling Leo his story. But Leo says nothing, forcing George, ever the salesman, to fill the silence. "I'm not gonna lie to you, kiddo," he says. "What Irma and I did was wrong. But we were scared. We're still scared. We figured if we were dead, then we'd get Weathers off our backs. You saw how crazy that sonofabitch is."

"Why not just disappear?" This is the first thing Leo says since George has sat down in the booth.

"Because he'd look for us and he'd find us like he's done before."

"What about the insurance money?" Leo asks.

"That? That's bullshit, one of Taylor's pipe dreams. We're never gonna see any money, not from an insurance company. But I can't say that to Taylor or his mother. All I want is for him to work the con long enough that it gets us the hell away from here. If Weathers thinks we're dead or too far away to bother coming after us, that's all I want. He has a record a mile long, so he can't screw around with people the cops are looking for. I'm sorry, Leo. I'm not proud of what I did, but we were on the ropes. We still are."

"You knew who I was all along." Leo says this more to himself than to George.

George plays with the tinny utensils on the table. "It was wrong," he says. "When Taylor came to us with the scheme, the whole idea of us thinking you were Taylor and you pretending to be him was nuts. But I thought what the hell? Why not try it? What's there to lose? To be honest, it was mostly Irma who kept saying that it'd work. And sonofabitch, look what happened: it did work."

"I did exactly what I was supposed to do."

"At first, you did." George's face lights up when he says this. "In my wildest dreams I never imagined you'd buy it. But, damn, I'm a good salesman."

"You're a con."

"You say potato. But then in the middle of it all, the strangest thing happened."

"Did it?"

"That's why I'm sitting here right now with you."

Leo is silent.

"Ask me what happened," George says to him. "Go on, ask me."

"What happened, George?"

"I started to believe in the product I was selling."

"What product is that?"

"You," George says. Leo doesn't respond, so George continues. "Us. You. Me. Irma. Well, not so much Irma, but you and me. Can you imagine how surprised I was? As soon as you moved in, I realized that this is what having a real son is supposed to be like. Like on the TV shows."

"You have a real son."

"That prick should've been drowned at birth."

"They never say that on the TV shows."

"Not on the network shows, no. On cable they might, though," George says. "But you, Leo, you touched a nerve in me. I connected with you."

"You're working me now."

"I'm not. I swear." George claims that he understands Leo. He tells Leo that he, too, lived in an abusive home. Alcoholic parents, a misdiagnosed learning disability, a father who abandoned them when George was a child, a mother who committed suicide, his own early struggles to make a living.

Leo doesn't want to hear any of it. "I have no idea where you're going with this, but one thing I do know is that it's all a part of your scam."

"It's not. I swear to God, Leo, it's not."

"Irma's trip to the hospital, was that bullshit?"

"We thought it would bond you to her."

"What about the visit to Dr. Frank's? What was that supposed to do?"

"Prove to an outsider that we believed you were Taylor." George says. "But forget all that. The point is I was moved by what you said in Dr. Frank's office, Leo, I really was. Couldn't you tell?"

"After your fight with Weathers. You gave me the hedge clippers so they'd have my finger prints on them."

George looks down at his coffee cup. "You're not so dumb."

"My polo shirt that Irma took inside to clean your blood off of. She didn't clean it, did she?" George shakes his head. "The police are gonna find those things, aren't they?"

George nods, ashamed. But, admittedly, a little proud. "I can't believe how well it came together. But that's all irrelevant now."

"So everything you said to me was a lie," says Leo.

"Not everything. That's why I'm here."

Leo stares at him and repeats what he said. "Everything you did and said was a lie, George."

George looks directly at Leo. "You lied to us, too."

Leo pounds his fist on the tabletop causing the plates and silverware to jump. "THERE'S NO COMPARISON."

The waitress and several customers look over when Leo yells this, so George leans across the table and, in a stage whisper, says, "Why would I lie to you now? I'm here looking out for you. I'm here to put an end to this mess. I had to punch Taylor's lights out just now so I could come here to see you. And let me tell you, it felt good doing that. Damn good. I don't want you to take the fall for a murder you didn't commit."

"A murder that hasn't happened," Leo says.

"Exactly. See? You're already on top of this. You're sharp. That's another thing I like about you."

Leo rubs his face with his hands. "What is it you want from me, George? Why didn't you just go to the police?"

George hesitates. "I was hoping before I did anything else, you and me, we could clear all this up between us man to man, put it behind us and start all over again. Like a family."

"We're not a family."

"But we could be."

"Is that what you want? For us to be a family?"

"With all my heart."

"There's only one way we can do that," Leo said.

"Tell me."

"Are you listening?"

"Loud and clear."

"We go to the police, you and me. We explain everything to them. Right now."

George sits back in the booth and grimaces. "See, that's the thing, Leo. I don't know if can I do that."

"Why not?"

"I got a record, Leo. I'm on parole. The least little thing and I'm back inside."

"This is what a real father would do."

George thinks about what Leo says. "You're right. It is. It's what Fred MacMurray would do, isn't it? Or Jimmy Stewart."

"We go to this guy, Detective Ford," Leo says, putting Ford's card on the table in front of George, "and tell him you had an accident in your car and you blacked out or something and now you and Irma are back all in one piece. End of story."

George considers this. "But what about you pretending to be Taylor and all that?"

"You tell him you knew all along that I wasn't him. I'll say the same thing. We were both playing some kind of psycho game. It's crazy, but we weren't breaking any law, were we? This is LA. Shit like that is part of the landscape. You and Irma are C-list celebrities. People expect you to be messed up."

George frowns. "You think we're C-list?"

"Who gives a shit what list you are? The cops will be happy to end this thing."

"So what do we do about Taylor?" George asks.

"Nothing. After you tell the police this, there's nothing Taylor can do. He can't try anything else because everyone's eyes will be on him."

George nods. "That's good, real good. See? You're a natural at this." George grins. "You sure you're not my kid?"

Leo doesn't answer him. "Let's do it right now so I can get out of here and live the rest of my life," he says. But as he stands up, George grabs his wrist. "What?" Leo says and sits down again.

George looks at Leo like a car salesman who's just come back from the manager's office with a new offer. "I had another idea."

"What?"

"We kill him."

"Kill who?"

"Taylor." George takes a pistol out of his pocket, puts it on the table and pushes it to Leo.

"Are you insane?" Leo says, covering the gun with his plate and pushing it back to George. "Where did you get that thing? Put it away. Now."

George sticks the pistol back in his jacket pocket. "The kid scares me. If he gets out of this unharmed, he's gonna come after me for screwing up his deal. And maybe you, too. In fact, I know he will. So do you. There's nothing people like him hate more than losing," he says. "Taylor's a very bad guy, Leo. The cops'll buy that you shot him in self defense."

"He's your son."

"Technically, yes, but there are extenuating circumstances."

"Forget the circumstances," Leo says, "I'm not killing anybody. Until I stole Taylor's passport, I'd never even broken the law before."

George holds his hands up in mock surrender. "You're right. I'm sorry. I don't know what I was thinking. See how messed up this whole thing has got me?"

Leo's angry. "A minute ago you wanted to clear me. Now you want me to murder your own kid. What's wrong with you people?"

"I'm not usually like this," George says. "Swear to God. Most of the time Irma and me, we're very likeable people."

The waitress comes and stands over them. "Anything else, gentlemen?"

"The check, please," Leo says.

She snaps it off her pad, slaps it on the tabletop and walks away.

"We do exactly what I say, George. It's the only way this happens," Leo says, sliding the check to George. "Pay this."

George takes off his sunglasses, puts on his reading glasses and looks at the check. "Did you have French fries?" he asks.

"Who gives a shit if I had French fries? Just pay the damn thing."

George takes money from his wallet and carefully figures the tip. "Tell me about yourself, Leo. I want to know everything. Taylor said you were brought up in foster homes."

"First we talk to the police," Leo tells him, "then I'll tell you whatever you want to know about me."

"Fair enough."

They pay the bill and leave the coffee shop. They walk up the motel's steps to Leo's room. Leo takes his cell phone out of his pocket and dials it.

"Who are you calling?" George asks.

"Ki. She's a lawyer. We'll need a lawyer when we go to the cops."

"Good idea," George says and then adds with a smile, "Are you sleeping with her?"

"What difference does that make?"

"There's something very sexy about her. Maybe it's the short hair. Irma doesn't like her, but she's just jealous. She'll get over it. Irma was sensational looking once. You should see her old photos."

"I've seen them," Leo says as Ki's phone rings. "They're all over the damn house."

"There was no one who looked like her."

Ki answers her phone. "Leo, where are you?"

"I'm at a motel with George."

"He's alive?"

"Very much," Leo says.

George speaks loudly so that Ki can hear him. "Hi, sweetheart, it's me, George. I'm fine."

Leo hands his room key to George to open the door. "Taylor's alive, too," Leo says to Ki.

"What?"

"Taylor's alive."

"How is that possible?"

"It was a scam," Leo says. "The whole thing."

"A big, fat scam, sweetheart," George shouts as he fiddles with the door's lock.

"I don't understand," Ki says.

"I'll explain it when we meet," Leo says.

"Where are you?" she asks and Leo tells her the name of his motel. "Come meet us here."

She hesitates. "You come and get me. I want to talk about this first." Leo hears a man's voice call out to her in the background. "I have a conference call. Meet me at the Oasis in an hour," she says and hangs up.

George finally opens the motel room door and they enter. "This is a first class shit hole, isn't it?" he says.

"Ki's gonna help us."

George watches as Leo gets a few things together and puts them in his backpack. "Do you love her?" he asks Leo.

Leo wonders if he does. Or have the recent revelations made it impossible for him to trust anyone again? He says, "I don't love anybody, George."

"Don't say that, Leo. Remember, in the end family is all we have."

"This from the man who just asked me to kill his son."

"Point well taken. But believe me when I tell you it's important that you find someone to share your life with."

"Like you did with Irma?"

"The woman has her good points. And she's fond of you. She doesn't want this to go any further."

"Does she want me to kill Taylor, too?"

"God, no. And when you see her again, I'd appreciate it if you didn't bring that up. I'd never hear the end of it."

"I'm gonna go meet with Ki now," Leo says.

"I'll go with you."

"You stay here. I have to explain all this to her first. We'll come back and get you and take you to the police so we can end it all."

Leo opens the door and George grabs his arm. "Wait," George says, "I need to ask you something." Leo doesn't know what to expect now. "Was Taylor right?" George asks.

"About what?"

"About what he said."

"What did he say?"

"That you were playing us, too. Is it true? Were you playing Irma and me this whole time just to get money out of us? Or did you mean what you said about us being like a family?"

Leo makes sure he has the room key in his pocket. "We'll talk about this later."

Leo starts to go, but George holds onto his arm. "I need to know now. Tell me."

"I guess so."

"You guess you were playing us or you guess you meant what you said?"

"I meant what I said."

George smiles broadly at Leo who thinks it pathetic how much people need to be wanted.

"I knew it," George says. "I told Taylor you can't fake shit like that. I know because it's what I do. When this is all over, you and me, we can go somewhere."

"Where?"

"Wherever fathers take their sons. Camping in the mountains. We can go to Idaho or Wyoming and do some fishing. Do you fish?"

"No."

"Neither do I. It'll be great."

Leo opens the motel room door. "Lock this door after I go and don't open it for anyone except me," he tells George.

"Can I call you 'son'?"

"Are you serious?"

"Please."

"If you want," Leo says.

"Good luck, son," George says to Leo who shuts the hollow, metal motel room door behind him.

26

Louis Ford visits his grandmother Evelyn twice a week at The Methodist Home for the Aged in Hawthorne. It's a clean, well-staffed facility, much better than the other places he scouted. Evelyn Ford had told her grandson it was a waste of time to look anywhere else because no place on earth would be as perfect as her church's home. She was right. The Methodist Home was ideal and she was as pleased to be proven correct as her grandson was pleased to be proven wrong. Ford's at the age when it doesn't bother him to be wrong, not about anything. Needing to be right all the time is for younger men. It takes too damn much energy.

Evelyn sits on a small sofa next to her closest friend, Martha Ellsworth, watching television in the day room. Both women hate daytime network TV with all those fools pretending to be judges ("just 'cause you put on a robe doesn't make you any smarter") telling those losers arguing about rent and dented cars and tattoos what to do with themselves.

So Evelyn does with Martha what Evelyn and her grandson had done in their home when he grew up. They watch old movies. The two ladies are addicted to Turner Classic Movies with its romances and its mysteries, its comedies and Westerns. The only genre neither woman can tolerate is pirate movies. ("Men look ridiculous in those shirts. How are they supposed to eat in them?") Today they're watching a movie with Jack Lemmon and his pretty young wife who are both drunks. Evelyn hasn't decided if it's a comedy yet. She wrongly assumes it will turn out to be, because Jack Lemmon is in it.

Ford has brought his grandmother a small coconut cake, her favorite. The three of them eat pieces of it on unmatched china plates and talk about the case that Louis is involved with. In the background, a drunk Jack Lemmon bounces crazily on a cheap motel bed.

"Tell me something," Ford says to his grandmother. "If you'd given me up for adoption when I was an infant, say a day or two old—"

"Why would I do that?"

"I'm speaking theoretically. If you did that and I came back to you, say twenty-five years later, would you know if I was your son or not?"

"You could be gone a hundred years," Evelyn says, "and I'd know you were you."

"What if some other guy my same age and who looked just like me came back and said he was me, would you know it wasn't me?"

"There's not a mother in the world who wouldn't know."

Martha chimes in. "Like that show about the penguins." The two women watch *Animal Planet*, too.

Evelyn agrees. "Out of the thousands of baby penguins standing there on all that ice, the mother knows exactly which one of those little birds is hers."

When Ford asks her, "What about my mother?" Evelyn looks up from her piece of cake. "You think she'd know me?"

Evelyn is uncharacteristically slow to respond. "Your sweet mother loved you more than anything in the world, Louis. She'd know you in a heartbeat." She takes her grandson's hand. "And no mother is gonna think a stranger is her son. Not a one."

Martha nods her agreement. "Amen to that."

Ford agrees with them as he pulls his hand away from hers so he can cut the ladies another two pieces of cake. But he's lying because he thinks it's perfectly reasonable that someone who hasn't seen their child since the day he or she was born wouldn't recognize them twenty-five years later. He includes his own father who abandoned Ford's mother six months before Ford was born to return home to Iceland. They never heard from him again.

But that doesn't matter because Ford came to the Methodist Home to hear his grandmother do what she just did: affirm that the belief in the family is the most unshakable principle people have. It's a myth so deeply imbedded in the culture that everyone's expected to believe it, even if they've not experienced it. Especially if they've not experienced it.

Was Leo Malone so damaged by his childhood that he doesn't know which parts of the myth are real and which aren't? Or is he perfectly aware of how the myth works? And, knowing that, did he come here so he could profit from George Merton's and Irma Stowell's guilt?

27

George locks the motel room door when Leo leaves. He looks around the seedy room. It's as bad as his cell at Danbury. Worse. When he and Leo and Irma are finished with all of Taylor's bullshit, they'll go somewhere nice together. They don't need Taylor's imaginary insurance money. If Irma Stowell For the Mature Woman takes off like George thinks it will, they'll have all the money they need. They can go anywhere. They can spend time in first class hotels and resorts in places like Hawaii or Switzerland.

Excited by the thought of this, George calls Irma. "I saw Leo."

"What do you mean?" George can tell that Irma's been drinking.

"I spoke to him."

"What did you do that for?"

"We cleared it all up."

"Cleared what up."

"The boy forgave us."

"*He* forgave *us*? We haven't done anything to him."

"We've been lying to him, Irma."

"He was lying to us before we were lying to him."

"Maybe. But here's the thing: he forgives us and we forgive him. Even Steven." Irma's silent. George hears the ice clink against the glass in her hand. He speaks quickly before she can argue any more and he tells her what Leo said about their going to the police and ending this whole thing the right way. "This was never gonna work, baby. You know that," George says. "And this way no one's gonna get hurt before it gets out of hand. Including Taylor." George knows that the thought of no one being hurt, especially Taylor, will calm Irma. She hates violence.

"Where's the kid now?" she asks.

"Leo? He went to get the lawyer so they can take me to the police and explain everything and put an end to all this bullshit. By the end of the day it'll be over."

"What about the money?"

"We'll figure that out. We always do, don't we?"

"And what about Taylor? What are the cops gonna do to him?"

"He'll be fine. He hasn't done anything wrong so far. Not legally speaking. He's the last person you need to worry about. He's not gonna hurt us."

"Of course he's not going to hurt us. He's our son, George."

"Yes and no."

"He's our goddamn flesh and blood. More than that rhinestone cowboy is."

"Listen to me, baby," George says, trying to quiet her by painting a picture of the four of them, him, Irma, Taylor and Leo reconciled and spending time together. Family trips, Thanksgiving dinners, Christmases, holidays. Irma softens at the thought of all this. The alcohol is helping George now.

"We'll finally be a family," he says. "All of us."

George is lying to her. He doesn't want Taylor anywhere in this loving family portrait he's painting for Irma. He never wants to see the prick again, dead or alive. Of course he says none of this to Irma. And he says nothing to her about asking Leo to kill their son in the diner less than thirty minutes before. George is upset with himself for doing that. But he's scared and it was an understandable slip any parent might make in a moment of fear and confusion.

"Stay where you are until I call you from the police station," George says. "I'll pick you up and we'll all go home together and laugh about this over a good bottle of wine."

"Taylor isn't gonna be laughing," Irma says. "Neither is Weathers."

"We'll cross those bridges when we come to them, baby. Stay there and wait for me to come get you. Everything's gonna be fine."

George hangs up. He's anxious so he turns on the little TV in the room. He surfs through the channels and settles on a show about golf. He wonders if Leo plays golf. George doesn't play the game himself, but he can learn. Then he and Leo could go out on the links together. Isn't that what people call them? The links?

George lies on the bed, shuts his eyes and goes over what he'll tell the police when Leo and Ki bring him there. He's been asked lots of questions by lots of cops before, so he knows what they'll ask him. His lawyers always tell him that the less he says the better, which is hard for a talker like George. Maybe he should do what Leo suggested and chalk the whole thing up to some psycho family game. Blame it on Irma and her drinking and medications. The cops would roll their eyes at these crazy celebrities (Was Leo right? Were they really C-list?), but be happy to see the backs of them.

George frowns when he thinks about Taylor's scheme. It's nuts, the whole damn thing. From the very beginning. Well, okay, some of it might have worked pretty well, but—

George's eyes open wide. "Holy shit," he says aloud to no one. He sits upright on the bed and begins to breathe heavily because what Taylor's planned to do all along has suddenly become clear to him.

George jumps off the bed and paces in the small room. Sonofabitch. How could he have not seen it? His son isn't as blinded by ego as George thought he was. Not at all. Sure, the boy's a sociopath, but he's a professional con, smart enough to know what George does: that the insurance people will never pay out money for bodies that are missing. That being the case, the only way to make his scheme work is to give the insurance company what they need: bodies. Real bodies. George's and Irma's bodies. And Taylor's going to make sure the insurance company gets those two bodies because he's going to kill them. Leo will be prosecuted for their murders and with good reason, but it's Taylor, their vindicated son, who'll end up with the twenty million. Why hasn't he seen this all along? Maybe it's because he's old like Taylor keeps telling him. Or has his hatred for the boy blinded him?

George grabs his phone. He'll tell Irma to clear out of the apartment and go to the cops. Maybe Taylor only plans to kill me, George thinks, and not his mother, too, but either way she should get out of there. She doesn't answer. George swears and blames himself for calling her earlier and telling her about his meeting with Leo. It's probably caused her to drink so much that she's passed out by now.

Afraid that Taylor might hear a message on her phone, he doesn't leave one for her. Instead, George calls Leo, but he doesn't answer either. No one answers their phone on a motorcycle, do they? So George leaves him a message, whispering dramatically into the phone as if someone in the room might be listening. "It's me, George. Call me as soon as you get this. I figured it out," he says lowering his voice even more. "Taylor's gonna kill us. That was his plan all along. There will be real bodies, not missing ones. Ours. Mine and Irma's. That's how he's planning to get the insurance money. Kill us and, ultimately, you, too."

George pushes the "end call" button and sits on the bed. He hopes that Leo's already picked up Ki, and is on his way back to the motel.

There's a knock on the door and George jumps up from the bed. "Hold on," he says and goes to the door and yanks it opens. Taylor stands there. It's too late to shut the door.

"Hey, dad."

"Taylor, I—I don't—I—" George says. "How'd you know where I was?" Taylor says nothing. "Your mother told you, didn't she?"

"That she did, old man," Taylor says and once in the room, he kicks the door shut behind himself. He sees George's pistol sitting on the bedside table next to his hat and sunglasses. "Why would you tell Malone about our plan, dad?" Taylor's tone is less theatrical, less precious than usual. He sounds like a boy, genuinely hurt that his father has lied to him. I know I said I was gonna take you to the ballgame, son, but something came up at the office. "Why would you undo everything I've tried to do for you and mom?" he asks George.

George denies that he "undid" anything. He's grown fond of Leo, that's all, and Taylor will, too, once this cockamamie plan of his is put to bed and they can go back to living a normal life.

Taylor walks over to the table that the gun sits on. "What's your idea of a normal life, father?"

"I want us all to be a family," George says.

"You gave me away once and now you want to do it again?"

That's exactly what George plans to do but, instead, he says, "It's not like that at all, son. Well, okay, maybe I—we—did give you away once. But it's different this time. There's a place for everyone at the table now."

"Is there?"

28

Leo waits for Ki at the bar where she and her colleagues eat lunch and drink after work. He's grateful that she's agreed to meet with him. He's eager to tell her that George and Irma are alive. It makes Leo look like a fool, but at least nothing Ki has done with him so far will hurt her career. Or, he hopes, their relationship.

When Ki approaches him, Leo stands up. She lets him kiss her on the cheek, but her manner is cool and all she says is, "Hey". Leo tells her everything George told him. Everything that's happened is part of a con that's come unraveled now that George wants to call it off and go to the police.

Ki's face brightens as she listens. "What can I do?" she asks.

Leo tells her about her going to the police with George, but she reminds him that she's not a lawyer yet. It doesn't matter because George doesn't need a lawyer. He's done nothing wrong. He's nervous because he's on parole and all Ki needs to do is to hold the man's hand. If she does that, George will confess and Leo will be cleared.

"What about your entering the country under a false name? That's a crime."

"Once Taylor's put under the eye of the cops, he'll drop all that," Leo says.

"How do you know?"

"That's how people like him think."

"The customs and immigration people might not think like that. What if they suspect that you entered illegally? They have cameras at all the airports now."

"No one can prove it was me. That's what started this whole thing: no one could tell the difference between Taylor and me. A camera's not gonna do that, either."

"You're right," Ki says and she relaxes more. "Any good lawyer could make that case for you."

"Once the cops know that George and Irma are safe they won't care about anything else." Leo isn't sure if this is true, but having watched his foster parents' problems with the law, he knows how eager police are to close a case as soon as they get it. Like most men, the police love their job. It's doing it that they hate.

"Do you believe what George said about the scam?" Ki asks and Leo says he does. He doesn't know how much of what else George said in the diner is true. Does he really feel about Leo the way he claims to? Did he really want Leo to kill Taylor? It doesn't matter. Leo tells Ki none of that.

"What about Taylor?" she asks.

"He's crazy."

"So are George and Irma," Ki says.

She's probably right. They played along with Taylor's scheme and, at least at the start, were willing to watch Leo be punished for a crime he wouldn't have committed. But that doesn't matter now. "Once George goes to the cops," Leo says to her, "Taylor can't risk doing anything. None of them can. I'm safe. We're safe."

"What about the guy they owe money to?"

"That's their problem, not ours," Leo says, surprised at how easily he's able to say this.

Ki smiles. "Then once I leave Carl we can go anywhere."

29

Louis Ford sits in his gray Ford sedan, parked on Stone Canyon Road below Vestone Way. The two cars he saw at the Merton's when he made his first visit there were a beat up Hyundai and a restored antique MG. He figures the Korean car belongs to the Filipino woman. He never liked the word 'maid' so he's written 'housekeeper' in his notes. He's not a political correctness freak, but for a lot of reasons he thinks the word 'maid' is insulting.

He hasn't been waiting very long when he sees George Merton's Mercedes 280 SEL pull out of the driveway and head down the hill. Taylor Hoffman's driving. The young man ignored Ford's advice to stay away from the place until Leo Malone's been found. That surprises the Detective because Hoffman seemed like the kind of man who would worry about things like that.

Ford also wonders if it's odd, or even telling, that the couple's son is driving a car that's recently been found with what might be his missing father's or mother's bloodstains in it? But maybe all it it proves is that Hoffman has nothing to feel guilty about.

Riccio checked Hoffman's record and she came up with two or three charges in New York and D.C. of identity theft, but the cases were eventually dropped. He'd worked a boiler room scam in New Jersey when he was in high school. He was a juvenile at the time.

A friend of Ford's in the New York FBI told him that something ugly had happened there in the 1990's, something a lot of New York cops knew about, but Hoffman's record was expunged. His adoptive parents had enough money to keep stuff quiet, but all that ended when that family lost most of its money and officially disowned the kid. Hoffman's mother left her adopted son nothing in her will.

Material on Leo Malone was easier to come up with, since he'd been in the system in both Texas and Oklahoma. His birth name is Leo Licklighter, and, as the surviving child of the notorious Baby Bandits, he was, for a short time, as famous as his parents were infamous. Did the families that chose him see him as a special challenge? Did his connection to his parents' crimes make him an unwitting celebrity? Whatever the reason, from the age of three until eighteen he'd spent time in no fewer than seven different foster homes.

Normally, that's not a good sign. But Malone has no criminal record, none at all. He's never broken the law and he even managed to graduate from high school and college where he majored in, of all things, divinity.

Riccio points out to Ford that sociopaths often compensate for their deranged personalities by working in places like churches and hospitals. She suggests that Malone might be what Hoffman said he was: a con who took off after getting all he could from George Merton and Irma Stowell. The other possibility, the one Riccio likes more, is that Malone and Hoffman are in on this together. Riccio's instincts are good and getting better all the time, so Ford considers what she says. In her favor is the common knowledge that con men almost never work alone. Her argument makes a lot of sense, but Ford's not persuaded. Not yet anyway.

The detective watches the Mercedes disappear down the hill. Hoffman's not the person he wants to see. It's the housekeeper he's eager to talk to.

He doesn't have to wait long, because in his rear view mirror Ford sees the woman walking down the road toward Sunset. The road is steep and she's carrying a large bag. Cars whiz by her, perilously close. None stop. A Lexus SUV honks at her. When she gets closer to his car, Ford opens the door and steps out. "Good evening, Ms. Incarnacion."

The short woman doesn't seem surprised to see him. "Good evening, Detective."

Ford takes the canvas bag from her and puts it on the back seat. She holds onto her purse. He opens the passenger door for her. "I'll take you where you're going," he says. She lives in Echo Park.

The first thing she asks after getting into the car is, "What took you so long?" She's been expecting to hear from Ford ever since his visit with the man she calls "the second Mr. Hoffman".

"You find out that the first boy is not their son, don't you?" she says. Her English is better now than it was when she was being questioned at the Merton's place.

"We knew that the day this second Mr. Hoffman came home," Ford says. "But in the beginning, Mrs. Incarnacion, did you think the other boy was their son?"

"No."

"Why not?"

"He's not like them."

"You mean he doesn't look like them?"

"He's too nice for them." She can tell good people from bad people right away, "the same as you police do," she says to Ford and smiles as if she were in cahoots with him. "The father, he likes the boy. The Missus not so much. She doesn't like his girlfriend."

"You remember the girlfriend's name?" The housekeeper shakes her head. "Is there anything else you can think of that might help us?"

"Maybe." She opens her bag and riffles through it. She finds what she's looking for and hands it to Ford. "First boy, he left this on the floor."

It's a card for a Doctor Janice Heller in Santa Barbara. From the letters after her name Ford figures the woman's a shrink. He hopes she's better at her job than Dr. Frank.

"I'll keep this," he says.

"That's why I give it to you."

"What do you think about the boy who's there now?"

She looks at Ford and nods. “He’s their son. He’s like them. Very much.”

On their way to Echo Park, Ford asks her more questions about the Mertons and the two young men who both said they were their son. She says nothing he didn’t already know or suspect. The Filipino woman’s main concern now is finding a job in the event the Mertons never come back. “In case they are dead,” are the words she uses.

“You could work for the Hoffman boy.”

She looks at Ford like he was crazy. “Not going to happen,’ she says.

30

Leo rides his motorcycle and Ki drives her car to the motel on Adams where George is waiting for them. Leo gets there first. His spirits are high. Ki parks across the street and walks through the motel’s empty lot. They stop at the bottom of the concrete steps where she lets him kiss her.

“You know what you’re going to say to George?” Leo asks her.

“I think so.”

“Remember that he’s scared.” They walk up the steps to the second floor room. Leo knocks on the door, but George doesn’t answer. He’s left the room unlocked, so Leo opens the door and he and Ki walk in. George lays on the bed where he’s fallen asleep watching the TV. An infomercial about a juicer is playing loudly.

Leo shuts the TV off. “George?” he says. “Wake up. Ki’s here to take you to the police.” Leo shakes George’s shoulder and his hand falls off the bed. His arm is drenched in blood. “Shit,” Leo says.

Ki hasn’t seen the blood yet. “What’s the matter?”

Leo turns George over. He’s been shot in the chest and the bed is soaked in his blood. He’s dead.

Ki screams. Leo grabs her and covers her mouth with his hand, frightening her even more. She screams into Leo's hand and struggles to get free of him. He can feel her wet teeth on the palm of his hand as he whispers into her ear. "It's all right. I'm not gonna hurt you. I promise. But you gotta be quiet."

When Ki stops struggling, Leo lets go of her and, as soon as he does, she backs away from him, pressing herself against the room's pale green wall. "Every time I go somewhere with you someone's dead," she says. "Then they're not dead, then they are." She points to George. "Well, that guy right there is dead, Leo."

George's gray hair is matted with blood, not unlike Leo's mother's hair was as she lay on the Oklahoma truck stop floor.

Ki can't look at George. "Did you kill him?" she says.

"Of course not."

She asks again, this time more forcefully. "Tell me the truth, Leo. Did you kill him?"

"I swear."

Ki must believe him because she calms down. "Then who did?"

"Taylor."

"What about the other guy? The one he owes money to."

"Weathers? No. If George is dead then Weathers never gets his money. Taylor must've figured out that his father was gonna go to the police."

"How?"

"Irma must've told him. George probably called her when I left and told her where he was."

"I have to get out of here," Ki says, crossing to the door, but she stops when she gets there. "I have to report this."

"Why?" Leo approaches her, but she moves away from him.

"Because I'm an officer of the court."

"Did you touch anything?"

"I don't think so."

"Then leave. I'll take care of this. Your name will never come up. This place doesn't have cameras. I checked. No one saw you. I'll never say anything. Just leave."

But she doesn't move. She stands there and stares at George on the bed while Leo searches his body for the gun George brought to the coffee shop. Taylor probably used that same gun to kill his father. And he must've taken it with him because Leo can't find it. Leo can't remember if it has his fingerprints on it.

"What if you went to the police?" Ki says. She argues that would be the smartest thing, the only thing, for Leo to do right now.

Leo's not listening to her. He takes his phone from his backpack. There's a message from George on it and he listens to it. "Leo, it's me, George. Listen, I figured it out," he says, "Taylor's gonna kill us. That's how he was always planning to get the insurance money. Kill us and probably kill you, too."

Leo shuts the phone off. Of course. It's obvious. Taylor was always going to kill his parents. Why hadn't George and Irma realized this themselves? They're not stupid. George especially. But Irma wants to believe her son, her flesh and blood, her family.

Ki finishes telling Leo her idea. "Or maybe it's better if you don't."

Leo looks up from his phone. He hasn't been listening to her. "If I don't what?"

"Go to the police. The evidence is stacked against you right now."

She's right. The cops will arrest him first and listen to him later. They've probably already found his polo shirt with George's blood on it.

So Leo has to find Irma, the only person who can prove his innocence—and Taylor's guilt—in all this. She can't defend Taylor once she knows that he's killed George. She'll tell the police that it's Taylor, not Leo, who killed his father. "I've got to get to Irma," Leo says. "Taylor's gonna kill her." He dials Irma's number. But Irma doesn't answer.

"So what?" Ki asks. "Let him kill her. What do you care? She's not your mother, is she? She set you up. She didn't care if you died in the gas chamber, did she? So let them all go." Ki doesn't sound like herself. She's tougher than Leo has ever seen her before. But maybe the lawyer in her comes out in a situation like this. Maybe that's a good thing.

"It doesn't matter," Leo says. "I can't let him kill her. She's the only person who can prove I'm innocent."

Ki moves to the door. "Do whatever you want. I never should've come here with you in the first place."

Leo reaches for her, but she pulls away. "Don't touch me."

"You believe me, don't you?"

"I don't know what I believe anymore," she says. "But whatever you do, don't call me again. I'm sorry, Leo, but you have to forget you ever met me. It could've been good for us, but not now, not after all this. You and me, it's like we're cursed. Wherever we are, things go wrong." She grabs a flimsy towel and uses it to turn the door handle. She tosses the towel on the floor and leaves the room without looking back at Leo. He can hear her heels on the motel's concrete steps as she hurries to the street below.

Leo opens the plastic blinds and watches her cross the parking lot to her car. It's the last time he'll see her. He'd left her once before, the night he stole Taylor's passport and sneaked into the country. Like it was then, breaking off with her now is the right thing to do, a sacrifice that will protect her. It will show his love for her. She'll understand that some day. Ki doesn't look back to the motel room. She gets in her car and drives away.

Leo pulls the grimy plastic bed cover off the floor and covers George's body with it. Was George being honest earlier when he spoke about his desires to connect with Leo like father and son? Leo wants to believe the old man was sincere and seeing him lying dead in this small, decrepit room saddens him. In his whole life there have only been two men willing to call him son. And Leo has seen both of their dead bodies, bullet-ridden and bloody.

Leo checks that he's left nothing behind in the room. He shuts the door behind himself. There's no point in locking it. He puts on his helmet in the motel parking lot, starts his motorcycle and drives off.

31

When Ford calls Dr. Heller and tells her that he wants to talk about Leo Malone she asks him why. He says he'll explain when he gets there in the morning.

He takes the Pacific Coast Highway to Santa Barbara instead of the faster inland route. It's a sunny, breezy day and the waves give the ocean an unsettled look. Ford pulls up in front of Dr. Heller's oceanfront home, a small, older house in a neighborhood where the brightly painted beach homes built in the 1950s and 1960s are being replaced by houses that look more like hotels. He's early, so to pass the time he leans against the hood of his car and looks out at the ocean.

Anyone seeing the suited, forty-eight-year-old Black man might find it hard to imagine that as a boy he loved surfing, not football, baseball or basketball, making him the rare Black kid among the Beach Boy clones that claimed the sand.

In high school, he was expected to try out for those other sports. But whenever he watched the teams' coaches, middle-aged men, running up and down the sidelines or the gym floor screaming and swearing during games he was embarrassed for them. What made them feel so small and shitty that they needed to win a game so badly?

So he took to surfing where the only competition was between himself and the ocean. There were remarks and jokes about his color. How could there not be? But there weren't many and they were rarely vicious. The ocean has no favorites. How good you were on your board is all that the mattered and Louis Ford from Fox Hills was very good.

Dr. Heller opens the front door. She holds a large tape dispenser she's been using to seal up the many cardboard boxes that clutter the house's entryway.

"Come in, Detective," she says. "I'm Janice Heller."

"Louis Ford," he says and shakes hands with her. He steps around the boxes. "Someone moving in?" he asks. "Or out?"

"Long story," the doctor says and then apologizes for her dog that jumps up to greet him. Its name is Ego. Ford says there's no need to apologize. He likes dogs. "During questioning," he tells her, "they often put their owners at ease."

"I feel the same way, although I don't call it 'questioning'. No officially anyway," Doctor Heller says, smiling.

She pours him a coffee and they sit in the living room. He likes her more than the shrink he visited the day before.

"Is Leo Malone a patient of yours, doctor?"

"He's not. I met Leo at a resort in Martinique where he worked as a guide for me. What's this visit about?"

Ford hands her an article from a 1981 Oklahoma newspaper about the deaths of Leo's parents Carly and Bobby Licklighter. "His parents were the Baby Bandits," Ford says as Janice skims the article, "the couple in Texas who in 1980 and '81 robbed more than a dozen service stations using their baby—Leo—as a shield."

"I remember this story," she says. "Who doesn't? It was everywhere. Newspapers, magazines, TV. It has all the right ingredients. An adorable little boy and his criminal parents shot dead right in front of him." She hands the Xeroxed page back to Ford. "Leo said that his parents were killed in a robbery, but he never told me that they were the robbers."

"Because he's ashamed?"

"It's more likely that he didn't want my sympathy. That's the key to a personality like Leo's, detective. Distance. He considers that his strength. His protection."

"From what?"

"From you. From me. From feeling anything." She tells him how when she met Leo she recognized the symptoms of emotional detachment disorder. She adds that many so-called normal people suffered from various levels of personality disorder, too. She laughs when Ford says, "Whose personality doesn't have a least a little disorder to it?"

"Would you consider Malone a sociopath?" he asks her.

"Like 'psychopath', that's a term not much used by professionals anymore," she says, "but even given its everyday usage, no, I wouldn't use it. Not in Leo's case." She tells Ford some of what Leo told her about his life in various foster homes after his parents' death.

"So he was abused."

"Probably sexually," she says, "but certainly physically and emotionally." While Ford writes in his notebook she asks, "Why are you here, Detective?"

"Malone stole the passport and airline ticket of a guest at the resort. A Mr. Taylor Hoffman. He used it to enter the country at LAX."

"And it worked?"

"The two men, Hoffman and Malone, look very much alike. Almost identical."

"So if that's the crime why is a Los Angeles policemen, and not a federal agent, coming to see me?"

Ford smiles. The woman has experience with the law. "This is where it gets interesting, Doctor." Ford tells her who Hoffman's parents are, their history and the planned reunion with them in LA. "Malone walked smack into the middle of that."

"You're saying the Mertons had no idea that Leo Malone wasn't their son?"

"That's what it looks like."

"What are the chances of that happening?"

Ford's asked himself the same question many times over the past couple of days. "Let's say that it is true, Doctor. What do you think would happen to a kid like Malone who suddenly finds himself in that situation?"

"If George Merton and Irma Stowell honestly thought he was their son, Malone would have to pretend he was, wouldn't he? Otherwise he'd be admitting that he'd committed a crime, several of them."

"Why didn't he leave the first chance he got?" Ford asks.

"He didn't?"

Ford shakes his head. "He stayed there several weeks. The housekeeper says that nothing seemed out of the ordinary. That both Leo and the Mertons acted as if they were two parents and a son, all happily reunited at last."

Doctor Heller gets up and pours herself and Ford another cup of coffee. "Maybe Malone's more damaged than I thought. There's no question the boy survived a brutal childhood and patients like Leo can be difficult to get through to. Their wall can be impenetrable. But once that defense is breached, the emotions people like Leo have held back for so long can flood out like a dam breaking. Emotionally speaking, they can go from zero to the speed of light in no time with no control or reason. Leo finding himself with these people—with parents for the first time in his life—was like a starving animal reaching for bait in a deadly trap. It sounds like it worked the other way, too. Given the Merton's history it makes sense that they'd want to believe Leo was their son, a boy who forgave them for abandoning him as an infant."

"You don't think Malone was conning the Mertons?"

"Not in the classic sense, no," she said. "It's possible that it was the situation that conned all of them. The Mertons need to believe that Leo's their son who forgives them. And Leo, given his background, wants desperately to be accepted as the couple's son. In the tired parlance of the day, it's the perfect storm." She pauses. "Why are you here anyway, Detective? Did the Mertons figure out that Leo was lying? And where is he now?"

"We don't know where he is. But do you think, Doctor, that Leo Malone is capable of killing anyone?"

"Are the Mertons dead?"

"They're missing."

This upsets Dr. Heller. She takes a moment before she answers Ford. "I don't think Leo's capable of killing anyone. If he were, he probably would have killed someone else by now. Someone from his childhood who he thought deserved it. Murder is the ultimate emotional attachment, isn't it? And that's exactly what Leo's spent his whole life trying to avoid."

"Until now maybe," Ford says.

When Ford says this, the Doctor hedges. "I suppose it's possible he could kill someone," she says. "After all, he broke from his usual patterns and made an emotional attachment with Hoffman's parents, didn't he?"

"That's the question," Ford says.

"I'd like to say no, that he's not capable of killing anyone. But maybe I'm wrong. Maybe he is dangerous." She shakes her head. "Still, I'd like to believe there's a basic goodness to him. And that somehow his goodness survived everything he's experienced. I want to believe that. I have to. Otherwise I couldn't do what I do.

"I understand," Ford says and he does. He pets her dog again and thanks her for her time. He gives her his card before he leaves.

Ford takes the PCH back to LA. He pulls his car into a parking lot and walks to the beach where he sits on a large log. He watches half a dozen seals cavorting not far off shore.

It's obvious that Dr. Heller has experience with police because instead of blurting out at the start what she knows about Malone, she waited until Ford told her what he came to say. She shared what she knew, but maybe not all of it at that. She's given Ford no new detailed information, but he didn't expect her to. What he came to learn was how she thought Malone might react to a situation like the one he might've unintentionally stumbled into on Vestone Way.

The detective looks at his notepad. Emotional detachment disorder. That's a lot of words to say that a person can't trust anyone. Ford had become withdrawn at first after his mother died, too, like many children who suddenly find themselves without a parent. He was hesitant to connect with people, but he never got put in the system because his grandparents adopted him and did everything they could to give him a normal childhood. Without them he might have ended up like Leo Malone. He makes a note to visit his grandmother twice this week.

Ford's cell rings. It's Denise Riccio. He didn't tell her about coming to see Dr. Heller, but she knows he's up to something.

"Where are you, Detective?" she asks.

"On the road."

"We got news."

Ford knows her well enough by now to recognize the tone in her voice. "I'm listening," he says.

"They found George Merton's body."

Ford's more disappointed than surprised. "Where?"

"A motel on West Adams. The manager identified Malone as the guy who rented the room."

"Interesting," is all Ford says. If this were another case, he might have congratulated Riccio about her being right about Malone. He might even have made a joke about it. But not this time. And, to her credit, she doesn't push it.

"Anyone tell Hoffman yet?" Ford asks.

"The Lieutenant went to the Merton's place, but he's not there. The maid said he never came back home last night. No one can reach him."

Of course the Lieutenant had gone to see Hoffman at his home. Now that there was a body in the case, a semi-celebrity's body, the department's chiefs have entered the picture. The Mayor will find his way into it, too, soon enough. That might piss off most detectives, but it makes Ford happy. While the higher-ups do their thing, he can do his own.

"They put an APB out on Malone," Riccio says.

"That's not gonna work."

"There's nowhere he can run to, Detective."

"Kids like Malone don't run, Officer Riccio." Ford uses her formal title because he's making a point. "They hide not by running, but by standing still. A boy like him, he's been hiding in plain sight all his life. We'll find him by accident or he'll turn himself in." Riccio says nothing. Ford's made his point and she's smart enough to take it. "I'll see you when I get back, Officer."

"Yes, sir."

Ford hangs up. He's disappointed. Maybe Riccio and the other cops have been right about the kid all along. Maybe Malone is working with Hoffman.

Ford reminds himself what he learned early on as a cop: to keep a distance between yourself and your suspects. Caring too much about a suspect is worse than neglecting them. You have to be especially careful around sociopaths because they know where your weak spots are. Whether this kid Malone is a perpetrator or a victim, things aren't looking good for him.

32

After he leaves George's body in the motel, Leo drives his cycle downtown where he gets a room in a seedy hotel. He's nearly run out of the money he took when he left Bel Air. He calls Irma. She's his out, the one person who can tell the police everything that's happened. But she doesn't answer. He collapses exhausted on the springy bed and sleeps through the night. He wakes up early in morning. Finding Irma is still his only goal.

Every cop in the city will be looking for him, so he puts on a baseball cap and sunglasses and goes to a drug store to buy hair dye. He's overwhelmed by the number of dyes sitting on the shelves. The pretty women on the many boxes seem to be laughing at him and the romantic plans he made with Ki. Those plans seem ridiculous now. Fairy tales like that don't happen to people like him.

Two streetwalkers sit in the lobby when Leo gets back to the hotel. On the TV is a breaking news story about a man's body discovered in a Mid-Wilshire motel. One of the prostitutes recognizes the motel. "That place a shithole, girl," she says to her friend and she all but cheers when the newscaster reports that the murdered man is George Merton, husband of the one-time celebrity and cosmetics magnate Irma Stowell.

Over the grimy sink in his fifth floor room, Leo dyes his hair an ashy blonde called French Champagne. While he waits for it to dry, he calls Irma again, but she doesn't answer. Has Taylor killed her? He needs both his mother and his father dead. That's how he'll get the twenty million. But at least George is dead now, so he'll get half the money. And if he can't manage to kill Irma, too, then the next best thing will be to kill Leo. A dead Leo Malone will be blamed for George's death and that will all but close the case. Leo will be seen by the media and the public as a natural extension of his parents, Carly and Bobby Licklighter, the Baby Bandits.

But killing Leo won't calm Taylor for long because eventually he'll expect his mother, under the influence of guilt, booze, pills, or a combination of all three, to break down and tell someone what really happened. Taylor knows that he's safest if all three of them are dead.

So Leo must find Irma and get her to go to the police. But he has no idea where she is. The only thing left that he can do is to call Ford and tell him he's coming in. The one time Leo met the detective at George and Irma's he seemed reasonable enough. Leo will explain the whole story to him and convince him that they have to find Irma before Taylor kills her. Leo grabs his backpack and digs out the card that Ford gave him that first night in Bel Air.

Should he ask Ford to meet him somewhere? Would it be safer if he went into the station accompanied by the detective? As he practices what he'll say to Ford, Leo's phone rings and he answers it.

"My darling George is dead, Leo," Irma says.

Leo's relieved to hear her voice. He asks her, "Where are you, Irma?"

She ignores his question. "George could be an asshole. He *was* an asshole, but I loved him."

"Where are you, Irma?"

"Did you kill him?"

"You know I didn't."

"I know, but I had to ask. People would expect me to, wouldn't they?" She's been drinking. Her words are slurred and her voice husky.

"We have to get you somewhere safe," Leo says.

"I want this all to end now."

"Tell me where you are."

"I'm in hell, Leo. Do you know what hell is like? It has shag carpeting and cottage cheese ceilings and not a shred of hope."

Leo tries steering the conversation back to reality. "Where are you calling me from, Irma?"

"In the apartment that Taylor got for us."

"Where is he now?" Leo asks.

"I don't know. I'm frightened of him. He killed his father. What kind of a boy kills his own father?"

Leo tells her to leave the apartment and go straight to the police. She can tell them everything about her, about George and about Taylor. She's done nothing wrong; she has nothing to fear.

But Irma's scared. "I can't do that."

Leo tells her to lock the door and call 911.

"What do I say to them?" Irma asks.

"Tell them who you are."

"I've done some very bad things."

"You've done nothing bad, Irma, but if you stay there, Taylor will find you and he'll kill you."

"I hate it when you talk like that. Will you come and get me, Leo darling? I'm scared. You're all I have."

Leo gets to Irma's apartment building on Normandie Avenue fifteen minutes later. He circles the block twice to see if any police cars are parked out of view, waiting for him to show. There aren't. He parks his cycle, crosses the street and rings the bell for apartment 6C.

Irma's voice is loud over the fuzzy intercom. "Who is it?"

"Leo," he says and seconds later the door opens with a buzzer blare so loud it causes several neighborhood dogs to bark.

Leo walks up the stairs to Apartment 6C. It takes Irma forever to unfasten the locks on the door. When she finally gets it open, the first thing she does is to hug Leo tightly. She's unsteady on her feet and Leo can smell the booze on her. Will this cause the police to question what she tells them? The best thing might be to stop on the way to the station and have her drink some coffee while they go over exactly what she'll tell them.

"Come on," Leo says, taking her arm, "we've gotta get out of here before Taylor shows up."

But Irma pulls away from him. She nearly stumbles, but Leo catches her and she takes a few steps back. "I have a new plan," she says.

Leo follows her into the apartment. "What new plan?"

"Don't be angry with me, Leo, darling." Irma's tone is sing-songy, like a bad actress trying to sound maternal, the way Leo's foster mothers sounded when caseworkers came to their homes.

"I'm trying to save your life, Irma."

"I appreciate that, Leo darling, I really do. But we thought of another way."

"We?"

Leo's not surprised when he hears Taylor's voice behind him.

"So nice to see you, Leo."

Leo turns and sees Taylor standing there, pointing a pistol at him. It's George's pistol, the one Taylor killed George with and took from Leo's motel room. "I'm not sold on the new hair color, though. A tad gay, no?"

Taylor's not the slacker Leo tolerated on the island. His body is taut and his movements are sharp and controlled. His voice is mature. "No hard feelings," he says to Leo, "but you were such an easy mark. Even you have to admit that."

It's true. Leo was an easy mark. But there are things about him and his life that Taylor never saw or could have imagined, things that made Leo fit even more perfectly into his scheme. Like so much of life, it's as much luck as anything that's made Taylor's scheme work so well. But you can't tell that to someone like Taylor who believes that the reason his plan has worked so far is solely because of his genius.

Irma looks at Leo, pleadingly. "Try to understand. He's my son, my flesh and blood."

"Issued from these very loins," Taylor says as he steps behind his mother and places his free hand on her hip, a gesture that's almost sexual.

"Put the gun down, sweetheart," Irma says to Taylor. "I'm from Wisconsin and I've seen accidents. Loaded weapons make me nervous." She throws her hands in the air like the exasperated character in a sitcom when she says to Leo, "What's a mother to do?" Leo half expects to hear a laugh track.

"He killed his father," Leo tells her.

"He explained all that."

"He explained it?" Leo says. "You explain how you dented the family car. You explain how you broke your mother's favorite vase. How do you explain how you killed your father?"

"With great regret," Taylor says.

“We can all agree it was a terrible thing,” Irma says, “but what choice did the boy have? It was self-defense. His father was going to open his mouth like he always does and ruin everything. It had to be done. Taylor’s very remorseful about it,” she says. “Aren’t you, dear?”

“From the bottom of my heart, mother.”

“While we were waiting for you, Leo, dear,” Irma says, “we thought of a way out of this. For all of us,” She finishes whatever’s in her glass and pours herself another drink from the almost empty bottle of vodka. “I’ve grown fond of you, Leo. I think of you two boys as brothers.”

“He’s going to kill me, Irma,” is all Leo says.

Irma scoffs at the idea. “He’s not going to kill you, you silly boy.”

“He’s going to kill you, too.”

“Stop harping on the negative for once,” she says to Leo. “Nobody’s going to kill anyone. That’s not how I built a cosmetics empire. I did it with strategy and conviction and, most important of all, optimism. I was a very rich woman at one time. And I will be again. Irma Stowell for the Mature Woman. Mark my words.” Taylor’s silent as his mother proudly considers what she’d just said about herself. “And Taylor and I came up with a plan in which everyone wins.”

“What plan is that?” Leo asks, knowing that whatever plan she’s talking about is not going to happen. But his goal is to keep Irma talking as long as he can to stall Taylor from shooting one or both of them.

“With the new passports Taylor got us, he and I will go to a country they can’t extradite us from, like Croatia or Cuba. Or my favorite, Cambodia. It’s so exotic, don’t you think? Once we get the insurance money for poor George, God rest his soul, we’ll go public. We’ll admit everything. Then you’ll be free.”

“That’s not how it’s going to happen,” Leo says.

“Of course it is. You can be such a goddamn stick-in-the-mud sometimes, Leo. I don’t know what George saw in you,” Irma says.

"Before we go, Taylor and I will even leave you some starter cash. Enough for you to hide out on until we come clean. And even if you do get caught and go to jail for any of this, it will only be for a short time."

"Until you go public," Leo says.

Irma nods. "Exactly. Until we go public." She turns to Taylor. "See, Taylor? Now he gets it."

"Tell your mother that's not how it's going to happen," Leo says to Taylor.

"That's exactly how it's going to happen," Irma says, annoyed.

"Leo's right, mother," Taylor says. "I tweaked our plan a bit."

This surprises Irma. "How so?"

"We *do* kill him," Taylor says.

"Oh, no, darling, no, no, no. You can't kill the boy, Taylor."

"I don't intend to."

Irma relaxes. "Of course you don't."

"You will, mother."

Irma waits for Taylor to tell her he's joking and, when he doesn't, she slams her now empty glass onto the wet bar. "I will not kill anyone. We had a plan and we agreed to it. Killing someone was not a part of it. Last minute changes like this are what destroy a good business plan."

Leo considers making a break while they argue. Irma didn't lock the door behind Leo when he came in.

"Leo broke in here after he killed dad and you shot him," Taylor explains to his mother. "So here, take this gun and shoot him. Now."

"You're not thinking this through, darling. How can I kill him? Hasn't he already killed me?"

"Obviously, he hasn't killed you," Taylor says impatiently.

Irma becomes more confused as things unfold. "Right. It's different now. Tell me again how we get my insurance."

"We don't. We get father's."

"Will that be enough?" she asks.

"We could get more if I killed you, but that means you wouldn't be able to spend any of it," Taylor says.

"Sarcasm is a very unattractive trait in a man."

Taylor raises his voice. "Stop trying to think, old lady. Take this gun and shoot him," Taylor says as he follows his mother around the room with the pistol in his own hand still aimed at Leo.

Leo knows that if he tries to run, Taylor will shoot him.

Irma keeps moving away from him, shaking her head. "I will not shoot him or anyone else."

"Take it!" Taylor says and forces the pistol into her hand. While she holds it, Taylor holds her hand and keeps the pistol aimed at Leo.

Leo trusts that Irma won't shoot him. Taylor will, but she won't.

"I don't shoot people," she says, moving away from Taylor and waving the pistol like the actress in an old movie might wave her cigarette. "I went to college. Junior college. Two years, anyway."

Taylor backs off, unsure now if his mother will do what he wants her to.

Irma keeps talking. "I was on the cover of *Rolling Stone*. Number five on *Time Magazine's* list of the most influential businesswomen of the 1980s does not kill people." With the hand that's not holding the gun she takes another dry gulp from her glass and turns to Leo. "He won't listen to me. What should I do?"

"Shoot him," Leo says.

"My own son? You can't be serious."

"In the leg," Leo says.

Taylor laughs. "She's not going to shoot me, are you mother?"

"Don't get overconfident. That's another unattractive quality in a man," Irma says before she turns to Leo. "The boy's right, darling. I can't shoot him, not even in the leg. He's family."

"Then he's going to kill one of us," Leo says. "Or both."

Irma laughs. "You've been watching too much TV. Let's all sit down and discuss this."

Leo makes a move for the door. He grabs the handle, but the door's warped and doesn't open completely. As Leo jiggles it, Taylor grabs the gun from Irma and crosses to him. He hits Leo hard on the head with the pistol. But because Leo turns his head in time, the blow isn't forceful enough to knock him out. It barely fazes him, but he falls to the ground anyway, as if he's been rendered unconscious by the blow, the same way he pretended to be unconscious when he lay in Jean-Paul's boat a few weeks before. The carpet stinks of pet urine and stain remover. Leo tries not to sneeze. He lays motionless on the floor not unlike his mother does in his dreams. He waits for his chance to make a break.

"Fine then. I'll shoot him," Taylor says and aims the pistol at Leo.

Leo closes his eyes and says a short prayer. Larry Buell's favorite saying was, "You never hear the shot that kills you." Of course that only applies if someone shoots you in the head.

Irma steps between Taylor and Leo. "You'll have to shoot me first."

Taylor pauses. "Good idea. I kill you with the gun Leo killed dad with. That means Leo came here and shot you after I left. He killed you both."

"That's not what I meant at all."

Taylor aims the gun at his mother and she finally realizes that Taylor does plan to shoot her. "My God," she says. In spite of the alcohol, or maybe because of it, everything makes sense to her now. "Leo's right. You always were going to kill your father and me, weren't you? Your father was right about you, too."

"And look where he is now."

On the carpet, Leo's face points at the door, but he hears Irma move away from Taylor and pick up and drop her cell phone. "I'm putting an end to all this right now," she says. Leo sees her hands as she bends over and picks her phone off the carpet.

"Put the phone down, mother."

"Hello? Police? Hello? My son is trying to – oh, for shit's sake, how do you work these damn things?"

Leo sees Taylor move toward Irma.

"Give me the phone, mother."

"Hello, police? My son is trying to kill me. Shit."

Taylor grabs his mother's phone and tosses it against the far wall of the room. He finds the remote and turns the TV on, adjusting the volume as high as it will go.

Still pretending to be knocked out, Leo waits to see if Taylor steps near him. If he does, maybe he can dive at his legs and knock him down.

Irma watches her son in disbelief and yells above the TV's noise. "All my life I wondered what was wrong with me because I gave you away. And when we finally met in Santa Fe, I felt guilty because deep down, no matter how much I tried, I didn't like you, I couldn't stand you and now I finally see that I wasn't the problem at all. It's not me. It's you."

"Shut up, mother."

Leo can't wait any longer. He readies to lunge at Taylor. He might get a shot off as Leo comes at him but, without having the time to aim the gun, he might miss Leo entirely or only hit him in an arm or a leg. But Taylor might get lucky, too, and hit Leo in the heart or the head.

Irma keeps railing. "Your father was right. You're the monster, not us, not me." She grabs the gin bottle. "I should've done what I wanted to all along and aborted you," she says. "I never should've had you."

Time's running out and Leo prepares to spring to his feet.

"And here's why," Taylor says and shoots his mother twice in the chest. She screams and collapses against the wet bar causing the bottles and cheap glasses on it to rattle and fall onto the carpet. She looks at the blot of blood on her blouse, breathing hard. "Do you have any idea who I am?" she says before she slumps onto the carpet.

Leo recoils when Taylor fires the shots. Everything's happening so fast. Leo expects to hear more shots, ones that will kill him, so he readies himself to get up to save himself, but Taylor's gun jams and Leo hears him say, "Oh, shit," as if he's no more annoyed at having jammed the gun that he just killed his mother with as not being able to find a parking space.

By the time Leo gets to his feet, Taylor's already dropped the gun on the carpet and run out of the apartment, leaving the door wide open. Leo picks up the gun and goes over to Irma who lies on the floor. One of Taylor's shots has gone through her heart and she's bleeding out, the hated shag carpet soaking up her blood like a sponge. She's dead. Leo's kept the promise he made to Irma his first night in Bel Air. He's stayed until she died.

He hears screaming in Spanish and turns to see a woman standing in the apartment's doorway. "Call 911," Leo yells to the woman before he bolts from the room.

He runs down the stairs, still carrying the gun. He hears the last words his mother said to him in his dream. "Run. Run like the devil, my little boy, run, run, run!"

33

Ford's happy he didn't have to attend the press conference the Mayor and the Chief held earlier that morning to discuss what the plans regarding Leo Malone and Taylor Hoffman were. The question most reporters at the meeting had is: now that George Merton's dead, where's Irma Stowell?

Publicly, the department plays down Leo's role in the two murders. He's a suspect and nothing more. First they need to find both him and Hoffman and figure things out. But Hoffman disappeared a couple of days earlier, telling the housekeeper at his parents' home that he doesn't trust the police to protect him from a psycho killer who's on the loose. So either Hoffman's in hiding or, as Riccio and most of Ford's colleagues think, he's dead, too, killed by Malone just like George Merton was.

Ford's torn. Everything points to Leo Malone being what people say he is. It's hard to argue with them. The only thing Ford definitely agrees with them about is that Malone should be found. But he disagrees about why. He thinks it's for Malone's safety, not for Hoffman's.

Ford has never gotten over how unfairly the dice rolls for different kids. Was the simple act of Taylor Hoffman being handed from his mother to a stranger in a hospital parking lot enough to cause him to become what he has? Whatever that is.

It took more time for Leo Malone to be damaged in a string of abusive foster homes, each family worse than the last one. By the time he got to the safe home in Texas, the teenaged boy's mistrust of the world had already been cemented. The psychiatrist in Santa Barbara thinks that Leo can overcome that damage. Ford isn't so sure.

Ford gets a call from Denise Riccio. "What now?"

"Hollywood responded to a call on Normandie," Riccio tells him. "They found Irma Stowell's body in an apartment."

"And?"

"The neighbor identified the man she saw leaning over the dead body as Leo Malone."

"Shit," is all Ford says. But what if it was Hoffman the neighbor saw? Don't the two men both look alike?

Riccio goes on. "They got an APB out on Malone. Designated armed and extremely dangerous."

"Makes sense," Ford says, aware that any miscue on Malone's part could end in his being shot and killed. In a case this big, it doesn't even matter that he's white. "What about Hoffman?" he asks Riccio.

"Still no word."

34

Leo waits on his motorcycle across the street from the Ki's office building. He keeps his helmet on so that no one will recognize him. The police must have found Irma's body by now and they'll presume, like Taylor's planned all along, that Leo killed both her and George. Now that his mother's dead, all Taylor has to do to remove any suspicion from himself is to kill Leo. So Leo will surrender to the police before Taylor can find him.

Leo hopes that Ki will come out of her office for lunch. But how will she react when she sees him? He's not here for any kind of reconciliation. He'll ask nothing of her other than that she introduce him to one of the lawyers in her office. Leo will ask that man or woman to represent him when he turns himself in. This is a big case and lawyers love shit like this, don't they?

In return for doing this, Leo will promise Ki that he'll never contact her again. But he would like to see her this one last time, if for no other reason than to apologize to her for putting her though all this.

But the lunch hour passes. It's nearly three o'clock and there's been no sign of her. Leo swears at his luck. He'll have to go to Detective Ford by himself and take his chances. But as he starts his cycle, he sees Ki's husband Carl exit the building. Leo's forgotten that Carl's office is in the same building as Ki's. It's how he and Ki met. Maybe Carl can tell him where she is.

Carl walks into the restaurant with several other men in suits. Leo shuts off his bike, takes off his helmet and puts on his sunglasses. He leaves the gun in the cycle's tank bag and locks it. Dodging traffic, he crosses Olympic Boulevard and enters the restaurant.

The place is crowded. The music's loud. Waitresses in short skirts and puffy blouses walk between the tables. Leo sees Carl and three other men sitting in a booth at the back of the room. He goes to their table and stands over it. He hopes they haven't seen his picture on the news or, if they have, that they won't recognize him.

"Carl?" Leo asks Ki's husband.

Carl looks up at him. "Yeah?"

"I'm a friend of your wife's," Leo says. He doesn't know how much Ki has told Carl about her relationship with him so all he says is, "I'm a client and I need to talk to her."

"You need to talk to my wife?"

"I'm having trouble locating her."

Carl looks at the other three men at his table and they each look at one another. "Are you the guy who's fucking her?" Carl asks Leo.

There's no point in lying now. "I am," Leo says.

Carl stands up. He's taller than Leo. "You're fucking my wife and you walk up to me in a restaurant in front of my friends and say it to my face just like that?"

"I have to see her."

Carl waits before he says, "Did Bruce send you in here?"

"What?" Leo asks. Carl's buddies stare at Leo, eager to hear where this goes.

"Bruce sent you, right?"

"Nobody sent me," Leo tells him.

"I don't know who you're looking for, bro, but I'm not married," Carl says. He points to a bearded man at the table. "Maybe it's Tom's wife you're fucking."

"Sleep with her," Tom says to Leo, "Please! I'll give you anything." The men laugh.

Carl puts a hand on Leo's shoulder. "You got me mixed up with some other dude, bro, because I ain't never been married."

Leo's confused. Did he pick the wrong man, someone else named Carl who looks like Ki's husband? Leo apologizes. "Sorry. I thought I met you at Michael's Restaurant with her and I—"

"Oh, right. You. That place. The guy with the father who made the crazy speech. I remember that bitch. The one with the crew cut, right?" Carl turns to his friends. "She comes up to me when I'm watching a Lakers game over there," he says, pointing to the bar.

Leo can hear Carl speaking, but it's only a jumble of words because he's trying to piece everything together.

"... and she starts asking me questions about the game and shit. Like she's really into me." Carl turns to one of his friends. "I told you about her. So damn hot, man. So I ask her out and she was like: 'We gotta go to this one restaurant.' I say there are better places, but she's like, 'No, we gotta go to this one or nowhere.' I say whatever. I'm thinking: anywhere you want as long as I can do you after, sweetheart. When we get there, she sees you with those other people and goes over to your table. It wasn't even worth trying to fuck her, so I drop her off in front of her place. I never saw her again."

Leo says nothing and leaves the restaurant.

"Fuck was that about?" Carl asks his friends after Leo leaves.

35

Leo parks his motorcycle at a 7/11 on Pico. He calls Ki's work number from the pay phone on the wall. The receiver's mouthpiece is filthy and chipped like it's been slammed against the wall countless times.

Ki's secretary answers. "Ms. Scott's office."

Leo pauses before he says, "It's Taylor. I'm at ..." and he gives her the pay phone number. "Ask Ms. Scott to call me. Right away. Tell her it's important," Leo says and he hangs up.

He only has to wait a few minutes, standing next to the flowers that fill the rack outside the store. The phone rings. He picks it up, but says nothing.

He hears Ki say, "Hello? Taylor, is that you? ... Taylor?"

PART FIVE

The Truth

36

The East LA neighborhood where Ki asks Leo to meet her is home to a mix of immigrants, legal and illegal. Asians have recently moved in on the historically Hispanic turf and not always peacefully. The Latinos were surprised how violent the Asian gangs could be. They weren't the obsequious, kowtowing servants of superhero movies or the rich Hong Kong millionaires who shopped Rodeo Drive. The Vietnamese, Koreans and Thais in this neighborhood had survived trips to the United States that made many of the Hispanics' journeys from the south look like theme park rides.

Leo steers his motorcycle along a street of small, older homes. Mexican, Salvadoran and Asian men work on their cars. Teenagers flirt, smoke and pose. Children play, infants cry. Dogs lay quietly together on the pavement waiting for someone to drop food they can fight over. Preparations for a quinceañera are being made in front of one home.

On the phone Ki begged Leo to come see her. She was relieved that he'd learned the truth and called her. She would explain everything if he'd give her the chance. She swore she wouldn't tell Taylor he was coming. She wanted nothing more to do with Taylor. "It was the biggest mistake of my life getting mixed up with that psycho," she says.

Leo said nothing as he listened to her, but he didn't hang up on her. He knew before he called her that if she answered he'd end up going to see her. What does he have to lose? Anything Ki might tell him about Taylor could be valuable evidence to give the police.

But it's more than that. He hopes by seeing Ki now he might learn something about himself, too. Would others have believed George and Irma? Would they have been so vulnerable to their scam? Or is what Janice Heller said to him true? Is Leo incapable of reading or trusting the motivations of others?

He knows that he'll want to believe whatever Ki tells him. His feelings for her, as misguided as they are, will make him susceptible. So he tells himself to be strong when he sees her and to doubt whatever she says.

Leo parks his cycle in front of a house that doubles as a beauty parlor. Through its windows he sees Latina and Asian customers, the older women too heavy, the younger ones too skinny, all begging their hairdressers to make them look like the impossibly beautiful women in the magazines that sit open on their laps. Theirs is a fool's dream, but how much more foolish is it than Leo coming here to listen to Ki's side of the story, hoping that it will change anything?

Leo locks the cycle's tank bag with the pistol in it and he approaches the house. Ki comes out to greet him, like she'd done in the reception area of the law office where she'd claimed to work. What had the receptionist in that office thought when this pretty, short-haired girl whom she'd never seen before shouted to her from the elevator that she'd be back in time for her two o'clock meeting?

Ki has dyed her hair a light blonde since Leo had last seen her. It's nearly identical to the color Leo has dyed his own hair and in another world they'd have laughed at that. This time they say nothing. She wears a thin green dress through which, when she stands against any light, Leo can make out her whole body.

She hugs Leo without any hesitation. "I'm so sorry, baby," she says and buries her head in Leo's neck. He can feel her breath the same way he did whenever she slept next to him. "I never meant to hurt you," she says. He wants to pull away from her, but he doesn't.

She takes him by the hand and pulls him across a rickety porch and into the shop. The hairdressers and their customers stare silently at Leo as he walks through the crowded room. One of these women has played the role of Ki's secretary Maria whenever Leo called her imaginary office. He guesses it's the one who's wrapping a young woman's hair in small pieces of foil because she's the only one who looks away when he passes her station.

Ki takes him through a rear door that leads to a smaller house, not much more than a shack, in the back yard. This is where she lives. The place is tiny and worn, but otherwise neat apart from the many children's toys scattered around the room. A makeshift kitchen with a sink and tiny refrigerator is on one side of the room. A portable, two-burner electric stove and a toaster oven sit on the once white countertop, now a shade of yellow. Ki shuts the door, dulling the noise that comes from the beauty shop and the street.

"Wait a minute," she says and goes into the other room. Once she's out of his sight, Leo realizes it was a mistake to have come here. He should've gone straight to the police after watching Taylor kill Irma or at least when he found out that Ki was a part of the scam. It's not too late to leave now. He turns to go. But before he can, Ki reappears holding an infant. The child, not two years old, wriggles in her arms.

"This is my boy, Brady," she says. "He's sick."

Ki reaches for medicine on the counter with her free hand. It's in a small, brown glass bottle with a teardrop squeezer top. She drops the bottle and says, "Shit." She speaks soothingly to the baby. "Mommy said a bad word, didn't she, sweetheart?"

Leo picks the bottle up and hands it to her. "He yours?"

"All mine. He's sick."

"What's wrong with him?" Leo asks.

"He's got this brain condition. Something he was born with. It's why he doesn't talk yet. It has to do with blood flow and water and stuff. He has seizures. I think he's about to have one now. Hold him while I get his medicine, will you?"

She hands her child to Leo who can feel the little boy's body heat through the jumpsuit he wears. His face is smooth the way Asian babies' faces sometimes are, but his illness makes him pale. He squirms at first, but because Leo has held many of his foster brothers and sisters, he gently bounces Brady and this calms the child down.

"You're good with kids," Ki says as she preps the medicine. "Check his eyes for me, will you?"

"Check them for what?"

"His pupils. Are they shaking?"

"How do you mean?"

"Like jumping back and forth," she says impatiently.

The child's eyes look normal to Leo. "No."

"We've got time then." Ki hands Leo a damp dishrag. "Hold this on his face. It cools him down. He likes it."

Leo does this and the child smiles at him. "Hey, little buddy," Leo says, "everything's gonna be all right."

Flustered, Ki searches the kitchen drawers. "I can never find a clean spoon in this place. Never mind. Here, hold him still for me." She gives her child a few drops of the medicine directly from the dropper onto his tongue. Brady calms immediately. "He likes you," she says. "You've held kids before, huh?"

"How old is he?"

"Seventeen months yesterday. Wait, eighteen," she says. "It goes so fast. Like one long day." She takes Brady from Leo and checks the boy's eyes. "I gotta get him to a doctor. Can you drive us?"

"Not on a motorcycle."

"Then I'll drive. We can talk on the way."

Leo rides in the front passenger seat and holds Brady on his lap. The child's calm while Ki maneuvers through the traffic, honking at and passing slower cars. At a red light she reaches over and rub her son's cheek. "He doesn't usually like strangers holding him," she says. Leo asks her who Brady's father is. "It's not Taylor if that's what you're thinking," she says. "I never even told Taylor about him."

"Why not?"

"I wouldn't trust his ass around any kid. Would you? Brady's father disappeared as soon I told him I was pregnant. Good riddance to that piece of shit, too."

Ki met Taylor while waitressing at a hotel restaurant in Beverly Hills. She met a lot of men that way, mostly married, mostly assholes and easy touches for cash when she threatened to tell their wives she was sleeping with them. She knew Taylor was trouble, but she thought he had enough money to make up for that. "I didn't have any money and I had Brady," she says. She never told Taylor about Brady because that would've scared him off like it did most men. Taylor hates kids anyway. "Most psychopaths do," she says, "except to molest them or kill them."

Taylor told her about his reunion with George and Irma in Santa Fe a few months before. He said they had a lot of Stowell Cosmetics money and each time Ki and Taylor got together he'd outline schemes how they could get it and what they'd do with it once they did. Taylor felt he deserved it. He said he was a great con man, a skill he admitted inheriting from his father. Taylor's plan involved a guy he'd seen in Martinique the year before, a guy who looked a lot like him. Leo. It sounded far-fetched to Ki, but what did she care if she got some money out of it?

"To him," Ki says, "grifting is like his religion. That's when he came up with his plan to use you. His parents didn't like it. Especially George. Neither did I. He never told them about me being involved either. The more lies he could tell his parents, the happier he was. But they were scared of this guy Weathers who's after them. So they went along with it. Like me, they figured what the hell?" She went to La Cachette with Taylor to help set up the scam. Her friend Naomi took care of Brady along with her own two kids. "That's why I was always taking the room service food that we didn't eat home with me. You always joked that I had a second secret family. I did. I gave the leftovers to Brady or to Naomi or whoever took care of him. I didn't have any money to give them."

Ki pulls into the parking lot of a hospital and takes Brady from Leo. "Wait here. That way I won't get another ticket," she says. She exits the car with her son and walks through the sliding glass doors of the emergency room.

Leo watches Ki approach the desk and speak to the nurse behind it. She and Brady follow a second nurse down a hallway. Leo feels sorry for the child, not only because of its illness but, because with a mother like Ki, its chances of ending up in the system like Leo had were better than good.

Leo believes Ki truly regrets what she's done to him. He still wants her and he imagines what might happen if they both get out of this mess unscathed. But he forces himself to stop thinking like this. Being cleared of George's and Irma's deaths is all that matters now. Ki comes back to the car holding her child and she gets in.

"What did the doctor say?" Leo asks.

"I didn't see a doctor. I don't want to take him in if I don't have to. I already owe so much money as it is, and if you don't have any insurance they make you feel like shit. One of the nurses, she helps me off the books. She steals medicine for him. He's gonna be okay this time. He's already better. I can tell. Here," she says and hands the child back to Leo. She starts the car and readies to pull it onto the street, but she brakes first. "You drive," she says, "I want to hold him." Taking the baby, she changes seats with Leo who drives them back home.

"All those mothers in the ward sitting there looking at me every time I go in," Ki says. "I hate it, the pressure everyone puts on you. The whole culture. I hate that the minute a baby's born everything and everyone spends all their time trying to make you feel like you're inadequate, trying to sell you shit. The pictures in magazines and the catalogs they send you. They're all the same. The perfect house, the spotless kitchen, the shiny new car parked in the driveway outside and the dimple-faced baby happily eating its oh-so-healthy meal. That's not what it's like. Not for me anyway."

Growing up Leo heard the same complaints from his foster mothers and their friends. The homes and the cars in the ads have changed, but the idea is the same.

"Did George and Irma ever find out about you?" Leo asks her.

"Taylor never told them. At first I thought it was because he was worried that Irma'd be jealous of me, which of course she is. But now I realize that it's because he planned on turning on them all along."

"And killing them."

"He thought if I knew that I would've pulled out of the whole deal."

"Would you have?"

"Of course. I'd never get involved with anything like that. I'm no angel. I'm the first to admit that. But I'm no killer, either. All I wanted was some money for Brady and me. And at first, everything was working like a dream."

"Because I was the perfect fool."

"I didn't say that."

"You don't have to. I fell for everything. That's how it works. People don't question things, do they?"

"People believe what they want to believe."

"The girls at the resort, Penny and her sister, you didn't know them, did you?"

Ki shook her head. "Of course not."

"What about your grandmother?"

"I'm sorry," Ki said and looked away. The old woman they saw in the home that day had no idea who the young man and woman visiting her were. Maybe she thinks they're people who'd died years before. Leo hopes their visit has made her happy for as long as she can remember it.

"In the beginning it was all working like a charm," Ki says, "but then you screwed things up. Taylor thought you'd go along with George and Irma believing you were him because you were gonna take them for some money. That's the thing with cons like Taylor.

They think everyone's as shitty as they are. He never figured you'd get involved with them the way you did. Neither did they."

"What about you? Did you think that I was scamming them?"

"No."

"Why not?"

"Because you're different than Taylor. You confused him because you're kind. You're good. It's like you and him talk in different languages. That blindsided his parents, too. George especially. Irma not so much. She likes Taylor. He couldn't do any wrong in her eyes."

"Until he killed her," Leo says.

"But George thought you were a gift from God. No one saw that coming, me included. Then the worst thing that can happen to a con happened to me." She pauses. "I fell for my mark. You."

George said the same thing to him in the diner earlier that day. "How did I know that was coming?" Leo says as they waited at a red light.

"I'm not expecting you to run off into the sunset with me."

Even after admitting everything she'd done, it disappoints Leo when she says this. "So what do you want?" he asked.

"Two things. The first is for you to get out of this clean."

"What's the second? The money?"

"Forget the money," she says. "All I want is to stay out of jail so I can keep Brady. The only reason I got into all this in the first place was to have enough money to take care of him. You have no idea how desperate you get with a kid, and a sick kid at that." She looks at Brady. "It sucks being poor, doesn't it, angel?" She holds the boy's forehead against her own and shuts her eyes like she's praying. "I've done a lot of bad things, Leo, but I'm a good mother. Brady's the only good thing I've ever done in my whole life. I can't lose him." She settles the boy in her lap. "I can't let them take him away from me. You were in the system. You know the shit he'd go through." Leo does know. The little boy turns and looks at Leo pleadingly as if it were a move he'd rehearsed.

By the time they park in front of the beauty parlor it's late afternoon. That evening one of the neighborhood girls will be celebrating her quinceañera and the whole street's getting ready for the party. Streamers hang from trees and bobbing in the breeze are brightly colored balloons tied to the eaves of the houses, looking as if they might be the only things holding the rickety structures up. Boom boxes play mariachi music and girlish pop songs. The neighbors sit on plastic lawn furniture and empty orange crates. They began drinking much earlier.

Leo wheels his motorcycle behind Ki's house and into the alley where no one can see it from the street. Brady sleeps soundly. Leo takes his gun from the cycle's tank bag and puts it in his backpack. "What are we going to do now?" he asks when they get into the house.

Ki sits on a small wooden chair with Brady in her lap. "We can go to the cops and tell them about Taylor. I'll back you up, but you gotta promise you'll back me up when I say I didn't know anything about Taylor's plans."

"Lying makes things messy."

"It's not a lie. And Taylor's so fucked up, he'll trip all over himself and give himself away."

"Do you have a record?" he asks her.

"No felonies. Think about it, Leo. Please." Ki says she's too exhausted to talk anymore. She needs to sleep. "You look fried, too," she says. Leo is. He's hardly slept for two days. She takes his hand and leads him into the tiny bedroom where there's a thin, stained mattress on the floor. Leo lays down on it.

Brady needs changing so Ki takes him back into the other room where Naomi, very young by the sound of her voice, has come in. Ki speaks in broken Korean to Naomi who takes the sleeping child with her. Ki comes back into the bedroom. Naomi will change Brady and, after he wakes up, she'll take him to the quinceañera and let him have some fun before she brings him home. That will give Ki a break she needs. She takes off her clothes and, naked, lays down with Leo who can feel the heat of her body against his and the hard nipples of her breasts pressed against his back.

"It means so much to me that you came here today," she says. "I don't expect anything from you. I want to enjoy this time with you right now before—" she stops there and says no more. Her hands move up and down his body and he doesn't stop her. He probably should, but he doesn't. They make love like two people looking for something neither one can find.

Ki falls asleep. Leo lays awake. Brady changes everything. The one thing he wants is to make sure the child makes it through all this safely.

He gets up and leaves Ki, still asleep, on the mattress. He walks out of the house and into the street where the quinceañera is in full swing. People drink and dance and argue. An older Hispanic woman smiles and hands him a bottle of Corona.

Leo walks through the many people. They look happy. These large families remain together in spite of the obstacles they face. They aren't the television families that George watched, trying to mimic them. These families accept the limitations they're handed and carry on in spite of them. Leo's own parents were criminals. His foster mothers sat at the dinner table after they'd been beaten. They forgave their husbands for having sex with other women. They welcomed their sons and daughters back into their homes even though they were felons, prostitutes, dealers and addicts.

Ki's made bad choices, driven by her son's needs. But she's not violent. If he stays with her, Leo will be stepping into an uncharted maze, but aren't all families a maze? Only in stories are they perfect. Janice Heller wrote that in her note. Is Ki a test for Leo? Is she a way to find out if he's capable of feeling what other, normal people did? Can he forgive her? Should he forgive her? Maybe it's too much too soon for him, like putting an infant behind the wheel of a car and expecting it to drive. But this is the hand he's been dealt.

Leo takes his phone out of his pocket and dials it.

37

Ford's relieved when Leo Malone calls him. He feels a certain amount of "I told you so", but there's no one he can say it to. And maybe it's too early to say that anyway. Malone only says that he wants to meet and talk. Ford tells him that it'd be better for everyone, safer, if he came to the Westside headquarters as soon as he hangs up. Ford would even go and pick him up, take his gun and drive him in. But Malone doesn't go for that. He'll only agree to meet the Detective somewhere on the East Side. Ford says okay. But when the kid lets Ford pick the place, the detective laughs. It shows how inexperienced Malone is.

Half an hour later, Ford sits at the same table in the small East LA taco joint he's been sitting at for twenty years. Carlos's Tacos is on South Atlantic close to where LA borders Alhambra. Lately, it seems like every neighborhood in the city is coming up with a name for itself. Will this neighborhood do that, too? And, if it does, what will it call itself and how would it change? Will it gentrify? Will Carlos's Tacos become a Starbucks? Or, worse, a nail salon?

Ford told no one about his meeting with Malone. The Irma Stowell case is getting bigger. Their murders bring these two middling celebrities back into the limelight, bigger than they ever were when they were alive. If any other officer had gotten the call from Malone, they'd have gone straight to the Chief. Take all the credit you can and let others deal with the details. But Ford knew as soon as he heard Malone's voice he wouldn't do that.

If Ford's superiors, or anyone else in the department, ask him why he agreed to meet with the kid, he can't give them a good answer. Not one they'd find acceptable anyway. All he'd say is that it felt like the right thing to do. Officially that wouldn't fly, but it's true. He has no interest in the promotion the department has been dangling in front of him. He plans to retire soon, although he hopes he'll be doing that on a full pension, not one that's docked forty or fifty percent because of an infraction like this.

Ford doesn't expect any trouble from the kid but, even so, he takes precautions. Malone's a suspect in two murders and the last time the kid was seen he was holding a pistol over the dead body of the second victim. So Ford loads his pistol, a small Berreta, and takes it with him to the meeting at the taqueria. When he gets to Carlos's, Ford wonders if he's done the right thing. But he's here now, so all he can do is eat the green corn tamales on the paper plate in front of him and wait.

He doesn't have to wait long. Through the restaurant's window he sees Leo pull up on his motorcycle. The kid doesn't get off his ride for several minutes. He sits on it without taking off his helmet. Has he decided that it was a mistake to meet? Does he think that Ford lied to him and brought Riccio and other cops to take him down here?

But Malone takes off his helmet. He's dyed his hair a blond color. He climbs off the bike and enters the nearly empty restaurant with his head lowered. Ford adjusts his position so that, if he needs to, he can easily get his pistol out of its shoulder holster.

Malone goes straight to Ford's table in the back corner of the small room and sits opposite him, facing the wall. The kid doesn't have to worry. No one other than Maria, Carlos's daughter who's cooking, could see his face that's been all over the TV since Irma's body was found earlier that afternoon. And even if Maria does recognize him she won't say anything to anyone.

"You want something to eat?" Ford asks when Malone sits down.

The kid shakes his head. "Thank you for coming, Detective."

Malone is polite. You have to give him that. Years in the foster system have trained him to use a person's official title as often as possible. Officer, Your Honor, Professor, Detective.

"Where's your gun?" Ford asks.

"It's not my gun, sir."

"Where is it?"

"I didn't bring it," Leo says. He pauses. "Is meeting with me like this gonna get you in trouble?"

Ford doesn't expect the question, a first for a suspect. "Depends on what you do after you leave this place."

Malone nods. "There's another person involved," he says.

"A girl?"

"A girl."

"The one in the guesthouse bathroom?"

"I didn't know she was involved in this, too. Not then anyway."

"But you know now?"

"Yes, sir."

Malone doesn't speak like the usual suspect. He hardly speaks at all. Most suspects you can't shut up. That's something you want because with the rope they make out of their own words, they usually hang themselves. But not this kid.

Ford takes a sip of his coffee. "Hoffman set you up, didn't he?" he asks and Malone nods yes. "I figured there was another person in all this besides him," Ford says. "Cons almost never work on their own. I don't know why, but I'm sure a shrink would be happy to explain it to us for two hundred bucks an hour." Malone grins. "That's why I thought maybe you and Hoffman were in on this together at first."

"I was," Malone says, "only I didn't know it."

Ford smiles. The kid's sharp.

"Where's Taylor now?" Malone asks.

"No one knows. He called that one TV show to say he's hiding because he's scared that the LAPD can't protect him."

"From me?"

"From you." Everything about how Leo Malone acts and what the kid says confirms the Detective's first instincts. The boy's not a criminal. He's a kid who's in way over his head. Ford feels sorry for him, but facts are facts and one of those facts is that there are two bodies in the city morgue with bullet holes in them put there by a gun the kid has in his possession.

"What do you want from me?" Ford asks.

"I want to come in with the girl."

"At what cost?"

"Only your promise we'll be treated fairly and that you'll listen to us with an open mind. Ki—" He stops when he says her name, but goes on. "She was in on the first part of the con with Hoffman, but not when it got out of hand. She had nothing to do with the killings."

The kid's starting to talk. He must really like this girl. She got to Malone. The shrink said that might happen. Once the gate was opened there could be a flood. "What's she like?" Ford asks.

"Korean. Part Korean. There's something else, too," he says. "The most important thing."

Ford worries that Malone's going to ask for something he can't deliver. "What's that?"

"She has a kid. Little. Less than two years old," he says.

"So?"

"You gotta promise me you'll have someone there ready to handle him when we come in. And that you'll let her give the kid to someone to take care of while this is all being sorted out. He can't go into the system. I can't let that happen to him."

"Okay," Ford says. He's lying because he's not sure he can keep the kid out of the system.

Leo goes on. "The girl misjudged Hoffman. That was her mistake. She's no saint, but she had no idea how crazy he was. He is. I'm going back to her now and get her and bring her in. She wants that. It was her idea. You can put us in jail if you want. I'd prefer it if you did. Both of us would. At least until you get Hoffman somewhere so that he can't come after me. Or her. Or her boy."

"Where is she now?"

"In a bungalow behind a beauty parlor off North Sixth. But let us come in on our own, okay? She'd freak if you showed up. And it'll look better for us that way, won't it?"

"Maybe. But call me before you come in," Ford says. "I want to make sure I'm there. I'll meet you in the lot and walk you in."

"Deal," Malone says and he stands up.

"Can I ask you a question?" Ford asks him. "Did you really believe that Hoffman's parents thought you were their son?"

"I did." The kid looks embarrassed to admit this. "It makes me look stupid, doesn't it?"

"Not really," Ford says. It makes you look like a normal person, he wants to say. Instead, he asks, "What was it like there? The three of you for all that time?"

"It was like a family."

"You took their picture, didn't you? The one on the desk in the guesthouse."

"I did." Leo reaches into his inside jacket pocket and takes that same photo of George and Irma out. Crumpled now, he puts it on the table in front of Ford.

Ford picks it up. "Why'd you take it?"

Leo shrugs. "They looked happy."

Ford looks at the photo. He could remember sitting in his own mother's lap as an infant while she read him a story. But who knows what we really remember or what we make into a memory from what others tell us? Witnesses will swear they saw events that never actually happened. What did Leo Licklighter remember about seeing his mother and father shot to death in an Oklahoma convenience store? And if Leo Licklighter had never felt wanted or loved, how good must it have been for him to suddenly find himself wanted by a family? Even one as unlikely as the Mertons?

"Thank you, Detective," Leo says and he shakes Ford's hand.

When Leo turns to leave, Ford holds out the photo of George and Irma. "You forgot this."

"You keep it," Leo says and leaves the restaurant. He puts on his helmet, gets on his cycle and heads north on Atlantic.

Ford eats his tamales that are nearly cold now. It's good that Malone is so naïve, so honest. He's not going to try and trick anyone. It's not good that this Korean girl he's involved with is a grifter. But it's like the shrink said: Malone doesn't have the skills to know if he's being used. And if the Korean smells blood, chances are she'll rip him to shreds. Ford will give the kid half an hour to call him. An hour tops.

He looks at the photo of George and Irma that lays on the table, a handsome and beautiful, all-American couple that any kid would want as their mother and father.

38

Ki's awake when Leo gets back from his meeting with Ford. Her short nap has restored her energy and she runs to Leo and hugs him tightly. "I thought you left us," she says.

"I needed to think," Leo says. "Where's Brady?"

"In the bedroom. Sleeping. Naomi fed him and took him to the party. She said he had fun and then she brought him back. You should've seen him. He was smiling from ear to ear." Her child's joy makes her happy and when she's happy she's more beautiful. She reminds Leo of his mother in the one short video he'd seen of her.

"Where'd you go?" she asks Leo as she cleans some dishes in the small sink.

Leo sits down. "I made a decision."

"About what?"

"We'll go see that cop, the one who came to Bel Air that first night."

"Why him?"

"I trust him."

She turns to Leo nervously. "Is that where you were? Meeting with him?"

Leo hates lying to her, but he does. He shakes his head. "No. I was just riding and thinking. You and I will go to him and tell him everything that we both did," Leo says. "If he offers us protection, we'll take it."

"Why?"

"It's better if we stay in jail until Taylor's caught."

Ki considers what he says. "Or …" she starts to say but stops herself.

"Or what?"

"I know it's crazy."

"What's crazy?" Leo asks.

"What if Taylor were to die?"

"How would he die?"

"We'd kill him."

Leo's shocked when she says this. More than shocked, he's angry. He shakes his head. "No, no, no. No," he says. This is the first time Ki's suggested their doing anything violent. Leo just promised Ford that nothing like that would happen. He told him that they'd come in peacefully. "Why would you even say that to me?" Leo asks her.

"Listen to me."

"No."

"Please."

"You're the second person today who's asked me to kill someone."

Ki looks sharply at him. "Who's the other one?"

Leo doesn't answer her. "Forget it."

"Hear me out, Leo."

"I'm not killing anyone," Leo says, walking away from her. But Ki follows him closely.

"I'm not saying we kill Taylor because I *want* to do it," she says. "I hate the idea of killing someone. Anyone."

"Good, because I'm not killing him. We have no reason to."

"We have a very good reason to. We have to do it to protect ourselves. What do you think is gonna happen now? Even if we turn ourselves in? Taylor's crazy and you know that if he talks his way out of all this shit which, if I know him, he will do, the first thing he's gonna do is kill you or me or both of us," she says. "And what's gonna happen to Brady after that, huh? Or maybe he'll kill him, too. Why not? Kill the kid. Get rid of everyone."

What she said about Taylor wanting to kill Ki and him is true. But Leo counters that Taylor will never get bail, not for murder.

Ki doesn't buy that. Taylor would find his way out of jail and come looking for her, for both of them. "You kill him in self defense. Or I do," she says. "You know that I'd never suggest something like this if he weren't crazy, but he is. Everybody knows that. The cops will buy it, no problem. I'll back you up. He set us both up, he killed his own parents, Leo. He came after us and we killed him. He doesn't deserve to live."

How can Leo tell her that what she's saying is wrong? They're almost free now. Should he tell her about his meeting with Ford?

Before he can say anything, she hugs him. "I love you so much. Look at me. I wasn't lying about that. You know that. And with Taylor dead we wouldn't have to worry about him anymore. We can take Brady and go wherever we want. We can start all over. Like we've been talking about."

Leo wasn't going to kill Taylor. He wouldn't let Ki kill him, either. But needing time to think through this new and unexpected turn of hers, he says, "How would I do it?"

Ki reads Leo's question as a sign that he's now considering killing Taylor. She perks up. "You could do it a million different ways," she says.

"One is enough," he says.

She takes his head in her hands. Her eyes are huge, like a child's. He remembers his mother looking into his face like this. "Think about it, Leo," Ki says. "It can work. You and me, we'll make it work," she whispers to him and out of her pocket she takes the gun Leo put into his backpack, the gun that killed George, the gun Leo took from Irma's apartment after Taylor killed her with it.

"Give me that," he says.

"You brought it with you for a reason, Leo. Everything happens for a reason."

Leo takes the gun from Ki. There are three bullets left in its cylinder. Of the three bullets already used, one killed George; the other two killed Irma. He has to convince Ki that killing Taylor is not the way to go. "Listen to me, Ki—" Leo starts to say, but Ki cuts him off.

She moves the curtain and looks through the window. "It's him."

Leo hopes it's Ford that she sees, that the Detective lied and followed him here with a dozen other cops. But it's not Ford.

"It's Taylor," Ki says and goes into the bedroom where Brady's sleeping.

The front door opens and Taylor walks in. Music and firecrackers from the quinceañera can be heard. When Taylor sees Leo and the pistol in his hand, he smiles and says, "Lucy, you got a lotta 'splaining to do," imitating one of George's favorite sitcom fathers.

Ki comes out of the bedroom buttoning her dress. "He knows," she says to Taylor about Leo.

Taylor grins. "And he's still here? Goddamn. The almighty power of the pussy. Men are such idiots, aren't we, Leo? We see our doom coming down on us like a freight train, but we stand right there on the tracks waiting, hoping it's not gonna hit us, don't we?"

Taylor isn't wrong about that. After all, Leo is here.

"We're getting out," Ki says.

"We?" asks Taylor.

"Leo and me."

"Seriously?"

"I love him."

Taylor looks at Leo. "First my parents love you more than me and now her. I'm lucky I don't have a dog."

"We're leaving," Ki says. "You can do whatever you want."

"What are you talking about 'leaving'? There are two dead people in the mix, sweetheart." Taylor points to Leo. "Two people everyone thinks he killed. Where are you going to go?"

"She had nothing to do with them," Leo says.

"He speaks," Taylor says about Leo and turns to him. "Is that what she told you?"

"I believe her."

"Of course you do. From the first minute she saw you on the island she read you like a book. *Leo For Dummies.* She's good, almost as good as me. But not quite. That's the genius of bitches like her. She knows what you're gonna do before you do." He turns to Ki. "Doesn't Leo have to take a piss right about now, sweetheart?"

"Shut up," she says.

"So what's the plan?" Taylor asks them. Leo keeps his pistol aimed at him. Taylor isn't worried; he knows that Leo will never shoot him and he's right. "Don't tell me," Taylor says. "She asked you to kill me." Leo's silence tells Taylor that he's right.

"Of course she did," Taylor says. "That'd be perfect. You kill me, they pin it on you, and that way she ends up with the insurance money."

"You don't know what you're talking about," Ki says.

"How would she get any of the money?" Leo asks.

Taylor looks at Ki. "Did you forget to tell him that part, sweetheart?"

"What part?" Leo asks.

"She's my wife."

"He's such a liar," Ki says to Leo about Taylor.

Taylor says, "We got married in Tahoe before we left for La Cachette."

"Don't listen to him," Ki tells Leo. "He's trying to confuse you. It's what he does. I've done a lot of stupid things is my life, but marrying this asshole is not one of them."

Taylor points angrily at Ki. "You are my wife in sickness and in health, for richer or poorer, whether you like it or not, you miserable cunt." He turns to Leo and smiles. "We wrote our own vows."

"Shoot him," Ki says.

"Leo's not gonna shoot me, sweetheart. You don't know him as well as I thought you did."

Leo turns to Ki. "How long have you been married?"

Ki closes her eyes and drops her head. "I'm sorry, Leo. I didn't tell you because I thought you wouldn't understand."

"How long?" Leo asks again.

"Six months," she says. "I only married him because I needed his health insurance which he lied to me about having anyway. Once all this was over I was gonna get an annulment. All I cared about was getting some money, getting the hell out of here and starting all over again. Then I met you. I fell in love with you, Leo. The three of us, we can be a family."

"The three of us?" Taylor says. "Are you including me in this happy family?"

"Shoot him!" Ki says to Leo, louder this time. "Shoot the shit out of him."

A string of firecrackers goes off in the next yard and in the bedroom the baby starts to cry. He's loud like babies can be when they wake up surprised by loud noises.

Taylor turns toward the bedroom. "What's that?"

"The baby," Ki says.

Taylor looks from Ki to Leo and back again. "What baby?"

"My baby."

"Since when do you have a baby?"

"Since I left Tulsa."

"What are you talking about?" Taylor asks.

"I didn't tell you," she says to Taylor, "because I didn't want you anywhere near him."

"I don't know whose baby that is," Taylor says to Leo, "but I can promise you it's not hers."

Ki yells toward the bedroom and the crying baby, "I'm coming, sweetheart." She turns to Taylor. "Why do you think I got into all this shit with you to begin with? Everything I did, everything I do, is for my little boy. Every single goddamn thing." Tears fill her eyes.

"This I want to see." Taylor walks toward the bedroom, but Ki grabs a knife from the kitchen counter and blocks his way.

"Don't you dare go near him."

Taylor stands in place. "She's playing you, Leo. She's punching your buttons with a sledgehammer."

Ki points the knife at Taylor and says to Leo, "Just shoot him. Do the whole world a favor and shoot the stupid prick between the eyes."

Even though Leo knows that most of what she'd told him is a lie, this plea of hers, the desperation of a mother protecting her child, affects him. Ki wants to keep her child safe from Taylor unlike Leo's own mother who'd used her child as a shield while she and Leo's father robbed gas stations.

"If you won't shoot him, I will," Ki says.

Here Brady appears unsteadily at the open bedroom door. He's crawled by himself across the bedroom floor and now stands up holding onto the frame of the bedroom door. He's not crying anymore.

Ki's face brightens. "There's my little cowboy," she says.

But Brady's diaper has slipped off and he's naked. He stumbles into the living room, grabbing onto the back of the small wooden chair for balance. But one thing becomes clear as he stands there: Brady is not a boy. He's a girl with the smooth crotch of a child her age.

Taylor laughs. "Looks like your little wrangler's missing a part, darling. Better check the manual."

Ki's face freezes. "You little twat," she yells and runs over and grabs the little girl who smiles at what she thinks is a game her mother might play, only with different words.

Leo realizes that after he called her that afternoon Ki had come up with the story about her kid. Given Leo's history, it was a smart tactic on her part. It was brilliant. But she'd forgotten that the child of the Vietnamese teenager in the house next to hers is a girl, not a boy. By the time she remembers—if she even did—what sex the kid is, she couldn't change her story. With a diaper on, who was going to know anyway? But the little girl's pants have come off.

Leo's not surprised or disappointed. He's relieved because now he has no more choices to make. They've been made for him. Nothing else that Ki or Taylor or anyone does or says now will matter. Leo's only purpose is to protect the child.

Leo aims his gun at Ki. "Put her down," he says.

But Ki keeps hold of the child and rests the knife in her hand against the little girl's throat. What she's threatening to do surpasses Leo's own mother's crime. The notorious Carly Licklighter might have held Leo in her arms, endangering him while she robbed stores with his father, but she never threatened to kill him in the process. Leo's always believed that the look on his mother's face as she lay dying on the gas station's linoleum floor was one of apology.

But Ki's reaction to Leo's demand is simple. "Put the gun down or I'll slit her throat wide open."

"Didn't I read that on a Hallmark card?" Taylor asks.

"Put the gun on the counter and walk away from it," Ki says to Leo. But he doesn't move. "Do it now or I'll cut her throat. I swear to God I will."

The child in Ki's arms laughs when she says this.

Leo says, "You wouldn't do that."

"She would," Taylor says and Leo realizes that he's right. Ki would slice the child's neck to save her own.

"Big mistake," Taylor says when Leo puts his gun on the kitchen counter and steps away from it.

Ki takes hold of a dishcloth and grabs the pistol with it. She tosses the knife across the room where it lands with a clank behind the sofa. "Give me your car keys," she says to Taylor.

"You can't get out of this without me," Taylor tells her.

She points the pistol at him. "Put your keys on the table."

Taylor drops his keys on the small table. He doesn't look afraid. It's not that he's hiding his fear. He doesn't have any to hide. Like most sociopaths, he doesn't experience that emotion. Leo sees that this time his inability is going to cost him.

Ki grabs the car keys, still holding the child who wriggles impatiently. "Quit moving," she says and jerks the child harshly.

"You can take the girl out of the trailer park," Taylor says, "but you can't take the trailer park out of—"

"You talk too much," Ki says and shoots Taylor once in the chest. The gunshot startles Leo as much as when Taylor shot Irma earlier. Taylor jerks backwards, but steadies himself by holding onto the wall. The look on his face isn't one of pain or anger. It's disbelief. He looks at the bloodstain on his shirt and all he says is, "Seriously?"

"Seriously," Ki says and shoots him a second time. Taylor collapses in a heap, landing on the floor in an awkward position.

This is the second time Leo's watched Taylor die. But this time it's real. Or is it? Could this be another one of his and Ki's cons? No, Taylor's dead. Blood begins to soak the floor beneath him.

The noise from the quinceañera's music and its firecrackers covers the sound of the pistol and even if it hadn't, a gunshot in this neighborhood wouldn't have surprised anyone.

But the gunshots have caused the baby to start crying again. "Shut up!" Ki screams into the child's face. But this only makes her cry more.

"You can go," Leo says to Ki, "but leave the kid with me. That's all I'm asking."

Ki backs to the door with George's gun in her hand, aimed at the child's head. "Nice try," she says to Leo, "but once they find this thing with your prints on it, the gun you shot George and Irma with, the same one you shot my late husband with, too, you're toast."

Leo knows that she's reaching. Her plans have taken her this far, but now there are too many variables and soon everything will be too difficult to keep in the air. Ki kicks the door open and walks through it backwards onto the shack's small front porch, staring at Leo the whole time.

Leo knows that everything that's happened to him in the last four weeks is because of this one moment. He was put here to save this kid who would return safely to her family because of what he's going to do.

Ki grins. "Maybe this would be a good time to get on your knees and say a prayer to that God you're so fond of, preacher," she says. Holding the child, she steps slowly backwards toward the worn wooden steps and onto the path that will take her to her car on the street. She doesn't notice yet that the sounds of the party, the music, the laughing and the yelling have all stopped.

What she hears instead is Louis Ford's voice. "Put your gun and the child down, Ms. Park," Ford says. Ki freezes. She swears under her breath.

When Ford came back from meeting with Leo, he asked Riccio to find anything she could on a female grifter named Ki who worked the Westside. Riccio didn't ask where Ford had been or why he wanted the information, but she came up with a woman named Jin Park who sometimes used the name Ki. She'd been identified by the manager of The Beverly Hilton six months earlier as the woman who'd skipped out without paying. She has a long rap sheet of fraud and petty larceny.

Ford repeats his demand. "Drop the gun, Ms. Park."

Leo steps onto the porch, his hands raised high in the air. Half a dozen policemen from the three squad cars parked in the street and on the lawn aim their pistols at him. Officer Riccio stands a few paces away from Ford. The quinceañera revelers are silent, watching this drama unfold from over the hedges and through the windows of the neighboring houses. The only sounds come from the child's mother who cries out in Vietnamese. She's held back by a Black female officer and another woman, a neighbor who speaks soothingly to her in Spanish. Hearing her mother's voice, the child stops crying and looks left and right to find her.

"You did go meet with him, didn't you?" Ki says to Leo.

"I thought once they got here," Leo says, "they'd figure out Taylor's part in all of this and that you and I would be cleared."

Ki shakes her head. "You're so naïve. How did you stay alive in all those places they put you?"

Denise Riccio takes a couple of steps forward. "Please, ma'am," she says, "put the gun down and give me the child."

"I'll give the kid to him," Ki says, gesturing with her pistol to Leo.

Ford and Riccio look at one another. Ford then looks at Leo who nods to the Detective.

"All right, Ms. Park," Ford says, "give the child to Mr. Malone, but do it slowly." Normally, Ford would never have agreed to this, but he trusts Leo. Ford yells to the policemen standing behind him. "Lower your weapons." They all do.

Ki walks back up the porch's steps to Leo with the baby in her arms. Its mother sobs the child's name while the policewoman and the neighbor hold her back.

"We'd have made a nice family, don't you think?" Ki says and she hands the baby to Leo. After taking the child, the first thing Leo does is turn his back to Ki in case she fires her gun. The bullet would have to go through him first before possibly hitting the child. Leo rocks the little girl. She stops crying and smiles at him.

"Drop your gun, Ms. Park," Ford says to Ki.

Ki does as she's told and tosses the gun onto the brown lawn. A uniformed policeman picks it up. Two others grab Ki, handcuff her and rush her to a squad car. Held tightly in Leo's arms, the child laughs as several other police charge the porch. Leo carefully hands the baby to Denise Riccio who, in turn, hands her to her mother.

Two policemen grab Leo. They cuff him and lead him to a second squad car, passing Ford who looks at Leo without saying anything to him.

The cops put Leo in the back seat of the squad car. Leo's relieved. He owes no one anything. Not George, not Irma, not Ki, not his foster parents or his own parents. No one. He's free from all entanglements, emotional or otherwise. This is how he'll stay from now on.

The police car pulls onto the road and leaves. The sounds of the quinceañera fill the neighborhood in no time.

PART SIX

Oklahoma

39

Evelyn Ford's funeral was held on an unseasonably cool August day. The doctor at the Methodist Home told her grandson that she'd died peacefully in her sleep. Louis Ford had watched several people die, none of them in their sleep. He didn't want to die in his sleep. He was awake when he arrived in this world and he intended to be awake when he left it. His own death was one event he didn't want to miss.

Ford had visited his grandmother two days before she died. "I told you, didn't I?" she said. "A momma's gonna know her baby. No way around that."

The Feds couldn't prove it was Leo who'd entered the country using Hoffman's passport. They were too busy dealing with possible foreign terrorists to bother with two dead celebrities.

Ford spoke on Leo's behalf at his hearing. He told the judge that Leo had been the victim of con artists and that he'd saved a child's life by putting his own in danger. Janice Heller came down from Santa Barbara to appear as a witness on Leo's behalf. She was persuasive.

The judge had trouble following the details of the case and the DA, who was now running for Congress, was eager to get Leo Licklighter or Leo Malone, child of the Baby Bandits, and the whole Irma Stowell affair off the front pages. The charges against Leo were dropped.

40

Leo stood in a dry Oklahoma graveyard and laid a bunch of daisies against the small headstone of his parents Robert and Carlotta

Licklighter who, as the stone informed the reader, died in 1981. The epitaph read: FORGIVEN BY THE LORD AND TAKEN HOME.

It was the first time Leo had visited their graves. None of his foster parents had ever brought him here.

Leo said a short prayer for his parents while Percy slept on the front seat of his car. Detective Ford had arranged for Leo to get the Merton's dog from the city animal shelter and he took Percy back to Oklahoma with him. For a few weeks now, Leo was working at a Caddo mission teaching second and third graders during the day and helping the reservation's addicts at night. He signed up for graduate school in the fall. He planned to get a master's degree in literature. He might be able to get a job teaching with that. Both Detective Ford and Dr. Heller wrote recommendations for him. Neither doubted that he'd succeed.

Leo heard from Detective Ford a couple of days before he visited his parents' graves. Ford was trying to find a girl. Her name was Sophie. She'd been living in a communal home and on heavy doses of medication for different psychoses. She'd run away and Ford asked if he could pick Leo's brain about the ways a kid in the system like her might think. Leo said he'd be glad to help him find the girl. He and Ford were planning to talk the next day.

A heavy-set older woman knelt in front of an ornate headstone with angels on it a few yards from Leo's parents' grave. She struggled to stand up. Leo hurried over and helped her to her feet. She brushed the dead grass from her skirt and thanked him. She saw the grave that Leo had been standing in front of.

"Those are the Baby Bandits," the woman said.

"I know."

"I was real upset at first when I found out they were going to be buried this close to my Clifford."

"They're dead," Leo said.

"I'm a Christian woman so I found it in my heart to forgive them. Like the stone says." The woman looked at him. "They your family?"

Leo nodded.

"Are you the baby?"

Leo nodded again.

"You don't say much, do you, son?"

Leo shook his head. "No, ma'am."

"I can't blame you." She walked to her car, a dusty blue Cadillac, but before getting into it she turned back to Leo.

"You want some advice, darling?" she said. "You didn't ask me for it, but I'm gonna give it to you anyway." She paused for effect. "There's nothing that gets you through life's rough patches like a family does. Nothing. Have you got yourself one?" She waited for Leo's answer. "Have you, honey? Have you got yourself a family?"

"I have a dog," Leo said and he walked back to his car where Percy waited for him.

ABOUT THE AUTHOR

Charlie Peters

Charlie Peters is a playwright and screenwriter who was raised in New York City and educated at Stonyhurst College in England, the University of Connecticut and Carnegie-Mellon University. His plays have been produced at La Mama E.T.C., Playwrights Horizons, The Edinburgh Festival, The Actors Theatre of Louisville and Primary Stages. Twelve of his screenplays have been produced and the casts in those movies include Sally Field, Bob Hoskins, Renee Zellweger, Burt Reynolds, James Caan, Morgan Freeman, Brenda Blethyn, Jeff Bridges, Michael Caine, Claire Trevor, Richard Dreyfuss, Diane Keaton, Frances McDormand, Jude Law and Maureen Stapleton.

CHECK OUT OTHER GREAT READS FROM

HENRY GRAY PUBLISHING

THE UNDERSTUDY by Charlie Peters

"Tell your boss that I have one of his employees."

With those words a kidnapping plot begins in the middle of a high-stakes corporate merger. But the kidnappers' plans don't unfold - they unravel.

"If you're thinking of committing the perfect crime, read Charlie Peters' **elegant new thriller** first. Find out just how many ways perfection can go wrong."—Dan Hearn, author, *Bad August*

VEIL OF SEDUCTION by Emily Dinova

1922. Lorelei Alba, a fiercely independent and ambitious woman, is determined to break into the male-dominated world of investigative journalism by doing the unimaginable – infiltrating Morning Falls Asylum, the gothic hospital to which "troublesome" women are dispatched, never to be seen again. Once there, she meets the darkly handsome and enigmatic Doctor Roman Dreugue, who claims to have found the cure for insanity. But Lorelei's instincts tell her something is terribly wrong, even as her curiosity pulls her deeper into Roman's intimate and isolated world of intrigue.

THE LAST STAGE by Bruce Scivally

Dying in his small Los Angeles bungalow, with his Jewish wife, Josephine, whom he calls Sadie, at his side, famed lawman Wyatt Earp imagines an ending more befitting a man of his reputation: returning to his mining claims in a small desert town, tying up loose ends with Sadie, and – after he strikes gold – confronting a quartet of robbers in a showdown.

For more info visit HenryGrayPublishing.com

...AND ENJOY OUR NEW RELEASES!

SHELBY'S VACATION by Nancy Beverly

Fantasy. Sex. Despair. (Hey, what are vacations for?)

Shelby sets out from L.A. on a much-needed vacation to mend her heart from her latest unrequited crush. By happenstance, she ends up at a rustic mountain resort where she meets the manager, Carol, who has her own memories of the past inhibiting her ability to create a real relationship in the present. Their casual vacation encounter turns into something more profound than either of them bargained for, as each learns what holds them back from living and loving.

"This is an uplifting and romantic novel about the power of love to heal hearts and minds."
 - Elizabeth Sims, author of the award-winning *Lillian Byrd* crime series

THE MAN FROM BELIZE by Steven Kobrin

A modern adventure in retro-70s paperback style!

Life-saving heart surgeon Kent Stirling lives in paradise, dividing his time between medical practices in the exotic Yucatan and deeply in love with the woman of his dreams. He has everything a man could desire... until enemies from his secret past as a government assassin convene to eliminate him.

Action. Adventure. Intrigue. Sex. Exotic Locations. All in one compact 4.25 x 7 inch, 214-page package!

Garner Simmons, scriptwriter of *BAYWATCH, SILK STALKINGS, V,* and *DEA,* says **THE MAN FROM BELIZE** "...captures the fast-paced action of Ian Fleming coupled with the intimate knowledge of this Central American Caribbean backdrop reminiscent of the thrillers of Graham Greene...If you crave action and suspense, **The Man from Belize** is the book for you.

Papa Rock's
WORD SEARCH BOOKS

PAPA ROCK'S ROMANCE MOVIES WORD SEARCH
by Rock Scivally and Jeffrey Breslauer

Here are Word Searches for 150 classic Romance movies made between 1921 and 1999, including *Gone With the Wind, Casablanca, Roman Holiday, Breakfast at Tiffany's, The Way We Were, When Harry Met Sally, Jerry Maguire,* and *Titanic,* among many others. Just remember—if this book closes before you've finished working a puzzle, you'll regret it, maybe not today, maybe not tomorrow, but soon and for the rest of your life.

PAPA ROCK'S HORROR MOVIES WORD SEARCH
by Rock Scivally

Sharpen your stakes - er, pencils - to solve these unique puzzles designed for anyone who loves classic horror films from the first Frankenstein film in 1910 to the giant bug movies of the 1950s. If you grew up watching scary movies presented by a local horror host, or collected plastic model kits of monsters or read monster magazines, then this is the Word Search book for you!

PAPA ROCK'S SON OF HORROR MOVIES WORD SEARCH by Rock Scivally

The 1960s. The 1970s.Two decades that encapsulated a shift in screen horror, from Dracula, Frankenstein, the Wolfman, and giant insects, to Blacula, Dr. Phibes, Regan, Damien, Carrie, a killer baby, and a rat named Ben. Pick up your pens, your pencils, or your blood-red highlighters and literally find all your horror film favorites from 1960 to 1979 within these pages. Happy Haunting!

If you enjoyed this book and think others will as well,
please leave a review on your preferred
bookseller's web page for

Too Much in the Son

For more information or to join our mailing list,
please visit:

www.HenryGrayPublishing.com

Granada Hills, CA
"Select books for selective readers"

Printed in Great Britain
by Amazon